In His Arms

By Robin Lee Hatcher

Coming to America Series

Robin Lee HATCHER

BESTSELLING AUTHOR OF *RETURN TO ME*

In His Arms

BOOK 3

A Coming to America Novel

ZONDERVAN®

ZONDERVAN.com/
AUTHORTRACKER
follow your favorite authors

This book is a work of fiction. The characters, incidents, and dialogues are products of the author's imagination and are not to be construed as real. Any resemblance to actual events or persons, living or dead, is entirely coincidental.

 ZONDERVAN®

In His Arms
Copyright © 2001 by Robin Lee Hatcher

Value Edition 978-0-310-28806-0

Requests for information should be addressed to:
Zondervan, *Grand Rapids, Michigan* 49530

Library of Congress Cataloging-in-Publication Data

Hatcher, Robin Lee.
      In his arms / Robin Lee Hatcher.
         p. cm.–(Coming to America)
      ISBN-10: 0-310-23120-5
      ISBN-13: 978-0-310-23120-2
      1. Irish American women—Fiction. 2. Armagh (Northern Ireland: County)—Fiction.
3. Sheriffs—Fiction. 4. Idaho—Fiction. I. Title.
PS3558.A73574 I5 2001
813'.54—dc21   00-140139

Interior design by Todd Sprague

Printed in the United States of America

08 09 10 11 12 13 14 • 20 19 18 17 16 15 14 13 12 11 10 9 8 7 6 5 4 3 2 1

To my cousin, Connie Burke Bunch, who loves all things Irish.
And to Mom, who told me I should use my great-grandmother's
name in a book some day.
So here is my story about Mary Emeline Malone from County
Armagh, Ireland.
I'm hoping you find her perfect altogether.

About the Author

Robin Lee Hatcher is the author of over thirty-five novels and novellas. Her books have won numerous awards, including the Christy Award for excellence in Christian fiction, the Romance Writers of America RITA Award, the Heart of Romance Readers' Choice Award, the Romantic Times Career Achievement Award, and the Favorite Author Award from Affaire de Coeur. For her efforts on behalf of literacy, Laubach Literacy International named their romance award "The Robin."

In those rare moments when she isn't working on a new book, Robin and her husband, Jerry, like to travel. Hobbies are nearly nonexistent since she sold her first book, but she enjoys the occasional golf game (don't ask about scores!), loves movies (both old and new) and live musical theater, and is a season ticket holder with the Idaho Shakespeare Festival. She also loves to spend time with her two daughters and three young grandchildren.

She invites readers to find out more by visiting her Web site at http://www.robinleehatcher.com, by e-mail to robinlee@ robinleehatcher.com, or by sending a #10 self-addressed stamped envelope to: Robin Lee Hatcher, P.O. Box 4722, Boise, ID 83711–4722.

Acknowledgments

No book is truly written alone. Everything that touches a writer affects her work in some way. Recognizing the truth of that, I'm grateful for the love of my husband, daughters, mother, and all the rest of my wonderful extended family. I'm thankful for the members of the LoveKnot, who have sustained me with their prayers and inspired me to reach ever higher, both in my writing and in my life. And I'm grateful to all the terrific people at Zondervan who have worked along with me on the Coming to America series. Thanks especially to Dave, Lori, and Sue.

Above all, I want to thank my faithful readers. I appreciate all the letters I receive and feel blessed when a reader shares how one of my stories has touched a heart in some way. Thank you for sharing yourselves with me.

For all of you, I pray that this old Irish blessing will come true:

May the road rise to meet you.
May the wind be always at your back.
May the sun shine warm upon your face,
And the rains fall soft upon your fields.
And until we meet again,
May God hold you in the palm of his hand.

Preface

To my readers:

In His Arms was written in 1997 for the general romance market and was published in 1998. Since then, God has called me into a deeper walk of faith, as well as calling me to use the talents he entrusted to me in a new and better way—writing novels that share my hope in Christ.

I was delighted when Zondervan expressed interest in revising and reissuing my Coming to America series, because I'm fond of these stories. While you will not find the faith message as overt in these books as you will find in the novels that I've written specifically for Christian publishing houses, I believe you will find the stories entertaining and uplifting.

One of my goals as a writer is to make my characters true to life, with all the faults and foibles that real people have. Unbelievers and Christians alike make mistakes, make foolish choices, fall into sin. I don't know any perfect Christians, and so I don't write about them. What I always hope to share is that we have Someone to call upon Who *is* perfect, Someone Who can take who we are and what we do and turn it into good when we trust in Him.

In His grip,

Robin Lee Hatcher

— Prologue

Ellis Island, New York Harbor
April 1897

With her heart hammering in anticipation, Mary Emeline Malone searched for her belongings in the ground-floor baggage room of the federal depot. The immigration process had been no worse than she'd expected and no better either. Long and stressful, to be sure, but bearable. Even though she was a woman traveling unescorted, Mary's admission to America had been granted with surprisingly little fuss. Of course, she had lied through her teeth on any number of questions—especially the one about her husband waiting for her—but she wasn't about to consider the right or the wrong of those lies now.

By some small miracle, she found her valise and satchel without undue delay. Then, with them safely in hand, she hurried outside into the fresh air, joining the flow of immigrants on their way to the ferry slips.

She looked about her for a glimpse of her friends, Beth Wellington and Inga Linberg. She'd become separated from them many hours ago, but still she had hoped to be able to see them one last time, if only to say a proper good-bye. Later today, if all had gone well for them inside, Beth would be taking the train to Montana, and Inga, her parents, and sisters would be leaving for Iowa. Only Mary would remain in New York.

A fearsome city, that.

She stared across the choppy waters of the harbor. Somewhere in that sprawling mass of humanity known as New York City, she would find Seamus Maguire, her fiancé and the father of her unborn child. When she found him, they would be married, just as they'd planned before he left England. Seamus hadn't expected her to join him this soon, but he would be glad to see her. He loved her, Seamus did.

Mary reached into her pocket, felt the scrap of paper with Ryan Maguire's address written on it. That's where Seamus had said he would stay until he found work, with his cousin Ryan. It was where she had sent letters to Seamus in the few months they'd been apart. Now it was where she would find him.

Faith, if she didn't believe her new life in America was going to be perfect altogether.

～One

New York City, July 1898

The door to the master's study swung shut behind Mary, causing her to gasp in surprise. But it was Winston Kenrick's soft chuckle that made her whirl about and her pulse quicken in dread.

"I wondered how soon you would get to cleaning this room, Mary."

"If 'tis a bad time, Master Kenrick, I could be coming back later. When you're not so busy and all."

He smiled, but the look was more feral than comforting. "I wouldn't think of causing you the trouble. Come in and be about your business."

Mary tried to disregard the ominous feeling in her chest. In the months she had worked for the Kenricks, nothing untoward had happened to her. Yet it seemed the master was always watching her. It seemed he was around every corner, in every room, waiting, observing, smiling. The truth be told, she didn't like him much.

"I'll be trying not to disturb you, sir," she said as she set down her bucket of soapy wash water. She pulled the feather duster from her waistband and walked to the bookcase, where she set to work, ignoring the man behind her.

The master chuckled again. "But don't you know, my dear girl? You always disturb me. You can't help it."

"I'm thinking I don't know what you mean," she replied without looking at him. But she was more than sure she did know.

Winston moved closer. "How is that little boy of yours, Mary Malone?"

Her heart nearly stopped. Her hand stilled, the feather duster resting on the spine of a book. "Me boy?" she whispered. She'd never told anyone in the Kenrick household about Keary. How did Master Kenrick know?

"It must be difficult, raising an infant on your own. What is he? Almost a year old now?"

She remained stubbornly silent.

"I could make it easier for you, Mary."

"I'm having no complaints as things are now."

His hands alighted on her shoulders. Slowly, he turned her to face him.

Winston Kenrick was a handsome man in his mid-forties. His hair was silver gray, but rather than making him look old, it added to his distinguished appearance. He had enormous power and influence among the wealthy members of New York society. He watched Mary now with eyes that said he knew exactly how to use his power and influence to get what he wanted.

"My dear girl, you have no idea what I'm offering."

Mary's infamous temper flared. "But I'm thinking I do know, sir, and I'll be having you know I've got no interest in the likes o' you. Not for any amount of your charm or your money."

His eyes narrowed. "Don't play the innocent with me."

"Oh, I'll not be pretending innocence, sir. You already know I'm not married and I have me a son, so there'd be no use to it. But I learned me lesson well with Seamus Maguire, I did. I've been betrayed, but I'll not be used. Not by you nor any other man."

She tried to push him away, but his grip on her arms tightened.

Winston grinned. "I think I can change your mind." He kissed her.

For a moment, she didn't fight him, too stunned to move. But then he chuckled low in his throat, pleased with himself and with what he was doing.

Her anger flared hotter. She bit his lip. Hard.

He howled as he stepped back from her. Mary used the opportunity to slip away, dashing to the opposite side of the master's enormous cherry wood desk. Winston, in turn, positioned himself between her and the door.

He touched his lip with his fingertips, then looked at them, as if checking for blood. "You Irish witch," he said softly. The words would have seemed less terrifying if he'd shouted them.

"Just let me go, Master Kenrick. I'll collect me pay and be gone from here."

"Are you aware that the authorities could deport you because you lied to get into the country? You told them you were married. They could send you back to Ireland." He paused a heartbeat, then added, "Without your son."

"They'd never do that." Fear made her mouth dry, her tongue thick. "They'd never do that."

"Do you dare take that chance?"

She shook her head, whether in disbelief or in answer to his question, she didn't know. "I can't betray Mrs. Kenrick nor meself in such a way."

He moved toward the door. "I have very powerful friends. Police officers. Judges. I can make certain you never see your son again. Never. Is that what you want?" With a click, he turned the key, locking the door. Then he faced her again. "Be careful what you decide, my dear. Be very careful. Your son's future is entirely up to you."

Keary. Me darlin' Keary.

Winston moved to the center of the room, then crooked his finger at her. With heart pounding, she came around from behind the desk. She told herself that no matter what happened, she'd lived through worse and survived.

"That's a good girl."

Winston stepped toward her.

Mary stepped backward.

He grinned, enjoying the game.

She bumped against the desk, stopping her retreat.

Winston laughed aloud. "Playing it coy, Miss Malone?"

"Don't do this, sir. Just let me go, and I'll be no more trouble to you."

"You're no trouble to me now."

For Keary, she reminded herself. To protect Keary she could bear anything.

Winston reached for her. Panic surged, and she instinctively tried to push his hands away.

"No!" she cried.

Irritation flashed in his eyes, and with unexpected swiftness, he rent the fabric of her blouse. "Let's be done with this silliness."

"Leave me be!"

He pressed her against the desk. She tried to brace herself, hoping for enough leverage to shove him away. Then her right hand closed around something large, cool, and hard on the desktop.

"You'll not be doing this to me!" she cried.

Mary swung her arm with all her might. The second after she hit Winston on the side of his head with the object in her hand, she saw a look of disbelief in his eyes. He stumbled backward a few steps, teetered drunkenly, and crumpled to the floor, lying in an awkward position on the Oriental rug.

Breathing hard, Mary took a step toward her employer. She nudged him with the toe of her shoe, but he didn't move. He made no sound. Then she saw the red stain spreading near his head across the elegant fibers of the carpet.

"Faith and begorra!" she whispered, her eyes widening. "Have I killed him, then?"

The answer lay before her, still and unmoving.

She would swing for this, see if she wouldn't. And then what would become of her wee Keary? She would have to get her son and run away before the master's body was found. She had little time to think about where she would go. She simply knew she must go quickly.

She felt light-headed and out of breath as she hurried across the room. It wasn't until she reached for the key that she realized she still held the weapon she had used against Winston Kenrick. She looked at the ornate box. It was real silver, she'd wager, and valuable. It was better if she took it with her. The police might think the house had been burglarized. Maybe they wouldn't notice the absence of one of the housemaids if they were looking for a thief instead.

Turning the key, Mary unlocked the study door, then turned the knob. She trembled as she looked out into the hallway. If one of the other servants were to see her . . .

The hall was empty. Now if she could get out of the house without being seen.

She remembered her bodice was torn down the front and knew she couldn't go running through the streets of New York, down Madison Avenue itself, looking like this. People would know she was guilty of something. They would summon the police and have her arrested. All would be lost.

Panic threatened to overwhelm her.

Use your head, Mary, me darlin' girl, her da's voice whispered in her head. *One hapless act may undo you, but one timely one will put all to right. Think, now.*

Mary forced herself to be calm and work things through in her mind. She knew Mrs. Norris, the cook, kept a spare apron hanging near the rear kitchen door. If Mary put it on, it would hide her ripped bodice. And her hat...She needed her hat. She needed to look like any other servant girl, out running errands for her mistress.

She glanced over her shoulder at the body of Winston Kenrick, and a shiver ran through her. He'd been an evil man, he had, but she would always be sorry she'd killed him. Because of it, she was certain she'd never know a moment's peace for the rest of her miserable life.

━

Blanche Loraine was going home to die. She'd seen all the fancy doctors her considerable wealth could afford—which meant, in her humble opinion, far too many of the educated idiots. She'd listened to their collective advice. And now she was going back to Idaho to spend what time she had left with the people she knew best. Not that she expected any of them to mourn her passing.

Her lapdog, Nugget, whimpered for attention.

"I know, boy," Blanche said as she stroked his silky coat. "I'm not looking forward to the trip either. But won't we be glad to get outta New York City."

Nugget licked her gloved hand.

A sudden coughing jag gripped Blanche. She covered her mouth with her handkerchief and tried to subdue the wretched hacking that seemed ready to rip her lungs right out of her body. Even as she fought for control, she noticed the couple opposite her get up from the seat and move to another part of the passenger car. She thought of a few choice—and most unladylike—things she could do. Of course, Blanche Loraine was no lady and had never pretended to be.

As she folded the handkerchief, she noticed the red stains on the white cloth.

"Miss Loraine," one of the doctors had said to her yesterday, "you should not undertake such an arduous journey at this time."

Idiot, she remembered thinking. He'd just finished telling her that her condition wasn't likely to improve. So exactly when was it she was supposed to travel home?

"Excuse me, mum. Would you be allowing us to sit here?"

Drawn from her musings, Blanche looked up at the prettiest face she'd seen in all her born days. And in her line of work, Blanche had more than a passing knowledge of what made a woman beautiful. "Of course," she said, waving toward the seat opposite her. "Sit yourself right down."

The young woman—in her late twenties, Blanche guessed—set her small child on the indicated seat, then, standing on tiptoe, managed to shove her satchels onto the rack overhead. As she sat beside the toddler, she adjusted her straw hat, which had been knocked slightly askew during her efforts with the luggage. Her ink-black hair was thick and curly, and long wisps had escaped her hairpins to coil at her nape. She had a heart-shaped face with a milky complexion that was absolutely flawless. Her eyes were dark brown, fringed in thick black lashes, and there was the look of a trapped animal in those eyes that intrigued Blanche.

"You going far?" she asked.

The young mother shook her head, shrugged, then quickly looked out the window, as if wanting to avoid the question.

"My name is Blanche Loraine."

After a long moment, she met Blanche's gaze again. "Mary Emeline Malone." Her eyes grew round, and she pressed her lips together tightly.

She's in trouble and didn't mean to tell me her name. But what kind of trouble? Aloud, she said, "Well, Mary, it's a pleasure to meet you. Who is this little man you've got with you?"

Again she was silent a spell before answering. "Me son, Keary Malone."

The boy bore more than a slight resemblance to his mother. He had the same wavy black hair and the same large brown eyes. But he knew how to smile, something Blanche suspected his mother hadn't done freely in quite some time.

Keary leaned forward, staring at Nugget, his arms outstretched.

"Oh, I see you like dogs." Blanche lifted her pet off her lap. "This is Nugget."

The child laughed and bounced his pudgy hands against the dog's back.

"Be careful, Keary," his mother said softly. Then she looked over her son's head, staring out the window with an anxious gaze. "I'm thinking we should be under way by now. Could there be trouble?"

"Trains hardly ever leave on time."

Mary worried her lower lip with her teeth. Fear was stamped on her pretty features as clearly as anything Blanche had ever seen. Oddly enough, it bothered her.

Blanche Loraine was not a charitable woman by nature. She knew the value of a dollar, and she didn't squander her money on anything she didn't believe might bring her a profit. Still, there was something about Mary Emeline Malone that tugged at her life-hardened heart.

"Tickets," a man called from the rear of the car. "Tickets, please."

Mary started as if she'd been pinched. Fear was replaced by an expression of near-panic as the conductor drew closer.

Blanche reached forward and squeezed Mary's knee, drawing her gaze. "Sit still and say nothing," she warned. "Do you hear me?"

Mary nodded.

"Give me your passenger ticket." She held out her hand. After Mary obeyed, Blanche continued, "Now, take that boy in your arms and turn toward the window. Rock him as if you're trying to get him to sleep. That way your face won't be seen, and no one will remember you were here."

By the time the conductor reached their seats, Blanche was ready for him. With one hand, she stroked Nugget. In her other hand, she held their tickets. "My good man," she said in her most authoritative voice, "someone has sold my niece the wrong ticket. As you can plainly see from mine, we are on our way to Whistle Creek, but she has been given one to Omaha."

The conductor frowned as he took the tickets from her. "She shoulda said something 'fore now."

"Well, don't you think she would have if she'd noticed? She thought she was dealing with competent people. Goodness, it isn't easy, traveling with a child and an irascible aunt. Now see that her ticket is exchanged for one to match my own. There'll be a handsome reward in it for you if you can do it quickly."

"I'll see to it, ma'am. Don't you worry."

As soon as the conductor was gone, Mary Malone turned from the window. "I'm wondering altogether why you did that, Mrs. Loraine."

"There's no missus in front of my name. Folks back in Whistle Creek call me Miss Blanche. You can, too." She cocked one eyebrow. "And to tell you the truth, I'm not sure why I did it. I suppose because there's a look about you."

"A look, mum? What do you mean?"

"Nothing really." Blanche lowered her voice so as not to be overheard. "Where in Ireland are you from?"

Mary's reply came softly. "I was born in County Armagh."

"How long have you been in America?"

"More than a year, just." She held her son more closely. "But you've not answered me question. Why did you do what you did? I can't be paying you back." She tilted her head, thrusting her chin slightly forward, the gesture filled with pride and a bit of bravado.

Blanche waved her hand. "I'm not asking you to pay me back, girl." Her own retort surprised her, and she wondered if she spoke the truth. She frowned as she sought a believable explanation. "I'm not a well woman, Mary. I came to New York to seek the advice of medical experts." She laughed sharply. Experts. Ha! "Now I'm headed home, and I need a companion to make the journey more enjoyable and to help me should my health worsen."

"But you know nothing about me."

"I know you're in some sort of trouble."

Mary paled.

Perhaps that was why she was helping her. Because Blanche remembered a time, many years ago, when she'd been in trouble and afraid, and there had been no one in the world who would help her. She'd fought for everything she'd ever had in this life. No one had cared about her, about whether she lived or died. Maybe she didn't want to leave this world without helping some other poor girl avoid what she'd been through.

"Where's your husband?"

A pause, then, "Me son's father is dead and buried these many months."

Ah, so he never married you, the blackguard.

Blanche's gaze dropped to the toddler in Mary's lap. The boy had fallen asleep. He looked cherubic. He was plump and well cared for. Loved, the way a child ought to be loved.

She looked at his mother again. "Let me help you, Mary Malone. If you decide you want to get off the train at any time, you're free to do so. You'll owe me nothing. But if you want to come all the way to Idaho with me, then you'll be welcome."

"Idaho?"

"Yes, that's where I live. Whistle Creek, Idaho."

Mary was silent for a long time, her dark gaze searching Blanche's face. Finally, she gave the smallest of nods. "I'll come and be glad of your help. May God bless you, mum."

—

Later that night, Mary lay on the top bunk in the sleeper car, staring at the ceiling that was hardly a foot from the tip of her nose. Beside her, Keary slept on his stomach, his tiny bottom stuck up in the air.

She wondered where they were now. It was well past midnight. How many miles from New York City had they traveled? Was it far enough?

Every time the train came to a stop that day, she'd feared the authorities would swarm into the passenger car and drag her away. Every time the train pulled away from a station, she'd breathed a fresh sigh of relief.

She closed her eyes and commanded her breathing to slow. Worrying would not help. She had locked the master's study from the outside, then slipped from the house without seeing another person. She'd worn the cook's spare apron to cover her ripped blouse. She'd forced herself to walk with unhurried steps along the sidewalks of Madison Avenue. No one could have guessed by looking at her that she'd killed a man. Besides, the wealthy rarely noticed servants on the street. It would be beneath them.

No, she was worrying needlessly. Even if the police wanted to question the missing housemaid, they wouldn't know where to look for her. In the few months she'd worked for the Kenricks, she'd never told anyone where she lived. She'd kept to herself, doing her work and then going back to the Dougals' apartment and her adorable baby son. She supposed most of the servants thought her unfriendly. Now she was thankful for it.

A wave of something akin to seasickness swept over her. Sweat beaded on her forehead.

May God have mercy. I've killed a man.

She hadn't meant to kill him. She'd hated Winston Kenrick for what he'd tried to do. She'd wanted to stop him, but she hadn't meant to kill him.

Truth be told, she hadn't meant for many things in her past to happen. She hadn't meant to lie with a man who wasn't her husband, a man who was destined to betray her, fool that she was. She hadn't meant to bear a child out of wedlock, although she loved her Keary more than anything. She hadn't meant to find herself a penniless immigrant, dependent upon the charity of strangers.

But all of that had happened to her, and there'd be no changing any of it.

In the berth beneath her, Blanche Loraine suffered another coughing spell. Mary had seen the flecks of blood on the woman's handkerchief, listened to her labored gasps for breath. She knew the signs of a dying woman when she saw them. She was sorry for her, to be sure, but she was thankful they'd met.

Idaho. Sure and it was nothing short of a miracle. Aye, a miracle, for her brother Quaid could be somewhere in that state. She'd not heard from him in many a year. She'd still been in service near Belfast, before leaving for England, when the last letter from Quaid had come. He was working in a mine in a place called Idaho, he'd written. True, he might not still be there. He might even be dead for all she knew.

But she'd not believe Quaid was dead. Not when a miracle was taking her to Idaho to find him. Though why God would help the likes of her—a fallen woman and a murderess besides— was beyond her. Still she wasn't one to spit into the wind.

It was to be Idaho, then. Mary had no idea where exactly that was, but she was given to understand it was far from New York City.

That made it a good place altogether.

Two

"Sheriff!" Young Todd Stover, the blacksmith's son, burst through the front door of the jailhouse. "There's trouble over at the Painted Queen."

Carson Barclay set the blue-and-white speckled coffeepot back on the woodstove. "Already? It isn't even noon yet." He reached for his hat. "What happened?"

"I don't rightly know. Pa just said there was trouble and sent me after you."

Carson strode toward the front door, moving swiftly and with purpose. When there was trouble at the Painted Queen Saloon—as there was on a fairly regular basis—it could quickly escalate into gunplay. And if there was one thing Sheriff Carson Barclay hated, it was folks getting shot up in his town. They could blow themselves to pieces elsewhere if they wanted, but not in his town.

The narrow main street of Whistle Creek was quiet this time of the day. The men from the Lucky Lady Mine's night shift were at home in their beds. The day shift was down in the bowels of the earth, chipping away at walls of rock, looking for the black-coated silver ore. As for the townsfolk, they were apparently going about their own business indoors. Other than a couple of horses tethered outside the boardinghouse, a wagon and team standing in front of the mercantile, and Abe Stover's motley wolfhound lounging in one of its favorite spots, Main Street was empty.

Everything was quiet, just as Carson liked it.

Except at the Painted Queen.

The saloon was the fanciest business establishment between Spokane and Missoula, and with the exception of the cavernlike buildings out at the mine, it was the largest, too. It boasted brass fixtures and spittoons, red velvet upholstery, and elaborate oil paintings. Three stories tall, the Painted Queen was home to some twenty or so females, most of them young and all of them pretty.

Carson frowned as he drew closer to the saloon. Truth was, he had more than a passing acquaintance with enterprises like the Painted Queen. He knew firsthand that nothing good came out of them. Not that he was innocent of his own share of sinning. In his past, he'd drank, gambled, and womanized like any other fool. Then, thank God Almighty, he'd found a better way of living. If not, he'd probably be dead or in jail himself, instead of serving the law.

It would have made things a whole lot easier if Blanche Loraine would take her business and her girls elsewhere. But that wasn't going to happen. The Painted Queen was as much a part of Whistle Creek as the mine and the stamp mill, the mercantile, the livery, and the Northern Pacific railroad line that ran between Mullan and Spokane.

The sound of shattering glass greeted him as he stepped through the swinging doors of the saloon. He saw Mac MacDonald, the card dealer, duck just in time to miss a flying beer mug as it hurtled toward him.

"Cheated me agin!" John Tyrell shouted, his words slurred. "By darn, ya cheated me agin, Mac!"

"That's enough, John," Carson said.

The young man spun, staggered, and nearly fell before catching himself against the bar. "He cheated me, Sheriff. Dadburned thievin' cardsharp. He cheated me agin."

"I don't hardly doubt that." Carson smiled good-naturedly at the dealer, a look that said no hard feelings. Then he approached John. "But I guess if you thought he'd cheated you before, you shouldn't've come in here again, now should you? Doesn't seem to me you've got money enough you can afford to throw it away playing poker."

John blinked his eyes as he leaned dangerously to one side.

"I'm afraid I don't have much sympathy for you, John. Nobody forced that liquor down your gullet, and nobody made you sit down at Mac's table either." He eyed the broken mirror behind the bar. "I reckon Miss Blanche isn't going to be none too pleased with what you did here this morning."

"But I'm tellin' you, Sheriff—"

"Yeah, I know." He took hold of John's good arm. "Let's get you over to the jail so you can sleep it off." He looked at Lloyd Perkins, the bartender. "I heard Miss Blanche is finally coming back."

"Yup. Matter of fact, she left New York at the first of the week. I expect her on the afternoon train."

Carson nodded, then led his prisoner out of the saloon. John struggled to keep up, stumbling along beside him, muttering about being cheated.

Carson didn't think John Tyrell had drawn a sober breath in a full three years. Not since the blasting accident down in the mines that left him, at the age of nineteen, with his face scarred and his right arm useless. No longer able to work in the mines and forced to live with his older brother, sister-in-law, and three nephews, John had taken to drink like an infant takes to its mama's milk.

"When are you gonna dry out, John?" Carson asked, a note of frustration in his words. "You're not the first man to be hurt in the mines. And you're sure not being fair to Wade and Dora and the kids."

John cursed in reply.

"Wade's money's hard enough to come by without you throwing it away in that saloon."

John remained stubbornly silent.

Carson shook his head as he opened the door to the sheriff's office and led his prisoner to the back room that held the jail cells. "It wouldn't hurt for you to think of someone besides yourself for a change." He unlocked the nearest cell and gave John a little push toward the cot. "Sleep on that thought for a while."

He didn't wait to see what the drunken man did. Instead, he turned, walked out of the back room, and headed for the stove and that cup of coffee he'd been wanting. As he took his first sip of the dark brew, he thought about the broken mirror at the saloon. Wade didn't have the kind of money it would take to replace it. That spelled real trouble for John.

Carson crossed to his office window and looked outside. Clanging sounds came from the interior of the livery. Abe Stover was probably shaping a horseshoe to fit or repairing a wagon wheel. Next door at the mercantile, Chuck Adams washed the dust off the shop windows while old Dooby Jones reclined on a nearby bench, smoking a pipe and, no doubt, reminiscing about the first gold strikes in Idaho and how he'd been there when it all began. Farther down the street was the small, whitewashed Whistle Creek Methodist Church, empty on a Friday.

Carson glanced in the opposite direction, toward the Painted Queen. Blanche Loraine was due back in Whistle

Creek today. She would want reimbursement for that mirror. Lloyd Perkins, who'd been running the place in her absence, would have let John work off the debt. Blanche was another story. She was a tough businesswoman who never wasted a red cent. She reminded him a little of Aldora Barclay in that regard.

Breaking off the uncomfortable direction of that thought, Carson set his jaw and turned from the window. He'd better get out to the Tyrell place and let them know John was in jail. Standing here wasn't doing anyone any good.

———

Mary stared through the soot-smudged window of the train. In the past four days and nights, she'd seen more changing landscapes than she'd have thought possible in one country. She'd seen a few big cities and many small towns that were not much more than the train depot. She'd seen prairies that stretched as far as the eye could see and mountains that touched heaven itself. She'd seen deserts and forests, antelope and rabbits, purple sagebrush and wide, muddy rivers.

For quite some time, the train had been winding through what seemed to be one long, continuous valley, mountains rising on both sides. Sometimes the valley narrowed to allow hardly more than the tracks and the river that ran alongside them. Other times it widened into lush meadows, occasionally dotted with a farmhouse or two. Since departing Tekoa that morning, they'd made stops in several towns with names like St. Joe, Kellogg, and Osburn.

"We'll be in Whistle Creek soon," Blanche said, drawing Mary's attention from the window and the scenery beyond.

Mary knew a great deal more about her benefactress now than she had four days ago. She knew Blanche Loraine owned a saloon, and Mary suspected she knew exactly what sort of women worked for Blanche inside that saloon.

But Mary had also discovered during the journey that she liked the no-nonsense woman who had befriended her, no matter how she made her living. Blanche had a way of speaking her mind that was refreshing. She didn't put on airs even if she did have plenty of money. Nor did she seem to feel sorry for herself, even though she was sickly.

"Here. Let me have the boy." Blanche held out her arms to take Keary, who was fast asleep in Mary's arms. "You look plum tuckered out."

Mary nodded. She was tired. Keeping an active toddler entertained in such a confined space for so many days hadn't been an easy task. Keary was a good baby most of the time, but even he was cranky and tired of train travel by now. Add to that the summer heat, making the railcar stuffy and close, and it was no wonder Mary was exhausted.

She handed Keary to Blanche. "Thank you."

"Nothing to thank me for. I enjoy holding him when he's asleep." Her expression softened. "You're a good mother, Mary."

She stared at her son and felt her chest tighten. "He's everything to me. I'd do anything for him."

"Mary?" Blanche's tone was thoughtful.

She met the other woman's gaze.

"Seems to me you've got a real good head on your shoulders. I'd like you to come to work for me."

Mary shook her head emphatically. "I couldn't be doing that."

"Oh, I don't mean as one of my girls." Blanche chuckled. "Although you'd no doubt make me even richer than I am now if you did." Her smile vanished. "No, I mean I'd like you to try your hand at managing the business. I don't know how long I'll be able to do it myself. I'd like to know I've got someone I can depend on helping me run things."

Mary was stunned. Manage a saloon?

"Lloyd's been looking after things for me while I was in New York. He's my bartender. But he's not exactly the brightest of men. It's been an enormous responsibility for him. I think I could trust you, Mary, to handle things as they should be."

Mary thought of Winston Kenrick, lying dead on the floor of his study. "I don't know why you'd say such a thing," she whispered. "You've no reason to trust me."

"I say it because I'm a keen judge of character." Blanche's eyes narrowed. "And besides, I like you, Mary Emeline Malone."

She smiled. "I like you, too, Miss Blanche. You've a kind heart, you have."

The other woman hooted a loud laugh. "That's not something I've heard said about me before. I'd just as soon you keep it to yourself. It wouldn't do for my reputation to be gussied up."

Mary wasn't certain she understood what Blanche meant. Still, she nodded in agreement.

"Now, back to my proposition. You need some way to make a living to support you and this boy here, and I need someone to keep my place running the way I want it to. You won't find any folks needing a maid in Whistle Creek. None of the wealthy mine owners live there. And I could use you for better things than dusting the furniture. Are you willing to give it a try?"

"Me ma would turn over in her grave," Mary muttered to herself, "were I to work in such a place."

Blanche heard her and chuckled. "I expect so. But will you do it anyway?"

Mary had already committed murder. She supposed her eternal soul would be no worse off because of this. And no matter what her other sins had been, she believed God still loved her fatherless son. He would want her to support him and make sure he had food to eat. So what choice did she have?

"Aye, I'll do it, Miss Blanche. Sure, and I'll be doing me very best, too."

"I know. I wouldn't have asked otherwise."

―

The train whistle echoed up the valley, announcing the arrival of the three-fifteen. And it was only a half an hour behind schedule, according to Carson's pocket watch.

Giving the brim of his Stetson a tug, he bid good afternoon to the gentlemen lounging outside of the mercantile and set off toward the depot. He'd promised Wade Tyrell he'd have a word with Blanche about the broken bar mirror. Not that Carson thought she would be any more sympathetic with the words coming from him. Nobody knew better than he did that the myth about the madam with a heart of gold was pure bunk. But he and Blanche did have a sort of mutual understanding. She didn't have much use for the law. He didn't have much use for her business. And they both knew the other wasn't going away.

He arrived at the depot just as the Northern Pacific rolled to a stop amid a hiss of steam and the squeak of brakes.

"Whistle Creek," he heard the conductor shout. "Next stops, Wallace and Mullan."

Carson saw movement inside the passenger car. He headed toward the rear exit.

His first glimpse of Blanche Loraine in six months told him everything he needed to know about her health. She must have lost forty pounds while she was gone, and there were dark circles beneath her expressive green eyes. She'd always been a handsome woman, but her sickness was destroying her looks as well as her lungs.

"Well, as I live and breathe. Sheriff Barclay." She flashed him one of her coquettish smiles. "Have you come to welcome me home?"

"As a matter of fact, Miss Blanche, I have. In a roundabout way."

"Will wonders never cease."

He stepped toward her. "I reckon not."

He held out his hand to help her down to the platform. Instead of taking it, she handed him that silly lapdog of hers, then descended unaided. Once down, Blanche turned and looked behind her. Carson followed the direction of her gaze.

A young woman, toddler in arms, appeared on the train's steps. A young woman prettier than any he'd ever laid eyes on—and that was saying something.

Angelic.

Heavenly.

A natural beauty, unspoiled by artificial adornment of any kind.

His mouth went dry.

"Sheriff Barclay, I'd like you to meet my friend, Mrs. Mary Malone, and her son, Keary. Mrs. Malone lost her husband a year ago. They're going to be staying at the Painted Queen while she manages the saloon."

His gaze swung to the madam. "They're going to what?"

"Yes, I agree, it is a shame to waste such a beauty on my books and ledgers."

He looked at Mary Malone again. She didn't appear quite so angelic or heavenly to him now. From the expression on her face, he didn't look too good to her either.

"Ma'am," he said stiffly.

"Sheriff," she whispered.

He showed the woman his back, saying to Blanche, "I need to talk to you."

"So I gathered. Well, walk along with us if you like. I've already asked the porter to see that our things are sent to the saloon." She held out her arms. "Here. Give Nugget to me. You're holding him all wrong."

Carson obeyed, glad to be rid of the animal. Then he fell into step beside Blanche, adjusting his stride to hers. He guessed Mary Malone followed behind them, but he refused to give into the urge to look.

"I take it there was some trouble at the Painted Queen," Blanche said, her tone all business.

"John Tyrell."

"Ah."

"He busted the mirror behind the bar."

Blanche frowned. "The young fool. Even when he was working for the mine, he couldn't make in a month what that mirror cost me."

"Look, I've got him in jail right now, but I was hoping you'd let him work it off. He doesn't have the money to pay for it, and neither does his brother."

"He'd probably just break into the liquor and get stinking drunk."

Carson couldn't argue with her. That was more than a slight possibility.

"I'm dying, Sheriff," Blanche suddenly said, her voice low. She stopped walking, looked at him, her expression grave. "But then, I guess you've already figured that out."

He didn't deny it.

"I turned forty last month. No spring chicken, I admit, but still plenty of years left that should've been mine."

He almost felt sorry for her.

As abruptly as she'd stopped, she started walking again. "All right, I'll let him work it off. But the first time he gets drunk on my time or my liquor, he goes right back to jail. Agreed?"

For a moment, Carson couldn't answer. He hadn't expected Blanche to consent to his plan. He didn't think she had a compassionate bone in her body.

"Is that agreed?" she persisted.

"Agreed."

Blanche slowed her pace while turning her head to look at him. "Believe it or not, I've missed you, Sheriff Barclay."

Once again she'd stunned Carson into silence. He couldn't do anything more than stare at her.

She smiled, and the humor returned to her green eyes. "Now if you'll excuse us, Sheriff, I need to get Mary and her little boy settled in, and then see how much money Lloyd's laziness cost me."

Carson stepped off the boardwalk and let Mary Malone pass him by.

Blanche had missed him? Blanche Loraine? What sort of thing was that for her to say? Her sickness must be eating away at her brain, too. That's the only reason he could think of for her passing comment.

As he stared after them, the younger of the two women glanced back over her shoulder. For a moment, Mary Malone's gaze locked with Carson's.

Blast!

She was going to mean trouble for sure, and just as always, Carson hated trouble in his town.

Three

A half hour later, Blanche backed out the doorway of Mary's room, saying, "You get yourself settled. I'll have your supper sent up in an hour or so. Tomorrow will be soon enough for us to start work."

The moment the door closed, Mary sank onto the bed and released a deep sigh. She didn't realize how closely she was hugging Keary to her chest until he objected.

"Sorry, love," she whispered, then set him on the floor and watched him toddle across the room, investigating their new surroundings.

Dread sapped any reserved strength Mary had. The moment she'd seen the sheriff standing on the train platform, waiting for them, she'd been overtaken by fear. Even after she'd realized he wasn't there because of her, she hadn't been able to rid herself of the oppressing sense of doom. Just the idea of being introduced to the sheriff made her sick inside. Now he knew her name. If he should learn the authorities in New York were looking for a Mary Malone...

The washstand wobbled, Keary's hands gripping its spindly legs. The porcelain pitcher and bowl atop it started to slide toward the edge. Mary jumped up quickly, just in time to save everything from crashing down on her son's head. Once the table was steady, she lifted him into her arms.

"'Tis a fine mess I've got us into," she whispered, her cheek pressed against Keary's down-soft hair. "We're in a bawdy house, to be sure, and me with a wee son t' look after. 'Tis no place for us. What is it we're to do?"

A knock interrupted her search for answers. She went to the door, cracking it open an inch or two.

"Hello." The girl on the opposite side was no more than sixteen or seventeen years old. Her appearance was at once innocent and carnal. "You must be Mrs. Malone."

"Aye." Mary opened the door a little farther.

"I'm Edith."

"Hello, Edith." She opened the door the rest of the way.

Edith's blue eyes, lined with black, turned toward Keary. "And this must be your son?"

"Aye."

She smiled. "I love babies. May I hold him?"

Mary hesitated, uncertain what to do. Although it was not yet five in the afternoon, Edith was dressed as if for bed, wearing a gauzy robe over what looked like a satin nightgown. Her hair, a lovely shade of gold, was pulled back from her face but hung loosely down her back in a cluster of ringlets. Her mouth was stained ruby red, and there were jeweled rings on several of her fingers.

"Please?" she said, meeting Mary's gaze again. "I won't hurt him. I've got six brothers and sisters of my own. All younger. I'll hold him while you get unpacked. That way, he won't be underfoot."

There was something touchingly painful about the girl and her plea, and Mary was unable to resist it. Wordlessly, she nodded.

Edith held out her arms to take Keary, smiling now. "I reckon you must be mighty tired after comin' all the way from New York City." She crossed the bedroom, carrying Mary's son with her, and settled on a straight-backed chair near the window. "This is one of Miss Blanche's best rooms, outside of her own, of course. Hers is almost like a house, all by itself. She's even got a private bathing room in there."

Edith stopped talking long enough to lift Keary over her head. He giggled as she lowered him quickly, then raised him up again, arms straight, elbows locked.

"You're gonna like workin' for Miss Blanche," she continued after a while. "She's got strict rules, but she's fair."

Mary frowned. "I'm thinking I'd like to know how long you've worked here."

"It'll be two years come July." The girl's pretty smile disappeared as she lowered Keary to her lap. "I had me a fella I was gonna marry. His name was Jack. But Pa didn't think much of him, and he told him to take his no-account self off our farm. Over in Montana, it was. Then I come up expectin'-like, so Pa told me to get out, too. Jack said he was gonna find work in the Idaho mines, so I came lookin'. Never did find him."

"And your baby?" Mary asked softly.

"She was stillborn."

"Faith, but 'tis sorry I am, Edith."

"I named her Ruth 'fore I buried her up on the hill there." The girl blinked away her tears and smiled at Keary once again. "I don't reckon it hurts so much now. Miss Blanche, she took me in, and she had the doctor see to me when the baby was comin'. He did everything he rightly could, but I don't guess she was meant to live. I couldn't've taken proper care of her, things being as they were."

Mary sat on the edge of the bed, anxiety forming a tight fist in her belly. The story sounded all too familiar. If circumstances had been a little different, her fate could have been the same as Edith's. "Did she...did Miss Blanche force you to work for her?"

"Glory, no!" Edith answered. "Miss Blanche never asked nothing of me."

"Then why..." She let her voice trail into silence.

"Why do I let men use me, you mean?" There was a hard edge in her voice that made her sound old beyond her years. "'Cause there ain't nothing else a girl like me can do to keep herself from starvin', that's why. I made a mistake. The kind there's no forgivin'. My own pa threw me out. Who else was gonna take me in? Men're gonna look at me as soiled goods whether I'm in a saloon or not, and respectable folks wouldn't give me the time of day, let alone give me work. You know what I mean?"

Mary thought of Master Kenrick. Somehow, he had found out about Keary, the son she'd borne out of wedlock. He'd thought that made his housemaid fair game. He'd thought Mary was soiled goods, as Edith put it. "Aye," she whispered. "I understand altogether."

"Miss Blanche, she's got real strict rules, like I said. She keeps us safe as she can. She's even had a fella or two arrested. And she don't hold the girls if they ever want to leave. Last year, Kitty got married to a farmer over near Spokane."

Mary rose from the bed and busied herself with unpacking her few belongings. Edith continued to chatter about the other girls and women who lived and worked at the Painted Queen, and about Lloyd the bartender, Mac the dealer, and Hank the hired man.

"Now, looky here. Ain't this pretty?"

Mary glanced over her shoulder. She felt the blood drain from her face when she saw what Edith held in her hand.

"Is it from Ireland?" the girl asked as she fingered the silver filigrees on the fancy box from Master Kenrick's study. "Is it a jewelry box?"

"No," Mary answered, sounding breathless. She reached out and took it from Edith. "No, 'tis not from Ireland, and 'tis not for jewels." Quickly, she tucked the offensive item in the back of a drawer.

Edith gave her a strange look, then continued with her prattle as if she'd never interrupted herself. "Can't say I know hardly any other folks in town. 'Cept some of the men, of course, and most of 'em that come in here work for the mines and don't have families to go home to." She shrugged. "We pretty much keep to ourselves at the Painted Queen. Let others come to us if they've a mind to."

Mary liked the idea of keeping to herself. It sounded safe.

Edith stood, balancing Keary on her hip as she stepped over close to the window, her gaze directed toward the street below. A smile curved her mouth. "Now if there was somebody in Whistle Creek I'd like to get to know better, that's him there."

Curiosity drew Mary to the window. Sheriff Barclay stood on the sidewalk opposite the saloon, talking to a man on horseback.

"I've never seen anybody more handsome than the sheriff," Edith concluded with a sigh. "Not even Jack."

Handsome? Mary hadn't noticed. She'd been too afraid to really look at him.

"He's got the bluest eyes I ever seen in all my born days," Edith went on.

The sheriff's face was shadowed by his black Stetson, but Mary remembered from the depot that he was a tall man, tall and lean and, she suspected, strong. He wore a set of pistols strapped to his thighs, like a gunslinger in a dime novel. She wondered how many men he'd shot.

"How often does he come to the Painted Queen?" she asked, afraid of the answer.

"Him?" Edith set Keary on his feet, then followed behind him as he toddled away. "Sheriff Barclay never comes here. Never drinks. Never visits the ladies. Never gambles." She laughed. "Well, he does have to come when there's trouble, so I guess he's here a few times a week."

The man on horseback rode away. Afterward, the sheriff tilted his head and looked straight toward Mary's window. Her breath caught in her throat, and a shiver ran through her. She took a step backward, hoping he hadn't seen her watching him. She didn't want to be noticed. Especially by the law.

"Something wrong, Mary?"

She turned, pretending a calm she didn't feel. "No. Nothing's wrong. But I am tired altogether. I'm thinking I'd like to lie down with Keary and see if we might sleep a wee bit before supper."

"'Course. I should've guessed. I'll leave you be." Edith moved toward the door. When she reached it, she glanced behind her. "But I hope you won't mind if I come to see Keary every now and again. It was real nice to hold him."

Mary nodded. "He'd like that, Edith. And I'm thinking so would I."

Carson saw someone move away from a third-floor window, and instinctively, he knew it was the Malone woman. But it was the lingering images of Aldora Barclay—not those of Mary Malone—that made anger boil in his chest, sudden and furious.

He turned on his heel and walked toward his office.

He didn't like remembering Aldora. His mother.

Mother? In a pig's eye. Even she hadn't let him call her that. She had always been Aldora.

Carson's earliest memory was of falling down the back stairway of the Golden Eagle Dance Hall in Idaho City. He'd been not quite four at the time. He still bore the scar from that fall. He touched the hairless spot in the center of his left eyebrow. He remembered one of the saloon girls, smelling of whiskey and cheap perfume, lifting him and carrying him upstairs to Aldora's room. He'd been crying. He remembered that, too, because it had made Aldora real mad. She'd hated to be bothered by the child she'd never wanted. She'd scolded him for crying, for not staying in his room, then she'd hauled him up another flight of stairs.

That was the first time Carson had been locked in the attic. It hadn't been the last.

He gave his head a brief shake, driving off the unwelcome memories as he opened the door to the sheriff's office. He walked through to the jail cells.

"John?"

His prisoner was lying on his right side, his back toward the cell door.

"John," Carson said, louder this time.

He groaned. "What?"

"I've got good news."

"Leave me be, Sheriff." John brought his left arm up, covering his ear and the top of his head. "Don't care about no good news."

"But you should." Carson put the key in the lock, turned it, and opened the door. "You're not going to have to stay in jail."

Slowly, John rolled over. He opened his eyes a fraction.

"You've got a job."

John groaned again. "A job?" He closed his eyes, as if the light of day hurt. "What sorta job?"

"Whatever Miss Blanche wants you to do, I reckon. You're going to be working over at the Painted Queen to pay off that mirror you busted. But first you need a bath and some fresh clothes. I'm taking you out to Wade's place so you can clean up."

"I'm not feelin' up to movin', Sheriff." He rolled onto his side again. "Maybe tomorrow."

Carson poked John in the ribs with an index finger. "Get up." When the young man didn't move, Carson took him by his left arm and gave a steady, firm pull. "Up, I said. Time's a-wastin'."

"You don't have no pity, Barclay."

"Yeah, well, you haven't got much sense."

John swore softly, but he didn't put up any more resistance. He allowed Carson to lead him from the cell and out through the office to the sidewalk. An hour ago, Carson had asked Abe Stover to hitch up a wagon so he could take John to his brother's farm. He found the buckboard waiting for them in the street.

"Get in," he told his prisoner. He waited behind him, in case John fell backward while maneuvering himself onto the seat. When the young man was safely in place, Carson went around to the other side and climbed aboard. As he picked up the reins, he said, "Listen close, John. If you don't work off this debt to Miss Blanche, you'll find yourself doing some serious time in jail. You've been in trouble before, but this time you could be sent down to the penitentiary in Boise."

John mumbled a nonsensical response.

Carson slapped the reins, and the buckboard jerked forward as the horse stepped out. "Miss Blanche is serious. You mess up, you dip into her liquor, you take something that's not yours, she'll have you locked up again in no time. How'd you like to be in one of those cells for years?"

There was a lengthy pause before John answered, "Wouldn't like it none."

"No, you wouldn't."

They traveled in silence for about fifteen minutes before the younger man spoke again. "How come you're so all-fired bent on helpin' me, Sheriff?"

"How old are you?"

"Twenty-two. . .I think. What year is it?"

Carson smiled without humor. "You're headed for real trouble, John. So was I once. But somebody stepped in and helped turn things around by showing me a better way. God didn't give up on me. I'm not giving up on you."

"Well, ain't that real Christian of you, helpin' the pitiful cripple." The words dripped with sarcasm. "You shoulda been a preacher man."

"You asked why I was doing it. I told you the truth."

"I need a drink."

Carson sighed. *Lord, how do I get through to him?*

He wondered if David Hailey had felt the same frustration, all those years ago. Carson had been a smart-mouthed kid, spoiling for a fight, looking for mischief, daring somebody— anybody—to do something nice for him.

A lot like John Tyrell, he reckoned.

As if reading Carson's thoughts, John said, "I don't want your help, y' know."

"Yeah, I know. But you're getting it, like it or not."

~ Four

Blanche frowned as she studied the ledgers in front of her. The story they told was worse than expected. The saloon had lost a considerable sum of money in the months she'd been back East. Could it be more than mere incompetence on Lloyd's part? She hated to think so. Lloyd Perkins had been with her for ten years. At one time, he'd been more to her than an employee.

A soft rap on the office door broke into her thoughts. "Come in," she said, looking up.

"Am I too early?" Mary asked when the door was open. She carried her son in her arms.

Blanche motioned her in. "'Course not. You're right on time. Close the door behind you." She waited until Mary took a chair on the opposite side of the desk, then asked, "Did you have breakfast?"

"Aye. Greta made us . . ." She frowned. "Now what was it she was calling them?"

"Flapjacks," Blanche offered with a chuckle. "They're what she does best. Greta's not a fancy cook, but she takes good care of the girls and me. Makes sure none of us go hungry, at any rate." She glanced at Keary. "How'd you and the boy sleep?"

"'Twas a wee bit noisy, don't ya know."

Blanche smiled. "You'll get used to it. Everyone does. Late hours come with the territory."

There was no return smile as Mary replied, "I'm thinking a body can get used to many things when forced to. Often as not, there's little enough choice in the matter."

Blanche leaned back in her chair, wondering about Mary's cryptic words. She had learned surprisingly few facts about the pretty Irishwoman in their days of travel together, other than that Mary was bright and had received some schooling, enough to read, write, and do sums. Yet Blanche believed she understood things about the younger woman that were far more important. Mary had walked side by side with trouble, Blanche was sure of it, yet she hadn't given into despair. She'd stayed strong. Perhaps most telling of all was the way Mary was devoted to her son.

"Mary...," Blanche began slowly, "I figure you know that I'm dying."

"Aye."

She rose from her chair and walked to the window. "I don't want the girls here to know. Not yet anyway. They'll guess soon enough."

"Aye."

Blanche's first-floor office at the rear corner of the saloon had a view of the railroad tracks, set about a hundred feet away. Beyond the tracks flowed the South Fork of the Coeur d'Alene River, and beyond the river were the mountains, their slopes garbed in pines and aspens. Beautiful beyond words. No denying this country was a whole sight prettier than New York City with its millions of people and tall buildings.

"I was right attractive when I was young like you," she said without looking behind her, feeling the need to talk, to explain, to be understood. "Even had me a fella of my own once. I was mighty bitter when he up and married someone else. A woman with more money and more class. I swore then that I'd never marry, and I didn't. I swore I'd never trust another man, not as long as I lived. Guess I kept that oath, too." She turned, waved her arm in an arc. "I built the Painted Queen, built this business, to take back from men what I thought they'd taken from me. Now that my time's short, I'm finding bitterness is cold company. I'm all alone."

"Sure and you're not alone. You have everyone here—"

"Honey, they aren't here because they love me." Blanche said it flippantly, but she was surprised how much it hurt to admit it. The urge to open up to Mary vanished. She returned to her desk and shoved the ledgers toward her newest employee. "Look these over. We've been losing money pretty fast while I was away. I want to know why. I have my own suspicions, but I want to know what you think. Can you do that?"

"Aye, I'll be doing me best."

"Good." Jerking her head toward Keary, she added, "You can fix a little play area for him in the corner if you want. Put some toys in here and whatever."

"Thank you."

"I'll leave you to your work." She picked up Nugget, who'd been lying in his bed beside the desk, and headed for the office door.

"Miss Blanche?"

She stopped, turned, met Mary's gaze.

"I'm hoping you know I mean that altogether. Me thanks, that is. For more than just saying I can bring toys into your office here. I fancy others have known your kindness, too, and are grateful for it. But none more than me." She offered a hesitant smile. "I'll be proving it the best I can."

Blanche had the awful feeling she was about to cry. "Just find out why I'm not making money the way I usually do. That's all the thanks I want from you."

With her dignity wrapped around her like a protective robe, she left the office.

—

Carson ate his breakfast at the Whistler Café, just as he did every day of the week except Sundays, when the restaurant was closed. Nobody rustled up eggs and bacon like Zeb Brewer, both chef and owner of the café, and his flapjacks were lighter than air.

The dining room was busy, filled with the usual breakfast crowd. Quite a few of the miners came here to eat on their days off. The Lucky Lady Mine employed over three hundred men. Most of them lived in the shacks the company had thrown up years ago. During their workweek, they ate at the company restaurant when they didn't cook for themselves, and they bought their supplies at the company store. But on their days off, you could count on many of them making their way into town. They ate at the Whistler Café and shopped at Chuck's Mercantile, and they gambled and caroused at the Painted Queen. Without the miners and their hard-earned wages, Whistle Creek would dry up and become another ghost town.

Carson only half listened to the conversations going on around him. His thoughts were elsewhere. He was thinking about John Tyrell, wondering how the angry young man was doing. John had been in a dour mood yesterday when Carson left him in Blanche's office. For all he knew, John had bolted and wasn't even there. There was no telling what bitterness, anger, and the want of drink might cause a fellow to do.

Carson pushed his empty plate back from the edge of the table, rose from his chair, and reached into his pocket for some money. He dropped the necessary coins beside his plate. "Thanks, Zeb."

"Sure thing, Sheriff. See ya later."

At the door, Carson retrieved his black Stetson from a peg on the wall. Once outside, he turned left and followed the sidewalk past the boardinghouse and to the door of the sheriff's office. He paused there, then changed his mind. He'd better check on John, or he'd just go on wondering about him the rest of the morning.

A few minutes later, he stepped through the front entrance of the Painted Queen. Lloyd was alone in the saloon, wiping the bar with a damp cloth. There was no sign of John. Mac, of course, would be sleeping in; card dealers, like the girls who lived upstairs, did most of their work at night.

"Mornin', Sheriff," Lloyd called to him.

"Mornin', Lloyd. Miss Blanche around?"

"In her office. Go on back. You know how to find it."

"Thanks."

Carson wound his way through the card tables that cluttered the spacious room and past the sweeping staircase with its plush red carpet and the small stage where some of the girls sang and danced nightly for the customers. In the center of the back wall was a door, camouflaged with red and black wallpaper. Even the latch was inconspicuous, but Carson knew where it was. He lifted it and opened the door.

The hallway was narrow and dark, but he didn't need light to find the way. He'd had more than a few meetings with Blanche Loraine in her office since he'd become sheriff of Whistle Creek back in ninety-two.

Blanche's office was located near the back stairs. Unlike the grand staircase in the main saloon, there was nothing sweeping about the narrow flight of steps used by the owner and residents of the Painted Queen.

Carson rapped on the door with his right hand while already opening it with his left. "Miss Blanche, I—" He stopped suddenly as Mary Malone shot up from the chair behind the desk.

Her eyes—dark as ground coffee beans—were wide with alarm as she stared at him. Then she glanced over her left shoulder toward the corner where her little boy was playing with some blocks of wood. As her gaze returned to Carson, she stepped sideways until she stood between him and the child.

"You'll not be finding Miss Blanche here." There was a slight quiver in her voice, but also a hint of defiance in the way she held herself.

"Do you know where she is?"

"Sure and I couldn't be saying."

Carson had never before found an Irish accent so appealing. The lilt in her words seemed musical. Unconsciously, he took a step closer to her. Mary let out a soft gasp and took a corresponding step backward.

He frowned, wondering if she was hiding something. He glanced toward the desk. "What are you doing in here?"

She didn't answer.

He looked at her again. Even dressed as simply as she was in a gray muslin gown, her face devoid of any rouge or powder, her thick hair swept into a smooth bun at the nape, she had a natural, earthy appeal that transcended mere beauty. It was almost perfection.

He pulled his thoughts up short, then forced himself to remember who and what she was. Perfection? No, she was just another fallen woman raising a neglected child in a saloon, and he should remember that.

"I asked what you're doing in here," he said, his voice harsh as he shoved away unwelcome memories from his own childhood.

He could see she was afraid of him, but she didn't back down. She stood her ground. He had to give her that.

"I'll be doing the work Miss Blanche gave me to do." Her chin lifted a notch. "If it be any concern of yours, sir."

"Mary is right, Sheriff," Blanche said from the doorway. "It isn't any of your concern."

He turned around.

"Is this what you do in your spare time?" the madam asked with a raised eyebrow. "Badger my employees?"

"I thought—"

"I know what you thought," she interrupted.

From the look in her eye, he was afraid she did know what he'd been thinking.

"Well, if it was any of your business, Sheriff, I'd remind you I've employed Mrs. Malone to see to my bookkeeping. I told you so before."

Carson turned toward Mary once again. Bookkeeping?

Mary blushed scarlet, but there was anger in her eyes, her fear of him apparently forgotten. "And you'd be thinking I'm not smart enough for bookkeeping, would ya now?"

"No, I—"

"Is it because I'm Irish that you feel this way, or because I'm a woman? I'm thinking that either reason would make you a fool, Sheriff Barclay."

Carson was saved from the need to reply by the child's sudden wail, brought on, no doubt, by his mother's raised voice. Mary immediately turned and whisked the little boy into her arms, murmuring words of comfort while keeping her back toward Carson and Blanche.

The madam chuckled as she entered the office and walked to her desk. When she looked at him again, she smiled and said, "I think Mrs. Malone put that quite well. Don't you, Sheriff Barclay?"

For her part, Mary thought she'd said far too much. She couldn't believe she'd actually challenged the sheriff. Whatever had possessed her to shout at him? The law, of all men.

Sure and it was her temper that had always been her undoing.

What am I goin' t' do with you, Mary Emeline? It was as if she could hear her dear departed mother's gentle scolding. *Will ya be fightin' like your fool brothers all your life, then? Why don't you use the sense God gave you? I'm thinkin' that'd be the better way altogether.*

Mary realized Keary had stopped his fussing and the room had grown silent. Drawing a deep breath, she turned toward Blanche and the sheriff.

Carson removed his hat, then with one hand smoothed back his thick brown hair, hair streaked with gold, as if kissed by the sun. "I owe you an apology, Mrs. Malone."

Edith was right. He did have the bluest eyes Mary had ever seen. Strange she hadn't noticed them before. And those blue eyes seemed capable of staring right into her most secret thoughts.

"'Tis sorry I am, too," she whispered.

For a breathless moment, their gazes held. Mary couldn't have looked away to save her soul. As the seconds passed, she felt a shiver—something akin to fear but very different at the same time—run up her spine.

It was the sheriff who broke the glance. "Miss Blanche, I came to ask about John."

Mary drew a breath at last, the odd spell broken. Without a word, she headed for the door, desperate to escape.

Blanche's voice stopped her. "You needn't go, Mary."

She sighed inwardly, then turned. She avoided looking at Carson. "'Tis a breath of fresh air we'd be needing, mum. I'm thinking the lad might sleep a wee bit after."

"All right. Come back to the office when you're finished with your walk. Keary can nap on my sofa. And Mary, stay within sight of the saloon. You're a stranger here. This town's got a few bad apples like any other."

Mary nodded, then left the office. She was reminded of the forced composure she'd worn the day she fled the Kenrick mansion. She'd felt anything but serene then, and it was the same now.

Sheriff Barclay was a threat to everything she held dear—her son, her very freedom. He didn't like her, didn't trust her. For that alone, he would watch her more closely. But there was something else about the way he looked at her, something about the way she responded inside herself to that look, that disturbed her most of all.

Mary followed a path to the river and made her way across on the bridge. Once on the opposite side, she carried Keary a safe distance from the water, then put the boy down in the long yellow-green grass. He giggled in delight.

"Oh, Keary," she whispered as she sank to the ground beside him. "Whatever will become of you if I'm found out? I swore I'd give you the life you deserve, and see what it is I've done, then."

She thought of the sheriff's blue eyes, of the way they'd held her captive. What if he could see into her soul? What if he guessed what she'd done? She would hang for it, and then what would become of Keary?

'Tis a man who is his own ruin, Fagan Malone used to say to his sons and daughter. *'Tis a wedge from itself that splits the oak tree.*

"Aye, Da," she replied, as if he'd spoken to her now, "I'll be keeping meself far from the sheriff. That I will."

⸻

Portia Pendergast Kenrick was not a foolish woman. She knew her husband did not love her. She did not pretend he had ever loved her. She knew Winston had married the plain, plump spinster for the Pendergast fortune just as Portia had married a feckless man ten years younger than herself for his good looks and the society doors the Kenrick name could open for her.

She also knew Winston had never been a faithful husband. His conquests had ranged from other society matrons to scullery maids in her and Winston's several residences. But, to his credit, he'd had the good sense to be discreet in his many dalliances. He had certainly never flaunted them before his wife. Of course, Portia was wise enough to keep Winston on a rather short leash all these years, an easy enough task when she and she alone controlled the purse strings to the wealth of Pendergast Industries. Knowing his wife could cut him off without a penny had kept Winston from being careless.

Twenty-four years after Portia and Winston had wed, she thought her husband was still a handsome man. As he aged, he seemed to grow more distinguished in appearance. She rather liked the tiny lines at the corners of his eyes and mouth. She approved of the mustache he'd grown more than fifteen years before, and she was especially fond of his silver-gray hair.

But she couldn't see his silver hair now. Not with his head wrapped in white bandages.

"We should allow the police to handle the matter, Winston." She sat on a chair beside his bed, watching as he sipped tea from one of her prized china cups.

"No!" He winced, jostling tea into the saucer, then closed his eyes. More softly, he continued, "This is a matter of pride, my dear. The girl didn't just strike me. She stole the only thing of sentimental value I have from my father."

Portia raised an eyebrow. Winston was not, nor had he ever been, a sentimental man. However, the ornate cigar box, finely crafted in silver, had sat on his desk throughout their marriage. She supposed there could be a grain of truth in what he said.

"I've hired a private investigator to help in the search," Winston continued, teeth clenched. "I will find the girl, and she will pay for this."

Portia sighed. "I rather liked Mary. She worked hard, and she never caused a moment of trouble."

"I told you we shouldn't hire Irish. You can't trust them. They're all thieves."

"Yes, you've said that, Winston." She rose from the chair, leaned over, and kissed his forehead. "But we would have less trouble with our Irish housemaids if you weren't so intent on getting into their skirts."

She smiled as she took the teacup and saucer from his hands, then left his bedchamber without another word.

～ Five

Sunday, 24 July 1898
Whistle Creek, Idaho

Dear Inga,

As you will be seeing from this post, Keary and I have left New York, and there is no sorrow in the telling of it. We traveled far across the country to Idaho, and I found employment with a woman named Blanche Loraine. Miss Blanche, as she is known, has enjoyed much success, but I cannot say everyone in this town is holding her in as high regard as I do.

It is not within me to be telling you the reason for our leaving New York City. I can only say it was a dark day that forced our going. My da always said it is well misfortunes come one by one and not all together, and to that, I would add my own amen.

Be that as it may, Keary and I are here, and I am thinking I will do well in Whistle Creek. For that I owe thanks to my mother's insistence that I study my numbers and letters. The truth is, I am not working as a housemaid as I have been doing in the past. It is a bookkeeper I am. Fancy that, would you now.

Keary and I attended the local church this morning. It was nothing like our long Presbyterian services in Ireland nor much like those in New York City, for that matter. The minister comes to Whistle Creek but once a month, this being only one of the churches he ministers to. Today it was the gentleman who owns the mercantile, Mr. Adams, who led the worship service. I cannot say I was sorry when it was over. Mr. Adams is not what I would call a stirring speaker.

Until this morning, I had met only the men and women who work for Miss Blanche in her business. Oh, and the sheriff of Whistle Creek. I have made his acquaintance, too. Sheriff Barclay is a handsome man, much taller than Seamus Maguire, but none too friendly. Which is not of great concern to me as I am content to keep to myself and have no interest in him at all.

It is the letters I receive from you and Beth, my dearest friends, that mean the most to me, so I beg you to write to me here in Idaho. I have kept all the letters you both have written since we arrived in America. I often take them out and read them again, trying to picture your life with Mr. Bridger and Beth's with Mr. Steele.

Today being my day of rest, I have decided to take Keary on a picnic. The town is surrounded by beautiful mountains, and today I mean to be doing some exploring in them.

From your affectionate friend,
Mary Emeline Malone

Carson let the dun gelding have his head. Cinnabar knew his way up the narrow trail. The two of them traveled it every Sunday afternoon during good weather. A quarter mile or so up the trail was Carson's cabin. He hadn't lived in it for several years, preferring to stay in the room above the jail so he would be close when needed in town. Still, he liked knowing the log house was there.

But he wasn't thinking about his destination as he rode. He was thinking about Mary Malone.

She'd come to Sunday services this morning. Carson couldn't remember ever feeling so much tension in church before. Heads craning. Furtive whispers. Unspoken indignation.

Gossip traveled fast in a small town. Everyone knew the Malone woman had come to Whistle Creek with the infamous madam, that Mary and her baby were living at the Painted Queen, that Mary was working there. The good people who attended the Methodist church knew what sort of work went on in that den of iniquity.

Carson figured it was only because they'd been so shocked that no one had gone over and demanded Mary leave. No, not shocked. Aghast and appalled. After all, none of Miss Blanche's girls had ever before entered the Whistle Creek Methodist Church, let alone sat down and participated in the worship service.

Carson hadn't paid much attention to Chuck Adams's dull preaching. He'd been too aware of Mary, sitting two pews behind him, and of the growing outrage of the parishioners. He'd felt the urge to tell them that she was the bookkeeper at the Painted Queen, but even if he had, no one would have believed it. He wasn't sure *he* believed it. Besides, even if it was true, she still lived in that saloon, she still exposed her son to everything that went on there. What sort of mother did that?

His jaw tightened reflexively at the thought. He knew what sort of mother did that.

Ain't he cute, Harrison? He may be just a little by-blow, but even I've got to admit, he's cute. All right, Car. Get on outta here now. You can see Aldora's got company. Find yourself something to do and stay outta trouble.

Stay out of trouble...

That hadn't been easy for a kid who didn't have a father, a kid who didn't have a last name to call his own, a kid who lived in a saloon instead of a house like the other kids. When Carson was in school, he'd gotten into a fight with somebody at least once a week. Aldora hadn't cared about the fighting, as long as he didn't come home sniveling or bleeding all over her nice things. What she'd meant was for him to stay out of her way, for him not to cause her any trouble.

He shook off the disturbing memories as the trail suddenly spilled into a small round valley. Near the clear-running stream cutting through the heart of the meadowland stood the log cabin Carson had built with his own hands back in the fall of ninety-two, before the first snows fell.

And seated on the grassy bank of the stream, not far from the house, was Mary Malone, her son in her arms. Her head was tipped to one side and forward as she stared down at Keary. Even from this distance, Carson could see the look of tender devotion on her face. There was a poignancy about the sight of mother and child that went straight to Carson's typically cynical heart.

He reined in, stopping his gelding. At the same moment, Mary noticed him. She quickly grabbed a small blanket and tossed it over both the child and her shoulder, holding Keary protectively against her.

Carson clucked at his horse and rode toward the woman who had intruded on his private valley.

Mary's face was flushed, her eyes downcast. As he drew closer, he could sense her discomfort. Perversely, he was pleased if he'd caused her to be flustered. It was nothing less than what she'd done to him ever since her arrival in Whistle Creek.

"Afternoon, Mrs. Malone," he said as he stopped his horse a second time.

She didn't look up. "Good afternoon, sir." She barely whispered the greeting as more heat flared in her cheeks.

"What brings you to my little valley?"

"'Tis yours?"

"Yeah." He dismounted, then stood near the dun's head. "I built that cabin when I first came to Whistle Creek."

"'Tis a fine house. But I did not go in." Finally, she lifted her eyes to meet his. "I swear to you, on me ma's grave, that I was not trespassing in your house."

Carson experienced a twinge of guilt. "Wouldn't have mattered if you did. Nothing much there."

Keary shoved at the blanket covering him, and Mary quickly turned her back toward Carson. It was only then that he realized she'd been nursing the child, and it was his turn to feel embarrassed.

While Mary closed the buttons of her bodice, Keary made his way toward Carson, his steps uncertain on the uneven turf. His eyes were wide with curiosity, and he was grinning.

"Faith and begorra," Mary muttered as she started to rise but was impeded by her tangle of skirts and petticoats. "Keary, come back here."

Instead of stopping at his mother's command, the little boy giggled and tried to walk faster. He stumbled and pitched forward at Carson's feet. Instinctively, Carson reached for him.

"Hello there, little man. Moving too fast for your legs, huh?"

Keary's grin disappeared, but he didn't seem to be afraid of the stranger holding him. Instead, the boy studied Carson with solemn brown eyes, as if not quite sure what to make of him.

"Here," Mary said as she hurried toward Carson. "Here. I'll be taking him now."

Carson frowned as he moved his gaze from son to mother. "I wasn't going to hurt him."

"Please, sir." Her voice was fearful. Her eyes beseeched him. She held out her arms in a desperate gesture. "Let me be having me son, and we'll be on our way. I was never meaning to trespass on your land."

Keary patted Carson's cheek with his right hand and giggled again. Carson glanced at the tyke and smiled in response to the boy's grin.

"Please, sir. I'm begging you."

"You don't have to beg, Mrs. Malone," he answered sharply, irritated by her choice of words. He passed the child into her waiting arms.

But his irritation vanished when he saw the stark relief on her lovely face. There was no doubting she loved her son. Whatever else he might think about her, he couldn't charge her with lack of motherly love.

He took a deep breath, then said, "You don't have to run off either. You weren't trespassing." He noticed the basket and the food set on a cloth. "Looks like you were having a picnic."

"Aye."

"Then maybe you'd let me join you, Mrs. Malone?"

"I'm thinking you shouldn't be seen with the likes o' me. 'Twould only cause more talk." She turned and walked toward her basket and picnic lunch.

So she hadn't been oblivious to the stares and whispers in church.

"Mrs. Malone, now I'm inviting you. Please stay. I wouldn't mind some company. And, if you've got any to spare, I'd like some of that cheese and bread I see there."

He figured she couldn't be any more surprised by his words than he was. He didn't know why he wanted her to stay. He just knew that he did.

Mary pondered the sheriff's request. It would be a foolish thing to do, and she knew it. The law could even now be looking for her. Even with three thousand miles between her and the Kenrick home, she wasn't completely safe. Not when the man she'd killed was as wealthy and powerful as Winston Kenrick. She should stay as far away from Carson as she could possibly get. The less she was known, the less she was seen, then the less likely she was to be discovered.

She turned to face him, intending to bid him a polite but firm good afternoon before taking her leave. But the words died in her throat.

Carson had removed his hat and was watching her with those startling blue eyes of his. She felt the uncomfortable urge to touch his cheek just as her son had done moments before, if only to see if it was rough or smooth.

"I'm supposing it wouldn't hurt to share a bite to eat with you, Sheriff," she said softly.

"Thank you." He led his horse to a nearby maple and looped the reins over a limb.

Keary squirmed in her arms, eager to be on the ground and exploring. Mary obliged.

It amazed her, watching her son as he tottered on his chubby little legs, how quickly he had gone from crawling to walking. But then he was always growing and changing. It seemed only yesterday that he'd been a wee babe in her arms, just under five pounds, and the doctor thinking he wouldn't live out the week. Now he was getting too heavy to carry for long, and a healthier lad Mary couldn't imagine.

"How old is he?" Carson asked as he stepped up beside her.

"Almost a year, just," she answered, her gaze still on her adventurous son. Keary was giving a yellow wildflower a close inspection.

"He looks like you, Mrs. Malone."

"Aye, there's little of his father in him." *And thanks be to God for that small blessing,* she thought.

"When did you lose your husband?"

My husband. She glanced sideways at the sheriff. To him and everyone else in Whistle Creek, she was Mrs. Malone. One more lie added to her list of many sins. She tried not to add to it. "His da was killed in the coal mines of West Virginia." That, at least, was the truth.

"I'm sorry."

She acknowledged his sympathy with a nod. "The worst of the hurt is over, and 'twould change nothing to dwell on it."

It was true. The worst was over. And besides, the pain of Seamus Maguire's death had been nothing compared to learning of his death from his American wife. Seamus had convinced Mary that to marry in America would be better, but to wait to share the warmth and comfort of each other's bodies was unnecessary. Aye, he'd been a smooth talker, Seamus Maguire. So he'd taken her to his bed while promising a better life in America. Then he'd sailed away with never any intention of sending for her, although she knew it not. If Seamus hadn't left her pregnant, Mary would still be in England, wondering why she'd never heard from him again. She wouldn't have known he'd played her for the fool she was and betrayed her heart in the bargain.

"You're lucky to have your son."

Brought back from the grim memories, Mary said, "Aye, I am that."

She went after Keary as he toddled closer to the gurgling brook. When she turned around, she found Carson reclining on the grass near her basket, his long legs stretched before him, his elbows supporting his torso. His black felt hat lay on the ground near his feet. He made an altogether disturbing picture. Too relaxed. Too handsome. Too...male.

As if she'd again be fool enough to fall for a man's charms!

"Mind if I just help myself?" he asked.

"No, sir."

Carson sat up, then cut off a chunk of cheese with a knife she'd brought with her. "I sure wish you'd quit calling me sir. Makes me feel like an old man."

"What would you have me be calling you, then?"

"How about Carson?"

She stiffened. "I'm thinking that would be too familiar altogether, sir."

"Then I suppose Sheriff Barclay will have to do."

Mary didn't like that much better. It would be a constant reminder of his office and what it could mean to her freedom. Still, there seemed nothing else to do except agree with him. "Aye, that will do."

"Tell me, Mrs. Malone, why'd you come to Whistle Creek? I mean, besides because Miss Blanche offered you a job at the Painted Queen."

She almost told him she hoped to find her brother here, then came to her senses before she spoke. The less Sheriff Barclay knew about her, she realized, the better it would be. The better and the safer.

She gave her shoulders a careless shrug. "Fate, I'm thinking. Nothing more."

He didn't reply. In fact, he seemed to be waiting for her to continue. There was something about the way his eyes watched her that made it difficult not to tell him whatever he wanted to know.

In order to resist the urge, she said, "Tell me something about the mine. Are there many who work there?"

"Yeah." He cut himself another chunk of cheese. "The Lucky Lady's got about three hundred or so miners. 'Course, there's bigger operations up here in the Panhandle. These hills are full of gold and silver and other ores. There must be thousands of miners in these parts."

Thousands? How was she to find Quaid when she was afraid to ask help of anyone?

Carson continued, "I guess if your husband was a coal miner, you've lived around mines before."

"No. In England, me husband"—the lie was becoming easier to tell—"worked in the stables, though he'd done some mining before I left Ireland and joined him there."

She was distracted by Keary again, this time as he scurried toward the sheriff's horse, arms flapping at his sides for balance. She ran after him, catching him beneath his arms and whirling him around in the air.

"Sure and 'tis into mischief you are, Keary Maguire Malone."

After she stopped and put him back on his feet, facing away from the horse, she glanced in Carson's direction. He was standing again. Standing and watching her with that piercing gaze of his. She was held captive by the look, afraid to move or even to breathe.

Finally, he said, "You're a riddle, Mrs. Malone."

"I wouldn't be knowing what you mean, sir."

He stepped toward her, hat in hand. "I mean, you're not the sort of woman who should be working in a place like the Painted Queen. That's not the proper place to raise a child, and you must know it."

Her temper flared. "Would you be saying I'm not a good mother, then? For I'll have you know there's nothing I wouldn't do for me Keary." *Even murder,* she finished silently.

"No," he said, his voice deep and low, "that's not what I'm saying. I can see you're a good mother. That's why I said you're a riddle."

Her heart was racing. She felt starved for air. Fear tangled with anger. She didn't know what to say to him. He frightened her, yet there was something that made her want to draw closer to him, made her want...made her want...

"I'm thinking I'd better be getting back to town. Good day to you, Sheriff."

Mary grabbed her son, balancing him on one hip while she hastily retrieved the remainder of her picnic, dropping food and cloth into the basket. Then, without another glance in the sheriff's direction, she walked away with as much dignity as she could muster.

~Six

Mary's escape from New York had seemed nothing short of miraculous, but she feared the miracle hadn't included the ability to keep the records of a saloon. No matter what she tried, she couldn't make the figures in the Painted Queen ledgers add up. Her da had once said his only daughter had more brains and good sense than all his sons put together. At the time, she'd taken enormous pride in the compliment. But now she felt nothing short of daft.

She rose and arched her back, stretching the taut muscles in her shoulders and neck. Then she glanced toward the corner where, moments before, Keary had been playing with pots from the kitchen. He was fast asleep on the floor.

"And isn't that always the way of it?" Mary whispered, thinking how wonderful it must be to fall asleep so easily. But Keary was a mere infant, free from guilt, while Mary had much to feel guilty about.

Last night before bed, feeling lost and more than a little lonely, she'd searched through her meager belongings for an old photograph of her parents and brothers. She'd needed a glimpse of a happier time, a time when she was still innocent and carefree. Instead of the photograph, her fingers had touched the ornate silver box she'd taken from Winston Kenrick's office.

Why did I keep it all this time? she wondered now.

She walked to the window and stared through the glass without really seeing.

Why don't I throw it away?

She'd awakened twice in the night, her nightgown damp with perspiration, her nightmares lingering even in wakefulness. They lingered still.

Laughter filtered through the window and into her dark thoughts, returning her to the present. A moment later, Edith came into view, soon followed by John.

Youthful joy brightened Edith's face as she turned to face her pursuer. She said something to John. He blushed scarlet. She touched his useless right arm, her expression suddenly sober. He flinched as if she'd slapped him, but she didn't let him pull away. Instead, she stepped closer, rose on tiptoe, and kissed him full on the mouth. John stood as stiff as a board.

Even from here, Mary could feel the young man's pain. She thought she understood the shame he felt. Her heart ached for him. Perhaps Edith could help him find happiness.

She turned from the window. It felt wrong to be watching the two young people, even unobtrusively.

As she returned to the desk, Mary thought of Sheriff Barclay. He had cared enough about John to try to help him. It would seem the sheriff was a kind man, not given to abusing the authority he had by virtue of his badge.

But the image that came suddenly to mind was of the Carson she'd seen yesterday. She pictured him in that meadow near the stream and the log house. She pictured him reclining on the grassy ground, leaning on his elbows, his legs stretched before him, his head bare and his hair mussed from the black hat he usually wore.

That memory was more disturbing than her nightmares had been.

As she regained her seat behind the desk, the office door opened and Blanche stepped into the room, carrying an armload of colorful gowns. She smiled as their gazes met.

"I've a surprise for you, Mary."

"A surprise?"

"Yes. I've decided to take stock of all of my possessions, and it seems I have more gowns than any ten women could possibly use. I thought some of these might do well for you. They would have to be altered, of course." Blanche laid them, one by one, over the back of the sofa.

Mary stared at the gowns—made from silk, satin, linen, crepe de chine, and velvet—and shook her head. "Faith but I'd never be able to wear anything so fine as those."

"Why not?"

"Because I...Well, I just couldn't, mum."

"Aha. It's because you don't think you're good enough. Is that it? It certainly isn't because they're not appropriately modest. Look at these high necklines. No, you think because you were a maid, always taking care of some English lady and her fancy clothes, that you're not good enough to wear the same things." Blanche picked up a deep blue satin gown with puffed sleeves and all sorts of draping around the skirt. "Well, you can put such nonsense out of that pretty little head of yours. It's... what do the Irish call it?"

"Blarney?"

Blanche grinned. "That's it! It's blarney."

Mary couldn't help smiling in return. "'Tis kind you are to me altogether, Miss Blanche, and I thank you for the offer. But I'm thinking I shouldn't be taking your gowns. They're too fine to be worn while I sit in this office, scribbling in your books. Who's to see what I'm wearing but me son? And he cares not at all."

"Where is it written you can't look nice while you do the most wearisome tasks?" Blanche's smile vanished. "You're pretty and you're young, Mary. Grab every minute you can. You don't know how many days are left to you. None of us do."

The last of Mary's objections died unspoken. She hadn't the heart to refuse. The woman had been too kind for Mary not to repay her in any way she could.

"If it means so much to you, mum," she replied as she took the shimmery blue gown from Blanche's hands.

"Try it on and let's see how much it'll have to be taken in. I used to weigh a good deal more than I do now, and I'm at least three inches taller than you. But Mrs. Wooster is an excellent seamstress. She's got the dress and millinery shop next door to the mercantile. I expect you met her at church. She'll be able to make it fit in no time."

Mary ran the fingers of one hand lightly over the fabric, feeling the rich texture of it. "'Tis truly too fine."

Blanche cupped Mary's chin in her right hand, tilting her face upward so their gazes would meet again. "My dear Mary Malone, let me tell you how different things appear when you're looking back on life instead of forward. The world is great for trying to make some folks feel better about themselves than those they're trying to keep down. Don't believe it, honey." She paused and lowered her hand, then gave her head a slow shake. "You've got just as much right to wear fancy clothes as the next woman. No more and no less."

As if disturbed by her torrent of words, Blanche moved away from Mary. She pretended to look through the other dresses on the sofa.

Mary heard a sound that was suspiciously similar to a sniff. She decided to change the subject. "Would you be ready to hear what I've found in your ledgers?"

Blanche sniffed again, then faced Mary. "Naturally."

"I'd have you be knowing I'm not able to make the entries balance. 'Tis possible Mr. Perkins will be able to help me understand them."

"Show me."

Mary carefully laid the satin gown aside, and the two women turned their attention to ledger entries made by Lloyd Perkins.

———

The chair squeaked noisily as Carson leaned back and put his feet on the desk. Showing a nonchalance he didn't feel, he laced his fingers together behind his head. "What brings you over from Spokane, Halligan?" He knew the answer wouldn't be good.

Standing in front of the sheriff's desk, Bryan Halligan looked every inch the wealthy mine owner, from the cut of his expensive suit to the gold watch and fob in his vest. He was as tall as Carson, but he weighed forty or fifty pounds more. A man in his thirties, Halligan sported a close-trimmed beard and mustache, sprinkled with gray now, like what was left of the hair on his head.

"There have been rumors of trouble at the mine," he answered. "I'd like you to look into it."

"Seems to me last time there was trouble at the Lucky Lady, you told me to stay out of it."

Halligan cleared his throat. "Perhaps I was a bit hasty. But we did handle that. This is different."

"Different how?" Carson slid his feet off the desk and sat up straight, ready to take the matter seriously.

"There have been threats to blow up some of the tunnels."

"Why?"

Halligan waved his hand in dismissal. "The usual complaints. Equipment. Wages. Work hours. You know these miners. They'll grumble about anything. Most of them are immigrants. Irish. Swedes. You know."

Yeah, he knew. He knew that Halligan kept as much money as he could for himself and his partners and put little of the profits into mine safety, let alone into decent wages or decent equipment or decent housing.

"I was hoping you might visit the mine, talk with the men there, see if you can figure out what they're planning. You've got a good reputation with them. They trust you. They treat you like you're almost one of them."

Carson briefly recalled the one time he'd gone down in a mine. That had been in Silver City many years ago. He remembered all too well the unbelievable heat. The lower he'd gone, the hotter it got, and he'd understood why hard rock miners stripped to their trousers and boots before riding the elevator cage down at the start of their shifts.

There had been nothing good about that experience. Only absolute darkness such as he'd never seen before or since and an endless maze of narrow tunnels and stopes. It had been his worst nightmare come true—ten times worse than Aldora's attic—and Carson had sworn he would never go down in a mine again. Not for any reason. Not even to save his soul. He'd kept that oath to this day.

Meeting Halligan's gaze once more, he said, "I don't plan on ruining their trust by spying on them." He rose to his feet. "But I'll do what it takes to maintain order in this town. I'll find out what I can."

"I knew I could count on you, Sheriff Barclay. I don't need to tell you what that mine means to the people of Whistle Creek. Without it, this place wouldn't exist."

It was a threat of sorts, and Carson didn't take to threats, especially from Halligan. He was about to say so when the door opened, and Blanche Loraine swept into the office, bringing a reluctant-looking Mary along with her. They came to an abrupt halt when Blanche saw Halligan.

"Afternoon, Miss Blanche," Carson said even as he took note of the way her eyes narrowed in dislike at the sight of the mine owner.

Halligan, on the other hand, was wearing a much different sort of expression as he stared at Mary. "Yes, good day, Miss Blanche." A blind man could have seen he was waiting for an introduction.

Blanche ignored him. "Sheriff Barclay, I must speak with you about a matter of some importance. I'll come back when you're free."

"It's all right. Mr. Halligan was just leaving. Our business is finished."

Halligan stepped toward the door—and Mary. "Yes, I was leaving. But I cannot do so until I meet this charming young woman."

"This is Mrs. Malone, my bookkeeper."

"Your bookkeeper?" Halligan took hold of Mary's hand and raised it to his lips. "Well, Mrs. Malone, I'm delighted to meet you."

Carson decided it would be a poor example of keeping the peace if he were to knock Halligan's head against the wall a half-dozen times.

"And since no one seems inclined to make the proper introductions for us," the man continued, leaning closer to Mary, "I'm Bryan Halligan, one of the owners of the Lucky Lady Mine. Does your husband work there, Mrs. Malone?"

"'Tis just me and me son, Mr. Halligan."

He smiled. "Ah. A shame. Well, perhaps I'll find more reasons to visit Whistle Creek now that you're here." With a jaunty motion, he placed his hat on his balding head and left.

As soon as the door closed, Blanche said, "You stay away from him, Mary. He's bad news."

But Mary didn't need to be told that. She'd once known a man who'd had the same soulless eyes as this Halligan. In fact, she'd killed him.

The memory of that horrible morning in Winston Kenrick's office washed over her unexpectedly. Her knees felt like rubber. Her throat seemed to close.

Since her flight from New York, Mary had been mostly successful in distancing her thoughts from the terrible deed itself. She had closed her mind to those dreadful images, mentally acknowledging she had committed a crime without letting herself remember the particulars. But today she couldn't stop the memories. She seemed to feel Kenrick's hands on her skin. Her heart raced now as it had then. She could smell both his lust and her own fear. She could hear the awful sound of metal meeting flesh and bone, the thump of a body striking the floor.

May God forgive me. I've killed a man. May God forgive me.

"Sheriff, Mary has discovered some serious discrepancies in my records that can only mean one thing. Lloyd has been stealing money in my absence."

It was Blanche's voice that drew Mary from the edge of despair. In that instant, she remembered her son. Keary depended upon her. He needed her. She had to be strong. She could not let herself be buried under guilt, no matter what. All her life, she would be forced to live with her sin. There would never be peace nor forgiveness. Not for murder. But for Keary, she must survive. She must be strong. He was all that mattered. Nothing else.

Mary glanced toward the sheriff and was relieved to see he wasn't watching her. She was sure he would have guessed the truth about her, for she knew her guilt must be written on her face.

Carson frowned at Blanche. "That's a mighty serious charge." His gaze shifted to Mary. "Are you certain?"

Mary wished she'd never told Blanche what she'd discovered. She never should have drawn the sheriff's attention to herself like this. She never should have gotten involved.

But she couldn't have done anything differently. Blanche had rescued Mary and Keary back in New York City. She had voluntarily placed herself in danger for a complete stranger. Mary owed her too much to not help her now.

"Aye." Mary nodded as she met the sheriff's gaze again. "I am that."

"How much has he taken?"

Blanche answered him, "At least four thousand dollars."

Carson whistled softly. "Four thousand? In six months?" He raised one eyebrow. "That would've put anyone else clean out of business."

"I'm not anyone else."

"No, Miss Blanche, you're sure not."

"Here's the proof, Sheriff." Blanche placed the ledger on Carson's desk. "I have no intention of leaving this here, so I suggest you study it now. Then I want Lloyd arrested."

Carson looked at Mary again, his blue eyes serious and searching. "Care to show me what you found?" He motioned for her to come around to his side of the desk.

Mary saw no way to avoid doing as he requested, although the last thing she wanted was to stand close to Carson Barclay. He made her too nervous. He represented the law, and Mary was a lawbreaker, a murderess.

She drew a deep breath and stiffened her spine with deter-mination, then moved to stand beside him.

"Show me," he said, his voice low but commanding.

Her throat went dry. She swallowed, trying not to move away from him as all her instincts commanded her to do. Instead, she flipped through several pages to the first suspicious entry. "'Tis here I found the first error."

"Could it be just an error, Mrs. Malone? Could Lloyd have made a simple mistake while entering the figures?"

She pointed to a column of numbers. "I'm thinking not."

He turned his head. She did the same. Their gazes collided. Her breath caught in her chest, and for a moment, she forgot why she was here or that she should be wary of him because he was the sheriff.

"Could you have made a mistake, Mrs. Malone?" he asked, his voice even softer than before, almost gentle.

She wanted to feel insulted by the question, but indignation wouldn't surface. She should have at least remained afraid and wary, especially with him standing so close. Especially with him staring at her with those blue eyes of his.

"If you're asking if I know what it is I'm doing, then I'll be telling you, I doubted it meself, Sheriff Barclay. At first I thought 'twas me lack of understandin' of your American ways, but then I was thinking 'twould take no genius to see what was done here." She took a quick breath. "If you would be looking at what's before you, you'd be seeing it for yourself."

She thought she would wilt with relief when he finally turned his gaze from her to the book on his desk. Once his attention had turned where it should, she was free to put some distance between them. She moved around the desk to stand beside Blanche.

It was a long while before the sheriff straightened, a frown creasing his forehead. "I see Mrs. Malone's point. This wasn't a simple mistake."

"So you'll arrest him?" Blanche asked.

"Yeah, I'll head over there right now."

"Good." Blanche retrieved the ledger from the desk. "Sheriff, I trusted Lloyd. We go back a long way." Her voice broke. She paused and swallowed hard. "I've paid him handsomely over the years. I never thought he would do something like this to me."

"The quest for money can make people do strange things, Miss Blanche." His gaze darted to Mary and lingered briefly, then returned to Blanche. "It's one of the things that keeps both you and me in business."

He didn't wait for a reply. He rounded his desk and strode across the office, where he grabbed his hat off the peg on the wall. Then he opened the door and left without a backward glance.

Mary suspected his cryptic departing words had been as much for her as for Blanche. She just wasn't sure what he'd meant by them. Did he suspect her of wrongdoing? Did he know who she was and what she had done back in New York City? Would she soon find herself in one of those jail cells?

"Well, come along, Mary. This unpleasant task is done."

Wordlessly, relieved and yet not relieved, Mary nodded, then followed Blanche out of the sheriff's office.

Late that night, with an angry Lloyd Perkins cooling his heels in a cell downstairs, Carson turned out the lamp and lay down on his bed. He didn't close his eyes right off. He'd always needed a few minutes to get accustomed to the dark. He'd learned the trick as a young boy. Once he felt comfortable with his surroundings, the sense of suffocating would diminish, the walls wouldn't seem to be closing in on him. Then and only then would he be ready to sleep.

But maybe his dread of tight places wasn't what was keeping him awake tonight. Maybe it was Mary Malone.

She was afraid, and he wanted to know why. He wanted to know why she'd come to Whistle Creek, why she'd chosen to live with her son in that saloon. This wasn't a woman who sold herself. Not for any reason. This was a woman who chose to go to church on Sunday, even when others shunned her. This was a woman who loved her child.

He closed his eyes now and remembered the sweetness of her lilac cologne. The fragrance had lingered in his nostrils long after he'd stepped away from her this afternoon, long after he'd brought his prisoner back to jail. In fact, it seemed to be lingering still. He also remembered the tiny fishhook curls that bordered her nape, the enticing curve of her neck, the way she held herself erect and proud, the lyrical sound of her voice, the soft pink color of her mouth.

He'd never had a woman take control of his thoughts before. Not like this. He wasn't sure what to do about it.

No, that wasn't true. He did know.

Lord, guess it's time I talked to you about this, isn't it? I always try figurin' things out on my own first. Wish I'd learn there's a better way. Reckon I will one day?

Lilac cologne…

Lord, it's about Mary Malone. I can't figure out why she troubles me so. First off, though, guess I'd better ask your forgiveness for settin' myself up as her judge. That's not my job. It's a weakness of mine, but you already know that.

An Irish lilt…

Beautiful women mean trouble in a mining town. 'Specially those livin' in a saloon. Now, I know she can't help bein' the prettiest gal ever to waltz into Whistle Creek, but…

He thought of David and Claudia Hailey. It was Sheriff Hailey who'd shown Carson that he could choose right instead of wrong, and it was Claudia who'd shown him a mother's love. For that he'd be eternally grateful. But it was David and Claudia's love for each other that Carson remembered now, and remembering almost made marriage look appealing.

Chocolate-brown eyes...

Carson sat up in bed. *Wait a minute, Lord. You can't mean for my thoughts to be going off in that direction. So I'm askin' you to help me stop thinkin' about Mary Malone. Just let me forget her. I'd be mighty thankful for it. Amen.*

He laid down and closed his eyes.

"Just gotta stop thinkin', that's all."

~Seven

Mary and Keary had eaten breakfast alone every morning since arriving in Whistle Creek. Therefore, Mary was surprised when she entered the kitchen the morning after Lloyd's arrest to find John seated at the table, sipping a cup of Greta's strong coffee.

"Good morning to you, Mr. Tyrell," Mary greeted him as she settled Keary into the high chair Blanche had purchased at the mercantile.

"Morning."

She looked at him, noting the changes a few days of sobriety had wrought. Although she hadn't seen John at his worst, she knew there was a clarity in his eyes that hadn't been there before. He carried himself with more confidence, and he wasn't so quick to turn the scarred side of his face away when he was speaking to someone. Mary thought Edith had contributed much to the transformation in this young man.

"And how is it you're finding yourself this fine day?"

He ignored her question and asked one of his own. "Is it true Lloyd was stealing from Miss Blanche?"

"Aye, 'tis true." Mary walked to the stove to pour a cup of coffee, then checked the pot of oatmeal that Greta kept warming there.

"Who'd've believed it?" John shook his head. "I thought the two of them were sort of...Well, you know. Together."

Mary glanced over her shoulder, her eyebrows arched. "Miss Blanche and Mr. Perkins?" It would never have occurred to her.

"Yeah. I heard they came here together. Hasn't ever been another bartender at the Painted Queen. Folks just assumed..." He let the sentence trail into silence.

Mary stirred the hot cereal. She wondered how much anyone really knew about someone else. Everyone seemed to have secrets of their own. Folks seemed always to be guessing and supposing, one about another. Of course, there were those rare few who could see through a facade to the truth beneath.

Those like Carson Barclay, for instance.

Her pulse jumped. What a terrible thing that would be, if he were to guess the secrets she carried in her soul.

She turned abruptly. "Mr. Tyrell, I'm understanding you used to work at the mine. Out at the Lucky Lady."

"Yeah," he said, unconsciously scratching his disfigured cheek.

"I'm looking for someone who might work there. Or maybe once did. How would I go about learning if he's there? I know only that he was mining in Idaho. I wouldn't be knowing where for certain. And 'tis long ago since I heard from him. He may have moved on to another place."

"Lots of men work in the Lucky Lady. Lots more have over the years." His brows drew together in contemplation. "I guess the best way'd be for you to go out there and talk to the manager. Fella by the name of Jeff Christy."

She repeated the name softly to herself, then asked, "And how would I be finding the mine and Mr. Christy's office?"

"Easy. The road north of here only goes to the mine. You can't get lost. But you shouldn't go alone, Mrs. Malone."

"Would you go with me?"

John shook his head. "Sorry. Can't."

She realized belatedly that she shouldn't have asked such a thing. It would no doubt be a place of bad memories for him. "'Tis all right, Mr. Tyrell. I understand altogether."

He opened his mouth to say something but was interrupted by the appearance of Edith in the kitchen doorway. Her blue eyes looked sleepy, her golden hair disheveled. As soon as John saw her, his face turned red. Edith, on the other hand, smiled prettily.

"Johnny, I didn't know I'd find you here."

"Miss Edith," he mumbled, his gaze falling to his coffee mug.

Mary returned her attention to her son's breakfast, feeling suddenly old and jaded. Once she'd believed in love and hope and the future. Once she'd been able to smile like Edith when she thought about a certain young man. But the innocent girl she'd been was gone forever.

⸺

Carson patted Cinnabar's side while looking over Abe Stover's shoulder. "What d'ya think, Abe?"

The blacksmith gently lowered the horse's leg and straightened. "I'd say he'd better rest it for a few days. Maybe a week. Swelling's bad, but nothing's broken. I'll treat it with liniment."

Carson nodded in agreement.

"When you takin' Perkins over to Wallace?"

"In the morning."

Abe rubbed the stubble on his jaw. "Sure never expected I'd see Lloyd Perkins in this sort of trouble. I've known him as long as I've lived here." He shook his head. "Stealing from Miss Blanche. Who'd've thunk it?"

Carson didn't comment. He'd been keeping the law for too many years to be surprised by what people would do.

"Hello? Is anyone here?"

Carson didn't have to look over the top rail of the stall to know the distinctive voice belonged to Mary Malone. It was a voice he'd begun to hear in his sleep.

"Right here," Abe called as he opened the gate and stepped out.

"Good day to you, sir. I'd be asking about the use of one of your fine horses and a buggy to go with it."

Carson looked through the rails and watched as Mary approached Abe. She was wearing a gown of indigo satin, and her midnight hair shimmered with the same shiny blue tones, looking like satin itself.

"You came to the right place, Mrs. Malone. I've got all kinds of rigs for rent. Reasonable rates, too."

"I'm sorry, but I wouldn't be knowing your name, sir. Have we met?"

"No, ma'am, but I seen you at church on Sunday." He held out a blackened hand. "I'm Abe Stover."

Carson noticed that Mary didn't hesitate to shake Abe's hand, even though it was sure to soil her pale gray glove.

"'Tis an honor to meet you, Mr. Stover." Her gaze drifted around the barn's interior. "I would need the buggy for several hours this afternoon. Miss Loraine said you are to put the charges on her bill."

Abe grinned. "Always glad to help out Miss Blanche. I can have the rig hitched up and ready for you any time you say."

"I'll be needing it in an hour."

"It'll be ready for you, Mrs. Malone."

Mary smiled, and the expression seemed to light up the livery stable. "Thank you, sir. I'll be seeing you then." She turned and walked out, a spring in her step.

It wasn't until she'd disappeared around the corner of the open doorway that Carson stepped out of the stall.

"Well, if she isn't the prettiest piece of calico I ever laid eyes on." Abe turned toward Carson. "I don't know where she's going, but she sure do look happy about it, don't she?"

"Yeah," he murmured, even as he wondered why Mary Malone would want to rent a buggy for an afternoon. Not that it should matter to him. The roads were open, and it wasn't all that many miles to Wallace to the east or Osburn to the west.

Before he realized he was doing it, he followed after her. It wasn't difficult to catch up, each of his long strides equaling three of her smaller ones.

"Mrs. Malone," he said when he was nearly close enough to touch her shoulder.

She gasped as she whirled about. Her right hand fluttered to her chest. Her eyes were wide. "Faith, but must you be sneaking up on a person? You scared me half to death."

"I'm sorry." There it was. Her lilac cologne. It floated around him and made him lose his train of thought.

"Was there something you'd be wanting from me, Sheriff?"

He gave his head a quick shake. "Yes…No…I'm not sure." His reply made her laugh—surprising them both, he suspected. For just that moment, she looked happy and at ease.

"I was in the livery," Carson continued. "I heard you renting a buggy from Mr. Stover, and I was wondering where you were going."

All signs of her laughter vanished. "Would there be some reason I'd not be free to go wherever I wished?"

Mary reminded him of a yearling filly he'd seen one time, cornered by a couple of men in a pasture. When the young horse had seen there was no other avenue of escape, she'd simply turned and charged through the barbed wire. He didn't want the same to happen with Mary.

Carson raised his hand, palm toward her. "No. Of course not. I just. . ." He cleared his throat and tried again. "I thought you might need some directions or something."

"I'm thinking I can find me own way to the mine."

"The mine?"

She took a small step backward. "Aye."

"You're not planning to go out there alone, are you?"

Mary's demeanor changed right before his eyes. Her chin lifted defiantly. Her shoulders drew back like a soldier at attention. "Am I not now? And why would that be, I'm asking? You've only just said I was free to come and go as I please."

"Women," he muttered.

"Aye, a woman I am." She leaned forward, eyes sparking. "One that will not be pushed about by the likes o' you, Sheriff Barclay."

Carson leaned forward, too, bringing his face mere inches from hers. "I'm not trying to push you around, Mrs. Malone, but if you go out there by yourself and get into some sort of trouble, it's me who'll have to take care of things afterward."

"And just what sort of trouble do you think I'd be getting meself into?"

He grumbled beneath his breath, then answered, "You're a beautiful woman, Mrs. Malone. That mine employs hundreds of men, and some of them have no more morals than a rutting bull elk. Just what sort of trouble do you think you'd be getting yourself into?"

Thick silence fell around them. Carson watched the play of emotions cross Mary's face as she considered his words, saw the widening of her eyes as she realized what he was implying.

"Oh," she whispered.

"Darn right, oh."

Mary glanced over her shoulder toward the saloon. "Maybe there's someone who can go with me."

"I'll go with you."

"You?" Her gaze swung back to meet his, suspicion in her wide brown eyes.

"Yeah, I've got business out there myself." He wanted to ask why she was going to the Lucky Lady, but he thought better of it. It wasn't any of his concern, just as she wasn't any of his concern.

Even though he'd been acting like she was.

He touched his hat brim. "I'll meet you at the livery in an hour." Then he turned and strode away.

———

Mary should have found someone else to accompany her to the Lucky Lady Mine. Anyone would have been better than Carson Barclay.

He was the law. He would arrest her, should her crime be found out. He would have to. He could be the very person who delivered her to the gallows, who would take her son and place him in an orphanage to be raised by strangers, strangers who would never love Keary as she did.

But it wasn't only fear of Carson's legal office that caused her distress as the rented buggy moved along the road toward the mine. It was also her growing awareness of Carson as a man. It was the way he caused her heart to quicken when he glanced at her. It was the tumble of emotions she felt when she looked at his hands, the leather reins looped through his fingers. Just sitting beside him left her feeling breathless.

Saints preserve her! The last thing she needed was to find herself caring for Carson. She'd made one grievous mistake in her life when it came to trusting a man with her heart. And although that mistake had given her Keary—and she'd not change having her son for anything—she was determined never to make such a mistake again. Never!

"'Tis grand country, this," she said, hoping to turn her thoughts in another direction.

"That's what I've always thought." He paused, then said, "The mountains are all part of the Bitterroot Range. This road follows Whistle Creek there"—he pointed to the ribbon of crystal-clear water—"from above the mine all the way down to the river south of town." He lifted his arm toward a place across the creek and midway up the mountainside. "That's the rail spur up there. Both it and this road only go as far as the Lucky Lady Mine. After that, there are trails fit for pack mules and not much else, but plenty of miners still trek into those backwoods, looking for their own fortunes instead of working for men like Halligan."

"And do they find it? Their fortunes, I'm meaning."

"Not often."

Mary felt his gaze turn toward her, and instinctively, she knew what he wanted to ask her: Why was she going to the mine? Who was she going to see?

Hoping to delay, if not completely avoid, the question, she quickly asked, "How did you come to be sheriff of Whistle Creek?"

"I sort of fell into the job." There was a note of amusement in his reply.

Curious now, she turned to look at him and was grateful to find him watching the road again. "What would you be meaning by that?"

"I worked cattle on a spread over in Montana for several years, but the owner was pretty near wiped out during the big winter of ninety-two. He couldn't afford to keep on all the cowboys he had working for him. I was one of 'em he let go. I'd met a fella who'd been over in Oregon, doing some logging, and he'd liked the work. I thought maybe I'd give it a try."

Carson removed his hat and wiped his brow with his shirtsleeve. He glanced up at the glaring sun, riding high above the canyon walls. Then he set his hat back in place.

"I was cutting through the mountains south of Whistle Creek when a rattler spooked my horse. Cinnabar was young and pretty green back then. He took off running like the Devil himself had ahold of his tail. Next thing I knew, the trail gave way and sent us both crashing to the bottom of a ravine. Broke my leg in two places, and my horse was mighty beat up, too. Even if I could've managed to get back on him, he couldn't've carried me far. Luckily, a couple of miners happened upon me the next day. They brought me into Whistle Creek."

"And your horse?"

He grinned as he looked at her. "Cinnabar's just fine, and thanks for asking."

It was difficult to break eye contact with him. There was something mesmerizing about the blue of his eyes, something all too endearing about his lopsided grin.

She moistened her dry lips with the tip of her tongue, then said, "Go on with your story, Sheriff."

He didn't immediately obey her request. He simply continued to watch her and smile. It was most disconcerting.

"Please, Sheriff Barclay, continue."

Carson shrugged. "Not much more to tell. While I was laid up, waiting for my leg to heal, they learned I'd been a deputy sheriff down in Silver City for four years. The folks here wanted their own sheriff, and somehow I found myself elected. I didn't mean to stay on long, but I discovered I liked it. I liked the country and I liked the people. And I took to sheriff's work better than I ever did cowboyin'. So as long as the townsfolk want me, I guess I'll stay." He nodded, as if to emphasize his words. "Now it's your turn. Tell me something more about yourself, Mary Malone."

She turned away from him, pretending to study the scenery. "Nothing I could tell would be so interesting."

Sure and that was a lie. He'd likely be most interested if she was to tell him about Winston Kenrick.

"I want to hear it anyway." He said the words in a low voice that vibrated straight into her heart. When she remained silent, he suggested, "Tell me about Ireland. I've never been farther east than the Dakotas."

Mary thought on it a moment, then decided the land of her birth was a safe enough subject. It would be a far sight safer than listening to the deep timbre of Carson's voice and feeling its effects upon her.

"Do you have family in Ireland?"

"No." She envisioned her parents, Fagan and Maeve Malone, and felt the stinging heartache that always came with missing them. "Me da was a tenant farmer, working the land of the English gentry. 'Twas a hard life, don't ya know, but 'twas not all bad. Me da was a big ox of a man with a laugh that could rattle the rafters. He and me brother Padriac both played the fiddle, and the rest of us would sing and dance when we had a mind to."

She smiled to herself, remembering the lot of them in front of one of the thatched roof huts they'd lived in over the years, dancing and acting the fools, as if they were as rich and grand as the landlord himself. Sure but those had been bonny times.

"I was the youngest of ten, but there was only six of us who grew to adulthood and me the only girl." She looked at Carson. "Do ya have any brothers or sisters yourself?"

"No." He frowned. "I grew up alone."

"Then 'tis sorry I am for you altogether."

"You said there was no one left in Ireland. What happened to your family?"

"Me ma died when I was fourteen." Poor Maeve Malone, made old before her time by poverty and hardship and heartache. "Da passed on after me twentieth birthday, just." Wonderful, laughing Fagan Malone, his fiddle silenced forever. "I was already in service to the Whartons by then. Ever since I was fifteen, to be sure. After Da died, me brothers went their own ways. Most went to England to find work. Padriac married a Scottish lass and moved to the Lowlands." *And Quaid came to America, but I'll not be telling you that, Sheriff Barclay.* "None o' me brothers was good at corresponding, and I don't know for positive sure where any of them are except Padriac. 'Twould be a miracle if I was to see any of the others again." But another miracle was exactly what she hoped for, although she wasn't telling the sheriff that either.

When she fell silent, Carson seemed content to leave it that way. He didn't ask more questions. Mary was relieved, for talking about her family had stirred up too many painful memories.

The Irish had a word for the act of leaving Ireland. It was *deoraí,* which meant exile, not emigration. Mary understood the word at this moment as she never had before. She could almost smell the sweet green of the Irish hills, could almost feel the crisp sea breeze upon her cheeks. The home of her birth, the land where she'd lived for twenty-four years before fate had taken her away, first to England and then to America.

"I'm sorry, Mary. I didn't mean to make you sad."

She blinked away the tears that blinded her. "'Tis nothing but a speck o' dust in me eye."

He was silent for another long spell, then broke it by saying, "The mine's around the next bend."

She was altogether glad of that, for hearing him call her Mary in such a gentle voice had wrought new havoc in her already confused heart. To continue sitting so close beside him without a few minutes to compose herself would have been unbearable.

Eight

The drive back to Whistle Creek two hours later took place in complete silence, both parties lost in thoughts of their own.

Mary had learned nothing from the mine manager. Jeff Christy had been friendly enough, but he hadn't been willing to open the mine records to her. He'd promised only that he would look into the matter, see if he could locate her brother's name among the hundreds of others.

Of course, she hadn't called Quaid her brother when talking to Mr. Christy. She'd said Quaid was her brother-in-law, the brother of her deceased husband. What was one more lie among many? she'd reasoned to herself.

Carson hadn't fared any better. While Mary was inside the office, conducting whatever business she had there, Carson had made small talk with some of the workers who were employed aboveground. If there were plans afoot to riot or blow anything up, no one had let it slip to him. Not that he was surprised. The miners might like him. They might trust him. But they also knew he was the law, and if they were up to mischief, they were smart enough to be cautious around him.

Shadows fell across the road in front of them as they came down out of the mountains. The heat of the day was already beginning to lose its grip on the valley below.

When the town came into view, Carson realized his stomach had been growling for the past two miles. Impetuously, he asked, "Would you care to have supper with me at the café, Mrs. Malone?"

For one brief instant, he thought she might agree. Then she shook her head. "I'm thinking I should be getting back to Keary. 'Tis"—she blushed—"'tis past time for him to be having his own supper."

Carson remembered his brief glimpse of Mary nursing her son. Why the lingering image of mother and child made him feel warm and content, he didn't know.

He turned off the mine road, crossed the bridge over Whistle Creek, and took the north road into town. He stopped the buggy at the corner of River and Main, then helped Mary to the ground.

"I'll be thanking you for taking me up to the mine, Sheriff."

"No trouble, Mrs. Malone. I was glad to do it."

"Good day to you, then."

He pinched the brim of his Stetson. "Evening, ma'am."

He watched as she hurried across the street and down the sidewalk toward the rear entrance of the Painted Queen. Then he hopped into the buggy and slapped the reins. He didn't have to turn the horse onto Main Street. The animal knew the way to the stables.

Carson was just entering the barn when a gunshot broke the peacefulness of early evening. It was followed by a woman's scream. He was out of the buggy and running before the sound faded away.

He found several of Blanche's girls huddled together outside the front door of the saloon.

"What happened?"

Ruby, a woman with bright red hair to match her name, turned toward him. "It's Lloyd. He's threatening to kill Miss Blanche."

"Lloyd? How'd he get out of jail?" The question was rhetorical. Carson didn't expect or need an answer right now.

He inched along the sidewalk toward the swinging doors of the saloon. Cautiously, he glanced inside in time to see Lloyd fire off another round, followed by another scream.

Cold fury swept over Carson as he took in the scene. Blanche Loraine was huddled behind the bar with two more of her girls, and midway up the stairs was young Edith, holding a squirming Keary Malone in her arms. Lloyd had safely positioned himself out of view of the doorway. Carson wouldn't be able to get a clear shot at him without exposing himself first.

"You there, Barclay?" Lloyd shouted, his voice slightly slurred.

He'd been drinking. That made him prone to mistakes. It would slow his reflexes. It also made him more unpredictable, more dangerous.

"I'm here, Lloyd. Why don't you put that gun down so we can get back to the jail and have our supper? Zeb always rustles us up some good grub."

"I'm not goin' back." He shot some of the bottles behind Blanche. Glass and liquor splattered everywhere.

A movement at the top of the stairs caught Carson's eye. Mary stood there, eyes wide with terror, hand over her mouth.

Lloyd saw her, too. "Get down here, Miz Malone."

"Go back, Mary!" Carson commanded.

Lloyd fired another shot, this one hitting the wall above Edith's head. Keary started to wail.

"I said, come 'ere!" Lloyd shouted.

Mary hurried down the stairs, quickly stepping in front of Edith and Keary, shielding her son with her own body.

"All the way down, Miz Malone. After all, this is your fault, ain't it? You're the one who told Blanche I was stealin' from her. Ain't that right?"

Blast! Carson couldn't stand there and watch Mary descend the stairs. There was no telling what Lloyd was going to do next. But if Carson went barging through these doors, Lloyd could fire several times before the sheriff would have a clear shot. Lloyd could kill both Mary and her son, maybe others, too, before Carson stopped him.

Just then, Abe arrived beside him, shotgun in hand. "What can I do?" the blacksmith whispered.

Carson glanced down the sidewalk to the northwest corner of the saloon. The Painted Queen had several windows on the street side ground floor, all of them made from stained glass. It let in light, yet hid the internal goings-on from passersby.

"Stay here," he answered Abe. "When I get inside, you come in. Ready to shoot if you have to."

"How will I know you're inside?"

"You'll know," Carson replied, then he ran in a crouched position toward the far end of the saloon.

—

"Hush now, Keary me boy," Mary whispered over her shoulder. "'Tis all right we are."

The sheriff is outside. He will help us.

Lloyd fired his gun again, this time toward the ceiling. "I said for you t' get down here, Miz Malone. I mean now!"

Mary wasn't sure her legs would carry her safely down the steps. "Mr. Perkins, sir, will you be letting me send the boy upstairs with Edith? He's just a wee babe and can do you no harm."

He replied by firing another shot, this one striking the wall over her right shoulder.

"For the love o' Mike!" Mary screeched, fear and anger mingling together. "Have you no pity? What has Keary ever done to you, I'll be asking?"

Lloyd downed another swig of whiskey, then rose from his chair. "The next shot goes right through you and into the brat's head if you don't shut up and get down here."

"Lloyd." Blanche stood and moved from behind the bar. "It's me you're mad at. Let the others go. This has gone far enough."

"Maybe I'll kill you now." He turned the muzzle of the gun toward her.

Mary held her breath. Even Keary quieted.

Blanche stopped and stared straight into Lloyd's eyes. "Shoot me then," she said in a calm voice, "if that's what you mean to do. Just quit terrorizing everyone else. This is between you and me."

Suddenly, there was a great shattering of glass. Lloyd turned just in time for Carson's first shot to tear through his left arm. Still, Lloyd managed to fire his own gun at the sheriff. Carson dropped, rolled, then was on his feet again, Colt revolver blazing. Another bullet hit the bartender, this one striking his chest dead center. An expression of surprise crossed Lloyd's face and was frozen there as he fell backward, dead before he hit the floor. Blanche let out a choked cry and rushed toward the fallen man, her hand over her mouth.

Keary started to wail again at the top of his lungs. Mary wanted to cry right along with him. Her knees gave way, and she sank onto the step, shaking all over as she took her son from Edith and hugged him to her bosom. She closed her eyes, shutting out the image of the dead man on the floor—an all-too-familiar image. She rocked back and forth, and after a while, Keary's crying quieted to an occasional whimper.

"Are you hurt, Mary?"

She opened her eyes, surprised to find Carson standing in front of them. She wanted to answer him but couldn't seem to form a reply.

"Are you hurt?" He leaned forward and placed a gentle hand on her shoulder. "Is Keary okay?"

She shook her head, then nodded. Her vision suddenly blurred.

"Thank God," he said softly. His hand left her shoulder as he straightened and looked behind him. "You don't belong at the Painted Queen."

She swallowed the lump in her throat and blinked away her tears. When she could see clearly, she followed Carson's gaze. Blanche was kneeling beside Lloyd's body and holding his hand as she talked softly.

"I must be going to her," Mary said as she rose.

He placed his hand on her shoulder a second time. "I think she'd rather be alone."

"'Tis true, then? Mr. Perkins and Miss Blanche?"

"Yeah, it's true. Long time ago." He took a step down, then grimaced and touched his right thigh. When he looked at his hand, it was scarlet with his own blood.

Mary's heart jumped at the sight. "Faith and begorra! You're wounded, you are." She looked behind her where Edith had been, but the girl had slipped away unnoticed. Glancing at the gathering of people inside the doorway of the saloon, Mary called out, "Someone send for the doctor. The sheriff is being shot."

"It's nothing," Carson objected.

"I'll be having none of it. Sit down, Sheriff Barclay, before you fall down." She tugged on his arm. "Do as I'm telling you." When he'd followed her order, she added, "Here. Hold Keary while I tend to you." She shoved her son into Carson's arms, then lifted her skirt to her knees and tore off a length of petticoat.

"It's nothing," he repeated as she knelt on the step and tied the white cotton strip around his thigh. "Just a flesh wound."

"You wouldn't be knowing that for certain. Now would you?" She glanced up. Her pulse skipped, this time not from alarm but because of his amused smile. In defense against the emotions racing through her, she huffed, "I'm not seeing anything to smile about, Sheriff Barclay."

"Can't help it, Mrs. Malone. You're mothering me like you do Keary."

She stood, then grabbed her son. "I'm doing no such thing. I'm thinking that wound has made you daft."

He laughed aloud. His skin crinkled near the outer corners of his eyes, blue eyes that sparkled despite the pain he was in.

She loved his laugh. She loved the crinkles near his blue eyes. She loved...

Faith and begorra! It was herself who was daft, and there'd be no mistaking it.

She was rescued from her unsettled feelings by the timely arrival of the town's physician. As Dr. Ingall set his black leather bag on the step next to Carson, Mary tried to escape up the stairs.

"Mary Malone," the sheriff called after her.

She stopped but didn't look back. "Aye?"

"I meant what I said. You need to move out of this place. It isn't safe for Keary." He paused. "Or for you either."

Heaven help her. The last thing she needed was Sheriff Barclay caring where she lived or if she was safe.

She continued upward without comment, not trusting her voice nor knowing what she would say if she tried to speak.

⌒

Tibble Knox squinted at the notepad in his hand. "Miss Malone stayed with a couple by the name of Nolan and Siobhan Dougal at the time she was employed by you. They've got a cold-water apartment on the Lower East Side."

Winston impatiently tapped his fingertips on the glass-covered surface of his desk. His head was pounding, and the stitches were beginning to itch. He wished the investigator would hurry up with his report. So far he hadn't told Winston anything he didn't already know.

"However, she was living with a Ryan and Cora Maguire when her baby was born. From what I could learn, Ryan was a cousin to Seamus Maguire, Keary Malone's father. Seamus left a widow in New York as well."

Winston cocked an eyebrow. Interesting but nothing more. "Go on, Mr. Knox."

"Keary Malone was delivered early, and for a time, the midwife didn't think the boy would live."

"Yes, yes, yes. But have you learned anything of value?"

Tibble Knox removed his spectacles and cleaned them with his handkerchief. "Actually, I have." He hooked the wires over his ears again and peered at Winston. "It seems Miss Malone formed a rather close friendship with two other immigrants during the voyage across the Atlantic. They've maintained a steady correspondence."

"Splendid!" Winston straightened in his chair. "Where do we find them?"

The detective shook his head. "Unfortunately, Miss Malone did not leave any of the letters behind, and I have yet to uncover the women's whereabouts."

"Then what good is the information?"

Tibble Knox rose from his chair, slipping the small notebook into his vest pocket as he did so. "Don't worry yourself, Mr. Kenrick. I will locate them. You can be sure of that."

"Let me remind you, Knox. When it's time to confront Miss Malone, I'm going with you. Is that understood? I will be the one to speak to her, not you."

"You made that clear at our first meeting. I haven't forgotten."

"Good." Winston reached for a cigar. He used to keep them in the box Mary had stolen, but it wasn't cigars that made the cursed thing so important to him. Without that box, his future would be ruined. It was crucial he get it back, and he had to get it back soon. Most important, he had to make sure that Irish witch hadn't discovered what was hidden inside.

—

Louise Schmidt drew herself up to her full, imposing height, her arms crossed over her ample bosom. "I'll remind you that I run a respectable boardinghouse, Sheriff Barclay. And besides, I'm all full up. There's no room here for that woman and her baby."

"But Mrs. Schmidt—"

"You heard me. There's no room available." With that, she closed the door in Carson's face.

Favoring his right leg—it was only a flesh wound, but it hurt like the dickens—he stepped off the boardinghouse porch and walked toward the jail. Evening had fallen over Whistle Creek, and shop windows were dark while residences had come to life with golden lamplight. At the far end of town, music and laughter spilled from the open doors of the Painted Queen Saloon. Except for the window that had been boarded over, no one would think anything unusual had happened there a few hours ago.

Carson stopped in front of his office, his gaze locked on the saloon.

Mary Malone didn't belong there. Keary Malone didn't belong there. They both could have been killed today. But if Mrs. Schmidt wouldn't rent Mary a room, what was she to do? She had a job and was being paid a wage for it. A better-than-average wage, more than likely, since Miss Blanche seemed to like her so much. If Mary was to leave the Painted Queen, what sort of work might she find? Nothing in Whistle Creek, that was for sure. She'd probably have to go clear over to Spokane.

But if she went to Spokane, who would keep an eye on her? Who would protect the widow and her son? Who would she turn to if Keary needed something? At least here, she had a friend in Miss Blanche. No, it was better that Mary Malone stay in Whistle Creek.

Better for whom he didn't allow himself to consider.

An idea came to him right out of the blue. His cabin. It was sitting empty. He could let her have use of it for free. It was no more than a quarter of a mile up the draw. It was an easy walk, and if necessary, he could help her get a horse and cart for transportation.

Of course, she would be out there by herself, but there were plenty of widow women who lived on their farms and homesteads all alone. He could show her how to use a rifle, just in case. He was convinced she would be safer out there than she was at the Painted Queen.

And Keary…What about the boy? Mary needed someone to care for her baby while she was working. Keary shouldn't be at the Painted Queen, watched out for by Edith or any of the others who worked there.

He remembered the blowzy Miss June back in Idaho City, a woman long past her prime with sagging skin on her throat and heavy makeup that caked in the creases of her face. Miss June had loved to cuddle and fuss over Carson. She'd smelled of sweat and greasy foods, and for a moment, it seemed he could still smell her body odor. He wrinkled his nose in distaste.

Miss June had looked after Carson whenever Aldora wanted her son out from underfoot. But Miss June, as kind as she'd tried to be, had been worse than having no one at all.

No, Keary didn't belong in that saloon, and if Mary Malone didn't have the good sense to get her son out of there, then Carson would do it for her.

With determined steps—and only a slight limp—Carson set off for the Painted Queen and a meeting with Mary Malone.

—

Holding a sleeping Keary in her arms, Mary sat in the rocking chair, humming softly. She stared down at her son's face, thinking how sweet he looked, how precious and beautiful. He might have been killed today. When she recalled the terror of those few minutes—minutes that had each seemed an eternity long—she felt a sick twist in her stomach.

"I'm thinking, Jesus, that you've no reason to hear me prayers, me sins bein' so great and all. But 'tis not here me Keary's meant to be. So for his sake, I'd be askin' for another small favor. Not for meself, mind you, but for the wee lad who's done no wrong to anyone."

The last words of her prayer were hardly spoken when a knock sounded at her door.

"'Tis open," she called.

She glanced over her shoulder, expecting to see Edith or Blanche. She definitely wasn't expecting Carson Barclay.

"Good evening, Mrs. Malone." He removed his black hat. "May I come in? I need to talk to you."

She held her son more tightly, feeling a familiar twinge of fear at his words. A sheriff's words. "Aye, you may come in, Sheriff Barclay."

Carson stepped into the room but left the door wide open. Then he walked toward her, stopping in front of the rocker so Mary didn't have to crane her neck to look at him.

"How are you?" he asked, his voice low and concerned.

"I'm all right, just." It was an honest reply. But would she be all right after he told her why he'd come to see her?

Carson slid his fingers around the brim of his hat, his expression thoughtful. "Mrs. Malone, you might tell me again that it isn't any of my business. I suppose it isn't. But I don't think you and this baby of yours should be living in this saloon. It isn't safe. It's one thing for you to work in the back office, keeping Miss Blanche's books for her. That's bad enough. But living in this place with Keary...Well, it's not the best situation."

Mary stiffened, but tried to swallow the anger that sprang instantly to life. "Would you be saying I'm not a fit mother? Haven't you said as much before?"

"No, that's not it. Maybe once I thought that, but no more, Mrs. Malone. I just want to help if I can. I've got that cabin sitting empty. It would suit the two of you mighty well, I think."

"Your cabin?" She pictured the log house and the pretty meadow filled with wildflowers. Then she remembered her prayer of moments before. *So for his sake, I'd be askin' for another small favor.* Had the Almighty answered so quickly, despite her sinful condition?

"Look," Carson continued, his tone more forceful now, as if arguing to convince her, "I don't know what Miss Blanche is paying you to keep her books. I'm sure it's fair, but it probably isn't enough to rent a house from someone else, even if there was one available. But I won't charge you rent. It would be better for me to have someone out there, looking out for the place, than have it standing empty. You'd be doing me a favor."

"A house of me own," she whispered. "I scarce can believe it."

"You can believe it."

She shook her head. If she moved into his cabin, she'd be beholden to the sheriff, the very man she needed to stay clear of. This couldn't be the miracle she'd been praying for...could it?

"Mrs. Malone, believe me, a saloon is not where Keary should be living. It isn't safe." The expression on his face was one akin to anger, but she suspected it wasn't really because of her. "Please, use my cabin."

He was right, of course. This wasn't the place she should be raising her son. As much as she liked Blanche and Edith and a few of the other women, she knew this wasn't where Keary belonged. He deserved better than this. It seemed her decision was made.

"Sure and I'll be thankful to you altogether, Sheriff Barclay. This is a kind offer you've made, and I'll be accepting it with gratitude." She rose from the chair, then cradled Keary with one arm long enough to shake Carson's hand.

A tingle raced up her arm the moment their fingers touched. It caused her pulse to jump and her breathing to momentarily cease. She was relieved when he released her hand and stepped back from her.

"I'll ride up there tomorrow morning. Make sure everything's in order." He placed his hat on his head. "Then I'll borrow a wagon from Abe Stover and help you take your things up there in the afternoon."

She thought to say he wouldn't need a wagon to help her move, her belongings being so few, but he left before she could speak.

Sure and she hoped this was the miracle she'd prayed for. If not, it was the Devil giving Mary her due for the crime she'd committed.

It was surely one or the other.

~Nine

Saturday, 30 July 1898
Whistle Creek, Idaho

Dear Beth,

It is less than a week since I posted letters to you and to Inga, but it seems longer as so much has happened.

First I would have you know I began searching for my brother Quaid. The manager at the Lucky Lady Mine, Mr. Christy by name, has promised he will ask about to see if Quaid ever worked at this mine. If not, I will be finding a way to visit the other mining operations in these mountains and be asking the same questions. I feel it in my heart that I am meant to find my brother, and there will be no changing that belief.

Last week there was a bit of trouble at the saloon. Keary might have been hurt were it not for the sheriff. I knew then and there that this was not the place for my baby to be staying, but I did not know where we would go.

Once again it was the sheriff himself who helped us. He has allowed us use of a small house he owns but has not lived in for some time. It is rustic, but far better than the places where my brothers and I lived in Ireland, to be sure. I have made new curtains for the windows, green to remind me of the land of my birth. There is a shed nearby that houses an artesian well. The water is cold and sweet tasting. The stove is a sad use of iron, but I am thinking I will be able to cook our meals on it without burning down this house made of logs.

Sheriff Barclay has visited us daily since we moved here three days ago. He is always bringing something he thinks we need. I would rather he did not continue to do so for I have no wish to be beholden to him or any other man, but I am not knowing how to tell him to stop. He has a real affection for my son, and Keary has taken to him altogether.

You would be surprised, Beth, were you to see me working with Miss Blanche's books and ledgers. My da always said I had a good head on my shoulders, and I am thinking he was right. Not that I would be bragging and puffing myself up. But it is pleased I am when the work is through at the end of the day. I like it altogether better than dusting handrails and mopping floors and carrying laundry up and down a back staircase, day in and day out.

Today I mean to plant some flowers near the house, and then we are going to search for huckleberries, for I am told they are delicious in a pie.

> I remain your affectionate friend always,
> Mary Emeline Malone

With her hair in a braid and wearing her most threadbare dress, Mary knelt in the dirt in front of the cabin and attacked the hard-packed earth with a spade. She'd been told in the mercantile that the growing season was half-gone. But she knew the wildflowers in the meadow would soon die, and she was determined to have a garden of flowers to enjoy until the first frosts.

Of course, she might not be in this house come winter. She might find Quaid, and then they would go away from here.

Her brother would take her to a place of safety, a place where she didn't have a sheriff lending her a house and watching over her all the time, where she was far away from anyone who might suspect her of committing murder.

Her hand stilled and a shiver raced up her spine. She hated remembering what she'd done. She liked it much better when she could pretend that nothing so horrible had happened. But even worse was thinking what would happen if she was found out. Keary would grow up in an orphanage. He might grow up mistreated and hungry. She would rather live with the knowledge of her sin weighing on her shoulders than have her child suffer as he might if she were arrested and hanged or imprisoned.

Which brought her thoughts directly back to Sheriff Barclay. How was she to dissuade him from taking on the role of protector? How was she to tell him she didn't need his help—especially when it was so obvious that wasn't true? She'd needed his help several times already. She would never have been able to start a fire in that miserable stove without his careful instructions their first day here. She wouldn't even have this little house to live in without his generosity.

"Sure and I'd like to know what it is I should be doing?"

Keary's cheerful jabbering caused her to sit back on her heels and glance to her right. Her son was seated a short distance away in the center of a child-sized corral Mary had made from some lengths of lodgepole pine. And with Keary was the mangiest-looking dog she had seen in her life. The large beast was brindled in color, tawny with spots of black and streaks of white, its long hair matted and its tail drooping. It had one blue eye and one black and an open mouth large enough to swallow Keary's hand and arm—which at the moment were painfully close to the dog's sharp fangs.

"Keary!" Mary jumped to her feet.

Her son squealed with laughter and pounded the dog on the head with both of his hands.

"Faith and begorra! Keary, stop!"

The dog lay down, pressing its chin onto the ground between its forepaws, and whined.

Mary hopped over the low barricade and whisked her child into the safety of her arms. She was preparing to race in the opposite direction when she took another quick look at the dog. What had looked so dangerous seconds before now looked pitiful. Her breathing slowly returned to normal as she took one step closer to the ugly canine.

"I'll be thinking you're a poor thing, you are. Look at you, will you now." She hunkered down, then tentatively reached out and stroked the dog's head.

It rolled its eyes upward, the better to see her leaning over it. Its tail flopped once in the dirt. Otherwise, it didn't move.

"Aye, 'tis starving you are beneath all that hair, or my name isn't Mary Emeline Malone."

"Ba, ba," Keary chanted merrily as he tried to touch the dog again. "Ba, ba, ba, ba."

"Do you think that's the name, Keary lad? Well, 'tis a bath for Baba before you'll be touching him...or her...again. But I'm thinking it won't hurt to share a bite to eat first. Would that be to your liking, Baba?"

The dog sat up, then cocked its head to one side, ears flopping forward. Mary couldn't help laughing at the expression on its face. She was quite certain no amount of soap, water, or brushing would improve Baba's looks by much.

"If you'll stay there, I'll be bringing you some food, Baba. If you've a mind to go on, then so be it."

She carried Keary into the house and set him in his high chair. Then she put together a plate of food—chunks of cheese and some scraps of ham and beef—for their guest. When she went outside, she found the dog sitting exactly where she'd left it.

"Come here, Baba, and fill your belly, for you look like you'd be needing it."

The dog immediately obeyed. It seemed she—for Mary could see now that the animal was female—was quick of mind even if she was a sore sight to look upon.

"I'll be putting a kettle on to boil, and when the water is hot, we'll rid you of the dirt and vermin, we will. If you've a mind to stay with us, then you'll not be dragging fleas into me house."

A half hour later, with Keary standing alongside the wash-tub that Mary had dragged down next to the stream and half filled with cold creek water, warmed slightly by hot water from the kettle, Mary set about scrubbing Baba. She knelt beside the tub, the front of her skirt tucked into her waistband to protect it from the dirt. Baba stood still, head drooping and without complaint, while Mary worked the soap into a lather, then rinsed several times. Keary stood on tiptoes and splashed merrily. When Mary paused to watch her son, Baba decided to shake off the water from her long coat.

"Stop, Baba!" Mary shouted, putting up her hands in defense of the flying beads of water and turning her face away.

In seconds, Mary and Keary were as soaking wet as the dog.

Mary would have laughed, but another beat her to it. The deep male laughter seemed to reverberate in her chest, making her heart leap.

She looked over her shoulder at her not-unexpected visitor. She knew the burbling brook and Keary's splashing had drowned out the sound of Carson's approach, but the reaction of her heart had little to do with her surprise at his sudden appearance.

"Quite a sight," Carson said, a chuckle lingering in his words.

Mary rose quickly and turned toward him. Too late, she remembered her skirt was hiked up, revealing her now-muddied petticoat and too much bare leg. Wet hair straggled around her face and neck. She was a sight to be sure, just as he'd said, and a poor one at that.

The sheriff, on the other hand, looked altogether too hand-some, standing there beside his horse, so tall and lean and whipcord strong, his golden brown hair reflecting the rays of the afternoon sun, his blue eyes twinkling with amusement.

"Will you be laughing at me, then?" she demanded, ready to be insulted, wanting to be insulted.

He shook his head. "Now be honest, Mrs. Malone. You've got to admit you couldn't be more wet if you'd all three jumped into the creek." He tried—and failed—to suppress his grin. "Aren't I right?"

Mary glanced at Keary and Baba, then down at herself. And then she laughed, too. "Aye, you are that."

"Where did you get that ugly mutt?" Carson left his horse's reins trailing the ground and walked toward Mary and the washtub.

"I wouldn't be knowing where she came from. Baba just showed up at me door, hungry and dirty."

"Baba?"

She lifted Keary into her arms. "'Twas me boy who named her." She felt her cheeks grow warm. "'Tis only babble, but I'm thinking he knows what it is he's saying."

"Ah." Carson stretched out an arm and ruffled Keary's hair with his hand. "I'm sure he does. You're a smart one, aren't you, Keary?" Then he looked at the dog again. "She probably belonged to some miner. Maybe he died or abandoned her."

"Aye, that's what I'm thinking. She seems gentle enough, though she frightened me at first, big and ugly as she is."

"Come here, girl," Carson said, patting his thigh with his fingers.

Baba didn't budge. Except for one side of her mouth, which twitched as if she was about to snarl.

"'Tis all right." Mary mimicked the sheriff by patting her own thigh. "Come here, Baba."

The dog immediately jumped out of the tub and came to stand in front of Mary. Baba sat and cocked her head to one side, looking up, as if waiting for another command.

"Looks like you've got a protector, Mrs. Malone."

I'm wishing you'd call me Mary. Her pulse skipped, and she felt short of breath. "Aye, 'twould seem so." *Carson,* her traitorous thoughts finished for her.

"Probably a good thing. I sometimes worry about you being out here alone, even though I know it's better than living over the saloon."

"And quieter altogether."

"Yeah, I imagine it is." The blue of his eyes seemed to darken as he stared at her. After a long moment, he cleared his throat. "Well, why don't I dump that water and carry the tub back to the house for you? It's plenty heavy for someone as tiny as you."

She longed for him to stay. She wished he would go. She wanted him to do everything for her. She wanted nothing from him ever again.

"I'm used to hard work, Sheriff Barclay," she said, trying to hide her confusion. "I brought that tub out here meself, you know. I'm not so weak I can't take it back the same way."

His smile returned, accompanied by his warm laughter. "Sometimes you're as prickly as a porcupine, Mary Malone.

Has anyone ever told you that before? I wasn't criticizing you. I was merely offering to help."

Softly, she said, "Maybe I'm thinking you've already helped enough."

Maybe she was also thinking she liked his help too much. Maybe she was forced to admit she looked forward to his visits. Maybe she knew she was not wary enough of this man of the law. Maybe she knew the danger was not in losing her freedom but in losing her heart.

Faith and begorra! It wasn't her heart she'd lost but her bloomin' mind!

—

Carson watched as Mary turned away from him and walked swiftly toward the house, her skirts flipping up just enough to reveal her bare feet. He had an almost overwhelming urge to go after her, take her in his arms, and kiss her soundly. The way a woman like Mary should be kissed.

A woman like Mary...

He wasn't sure what he meant by that. He didn't know Mary. Not really. She was a widow woman who needed a bit of help. That's all she was to him. Nothing more.

He thought of the way she so often faced off with him, head held high, her eyes sparking in defiance, her knuckles resting just above her pleasantly rounded hips. Even when she was afraid, Mary Malone didn't back down. She was full of spit and fire. She was beautiful and smart. She was gentle and loving. She was many things, and most of them were still a mystery to him. A mystery Carson wanted to solve.

He grabbed the washtub and set it on its side, watching as water spilled onto the ground and rushed in a dozen rivulets toward the mountain stream.

So the truth was, he admitted silently, that Mary had become more to him than a widow needing assistance. He just didn't know what that "more" was. Was it merely a response to her beauty? Or was it something less definable—and more disturbing?

He looked toward the house. Mary and Keary and that mongrel dog had disappeared inside. The door stood open, as did the windows. New green curtains, the color of a Douglas fir, fluttered in the gentle summer breeze. Mary had accomplished much in three days, turning a bachelor's cabin into a woman's home. Carson had always been proud of the one-room log house. He'd built it with his own hands. It was the first place he'd been able to call his own, and he'd liked living there. But it had never looked like it did now. Now it looked like a home.

As Carson picked up the washtub and strode toward the cabin, he wondered about the absent Mr. Malone. Mary never spoke about her deceased husband. He'd never heard her say how long they'd been married. He wondered if she'd loved him. He wondered if she still mourned him. He wondered what had caused her to leave her home in the East and come to Whistle Creek, Idaho, to work at the Painted Queen.

In the open doorway, he paused a moment, letting his eyes readjust to the dim light of the interior. Mary had curtained off the sleeping area of the cabin, and over the top of the blankets and rope strung from wall to wall, he saw her arms rise above her head as she donned a clean gown.

He cleared his throat loudly. "Here's the washtub, Mrs. Malone."

Baba nosed her way through the curtain and growled at him.

Carson decided he wasn't going to like that dog.

"'Tis all right, Baba," Mary said softly.

The sound of her voice flowed over Carson like warm honey, and he knew it would be better if he took his leave before he did something he'd regret later.

"Listen, Mrs. Malone, I need to get back to town. I came to bring you a rifle. I thought you should have one handy."

The curtain moved aside. "A rifle?"

"Yeah."

"Are you thinking I'll be needing one?"

"You need to be able to protect yourself and your boy if you have to." He shrugged. "Like I said before, I wouldn't have brought you out here if I didn't think you'd be better off, but all the same, you should know how to use a rifle."

Her voice had an odd, strained quality as she replied, "I would protect meself and Keary if I had to, Sheriff. Make no mistake of that."

"So do you know how to use a rifle?"

She shook her head.

"Like I said, I've got to get back to town. How about if I leave the rifle with you, and I'll come out tomorrow after church and give you lessons. Would that be okay?"

"I'm thinking that would be all right."

"Good. I'll get the rifle. It's on my saddle." He headed for his horse.

"Sheriff?"

He turned, saw her standing in the doorway. Her hair had been freed from the braiding, and it spilled over her shoulders like a black waterfall, damp and shiny in the afternoon sunlight. Her dress was a dark lavender calico that emphasized the narrowness of her waist and her womanly shape.

"Would you be staying for dinner tomorrow?" Her smile was hesitant, unsure. "You'd be welcome for all that you've done for Keary and me."

I'm not sure that's a good idea, Mrs. Malone, he thought, knowing he should refuse the invitation. *For either one of us.*

"I'll be frying a chicken," she added.

"Thanks, ma'am. I'd be obliged."

~Ten

Mary awakened on Sunday morning to a sky covered with dark rain clouds and a chilling wind that felt more like November than the last day of July. Staring out the window at the gloomy weather, she suspected her shooting lesson with Sheriff Barclay would be canceled. Which was probably just as well.

"I'll be losing me mind altogether," she whispered as she turned toward the stove and the breakfast she was preparing.

You need to be able to protect yourself and your boy...

The sheriff's words had been fulfilled before she came to Whistle Creek, and that was just one more reason to discourage him from coming around. She needed to make it clear that she preferred to do for herself, that she didn't want his help or even his friendship.

And what if he was wanting more than friendship?

She felt the flutter in her stomach. Merciful heavens! Love between them would be a dreadful thing were it to happen. Him the law itself and herself in hiding from the law. It was one thing to lie to protect her son, but she had no right to involve a good and honest man like Sheriff Barclay in her deceptions.

Well, then. It was up to her to make sure Carson understood she didn't want him in her life. Seamus Maguire and

Winston Kenrick had taught her all she cared to know about men.

With her thoughts still churning, Mary fed herself and Keary, then got them both dressed and ready for church. She was thankful Blanche had included a warm cloak with a hood among the clothes she'd given her. Mary suspected she would need it to stay dry until they were home again.

When she set off walking toward Whistle Creek, Baba insisted on following at her heels. Mary tried several times to order her to wait at the house, but for the first time since the dog had appeared, Baba refused Mary's commands.

"If 'tis sitting out in the rain you want to be, then you'll be getting your wish," she muttered as she quickened her stride, Baba continuing to follow along.

Mary's pulse accelerated as she entered town and walked toward the church. Last week, the members of the congregation hadn't been all that welcoming. Mary had known it was because she was living at the saloon, but it hadn't made their rejection hurt any less. Still, she wouldn't be missing church just because there were those who turned up their noses at her. She had sinned enough in her life without leaving the church altogether.

Mary, girl, there's nothing that can't be forgiven if you'll be but asking.

"Not murder, Ma," she whispered in reply, as if her mother were actually there with her. "Maybe for giving birth to Keary with no husband in sight, but not for murder." She was quite certain the glowering, hellfire-and-brimstone-shouting minister back in County Armagh would agree with her.

Mary was one of the first to arrive at the church that morning. After telling Baba to lie down at the side of the building beneath the shelter of the eaves, she went inside and slipped into the back pew, sliding over to the far corner. She didn't turn her head or watch as others entered the small sanctuary. She'd decided she would mind her own business and let them mind theirs.

But when she heard a sharp gasp and saw the heads craning from those seated at the front of the church, she couldn't help looking to see what the commotion was all about. And there was Blanche Loraine, her brassy orange-red hair piled high on her head in a cluster of curls more suited to a girl than a middle-aged woman. She had forgone the use of face paints, which made her look more sickly than ever.

Blanche smiled faintly when she found Mary. Then she slid into the same pew. "Good morning. I hope you don't mind if I join you."

"Sure and you're welcome, Miss Blanche. But 'tis mighty surprised to see you, I am."

"I'm a bit surprised myself. I saw you coming into town this morning, and all of a sudden, I decided it might do me some good to see the inside of this place at least once before I go."

Mary heard the low murmur of voices. It wasn't hard to catch the words that were meant to be heard. *Harlot... Scandalous... Jezebel...*

Anger flared in her chest. Shouldn't they be making her feel welcome? Shouldn't they be showing a wee bit of charity?

"I don't mind, Mary," Blanche whispered.

"But I'm thinking I do."

"There's nothing they can say that isn't true, I reckon."

"Miss Blanche—"

The other woman shook her head slowly as she laid her right hand over Mary's left. "I've never claimed to be a saint. In fact, I've had a right good time being a sinner." She offered a half smile. "But a body gets to thinking and..." She shrugged. "Anyway, I'm here."

Mary nodded, a sudden lump in her throat making it impossible to reply.

"Here. Let me see the boy." Blanche held out her arms for Keary. She made a funny face, then rubbed her nose against the toddler's. "You two still like it out at that place of the sheriff's?"

"Aye. You should come see us. We even have ourselves a dog now."

"A dog?"

A door behind the pulpit opened at that moment, stopping Mary's reply, and a black-garbed minister stepped through. He was an elderly gentleman, thin and short, with a shock of pure white hair combed back on his head. He wore spectacles on the bridge of a hawklike nose.

"Good morning," he said in a whisper-thin voice while his gaze scanned the congregation, pausing briefly on the two women in the rear pew.

Mary wondered if he would ask them to leave.

But before he could open his mouth again, a tall teenage boy burst into the church, stopping in the aisle near Blanche. "There's been a cave-in at the mine!" he shouted. "There's men trapped below."

In an instant, all the men—including the minister—were running out of the church. They were quickly followed by women and children.

"Come on, Mary. Even I'm tolerated when there's trouble like this. They'll need everyone's help. We'll get back to the saloon and gather up blankets, food, and lanterns."

For a moment Mary couldn't move. She thought of Seamus, who'd been killed in a cave-in back in West Virginia. Then she thought of Quaid. What if her brother was working at the Lucky Lady? What if he was trapped in that mine? Maybe Jeff Christy hadn't checked the records to see if her brother was working there. What if...

"Come on," Blanche repeated. "Time's a-wasting."

As Mary followed the other woman, she tried to reason with herself. She'd learned there were many mines in this region known as the Silver Valley. Quaid could be anywhere, in any one of them. He might not even be in Idaho. There was no cause for her to think the worst.

And yet her heart wouldn't stop pounding in dread.

—

Carson broke into a cold sweat just stepping close to the elevator cage filled with volunteers, their hands grasping picks and shovels. As the hoist engine fired up and the cage disappeared into the adit, Carson felt the same shortness of breath that he imagined those ten miners trapped below—at the two-thousand-foot level, he'd been told—were feeling. He watched the cable slide through the pulley and silently called himself every name for a coward he could think of.

"We'll get them out," Jeff Christy said, but he sounded cautious rather than confident.

Carson glanced at the mine manager. "Do you know what happened?"

Jeff shook his head. "They were driving another horizontal tunnel off of number nineteen. They weren't blasting at the time. The wall just gave way."

"Are you sure any of them survived?"

Again the other man shook his head. "Too much came down. Can't hear a thing. It could take us several days to reach them."

Carson didn't need to be a miner to envision what had happened. He'd spent most of his life in mining towns. Most of his friends and acquaintances had been or were miners. His one brief experience in a mine filled any gaps that their stories left unexplained.

There would have been the sounds of breaking timbers and a grinding rumble. Then there would have been a violent rush of air, followed by an eerie silence. Any survivors—and God willing, there were survivors—would have been plunged into total and complete darkness, their carbide lamps extinguished.

Carson smelled the smoke from the day's blasting, just as the men below must smell it. It seemed he could also hear the water dripping from the ceiling of the tunnel and trickling out of the walls. The miners' clothes would be uncomfortably damp. The heat would be unbearable. Whatever food they had with them, if uneaten, would quickly spoil in the moist, hot air. Whatever matches and candles they had with them would be gone in a few days. Then they would be trapped in darkness again, listening to the dripping walls and the beating of their own hearts.

Suddenly, Carson needed air. He quickly strode toward the mine entrance. Once outside, he paused and took several deep breaths. A measure of strength returned to his legs, and his pulse slowed. He was thankful for the cool, fresh air that brushed his damp, perspiring skin and filled his starved lungs.

It was hard for him, this weakness in his character. He had a healthy respect for fear in its proper place. He'd never gone up against a man with a gun without knowing he could die, but fear in such instances only seemed to sharpen his thinking.

His terror of close, dark places was another matter entirely. It left him feeling helpless. It numbed his mind. It was cowardice, pure and simple, and he hated being a coward.

He removed his hat and wiped his forehead with the sleeve of his shirt. As he placed the Stetson back on his head, he heard someone calling his name. He turned and saw Edith, the young girl from the saloon, hurrying toward him.

"Sheriff Barclay," she said in a breathy voice, "have you seen Johnny?"

"Tyrell? No."

She glanced toward the mine entrance. "He was coming out here this morning. He was gonna talk to a friend of his about something important, he said." Her gaze swung back to meet Carson's. "His friend is one of them trapped below. I just heard. Do you. . .do you think Johnny went down into the mine with him? His friend, I mean. I. . .I can't find him anywhere."

Carson would have had to be blind not to see what Edith was feeling. And in that moment, he also saw that she was more than just one of Miss Blanche's girls. She was a young woman with a heart, a girl able to love and care like any other. The notion surprised him, for he'd never thought it possible. Not just about Edith. About any of the women like her. Certainly it hadn't been true of Aldora.

He put his hand on Edith's shoulder. "I'll ask Jeff if he knows anything about John. But I doubt he'd have gone down into the mine. He's probably up here somewhere. Or maybe he's with the volunteers."

"I hope so," she whispered, furiously blinking as she fought tears.

Briefly he wondered what it would be like to have someone worried about him the way this girl was worrying about John. And then, for some reason, he thought about Mary Malone with her wild mane of black hair and her flashing dark eyes. What would it be like to have Mary worry about him?

As if summoned by his thoughts, Mary broke free of the crowd of those waiting for word of the miners and hurried toward Carson and Edith.

When she arrived beside them, her gaze met with his only for a moment before she turned her attention to Edith. While balancing Keary on her hip, she put her other arm around the younger woman's shoulders.

"Would you be helping us, Edith? We're putting together food to send down to the volunteers, and Greta is complaining she's only got two hands."

Edith nodded, her lower lip quivering.

Mary glanced at Carson once again. "You'll be looking for John, Sheriff?"

"Yeah, I'll look for him."

"Thank you," she said, then gently guided Edith away.

Carson seemed unable to tear his gaze away from Mary's back. He'd never known anyone like her before, but it was hard to define what made her different. Except that whenever he thought about her lately, he pictured a home, a family. He thought about love—which was a crazy thing for him to think about!

Other than Claudia Hailey, who'd been a surrogate mother to him in the years he'd lived with her and David, Carson had believed himself incapable of loving any woman. Besides, he'd seen how Claudia suffered when her husband was killed by a drunk with a gun. Carson had decided the night David died that lawmen shouldn't have wives, because then they wouldn't leave behind widows.

He gave his head a swift shake. He didn't know what had gotten into him, but this sure wasn't the time to be mulling over his personal philosophies. Not when there could be men dying two thousand feet beneath him.

Rain started to fall in the early afternoon and didn't seem inclined to ever let up. Blanche and Mary handed out many cups of coffee from beneath a canvas shelter held up with poles, ropes, and stakes, while Edith watched Keary within the shelter of a tent.

At first the women among those waiting for news—most of them miners' wives—refused to come near Miss Blanche and the others from the Painted Queen. But as time went on, even the most self-righteous among them needed the warmth of a cup of coffee to ward off the chill.

It was odd, the way she was feeling, Blanche thought as she filled another tin cup with the black brew Greta kept boiling over the campfire. There had been other disasters in Whistle Creek through the years, and Blanche had helped then, too. But she had done it with an angry attitude, a sense of flaunting who she was and what she did in the faces of those women who judged her and her kind. Today, there wasn't any anger on her part. She felt only sympathy for them.

Blanche supposed it was because her end was near. It changed a person's perspective, made one look harder at the things that were important and the things that weren't. It also probably had something to do with Lloyd's death. She'd been hurt by his stealing from her, but she hadn't been surprised. She'd loved him once, more than a woman like her had a right to love. She supposed there was a part of her heart that would always love him.

She glanced to her right and saw Mary speaking softly to a woman who was weeping. "I'm thinking you must be strong," Mary said. "Don't go losing your hope."

Mary had made a difference in the way Blanche looked at things, too. The young woman was a strange combination of fiery temper and gentle spirit, and she was like Blanche in a few ways. She wasn't defeated by the hand life had dealt her. She just took the cards and played them the best way she knew how.

"I'd be most grateful, Miss Loraine, for a cup of your coffee."

She turned her head toward the voice, and there stood the Reverend Mordecai Ogelsby, whom she'd never spoken to once in all the years she'd been in Whistle Creek. Not that their paths had crossed. He'd sure never walked into the Painted Queen, and until this morning, she'd never darkened the door of his church.

"It was good to see you at services." He had a thin, parchmentlike voice. "I regret you didn't have the opportunity to hear the sermon I'd prepared. It was one of my better efforts, I believe."

Blanche wondered how he could be heard from the pulpit with such a soft voice, even in a church as small as the one in town.

"It's good of you to do this, Miss Loraine," he continued. "I'm afraid we're in for a long wait."

She shrugged, uncertain what to say to this man of the cloth. A year ago she would probably have said something crass, would surely have tried to embarrass him. She wasn't tempted to do anything of the sort now.

He reached out, touched her shoulder lightly. "If ever you wish to talk to me about anything, I would consider it a privilege."

Blanche was suddenly overtaken by a fit of coughing. It took several minutes before she could control it and draw a relatively peaceful breath. By that time, Mary had come to stand beside her, watching her with a concerned gaze.

"I'm all right, Mary," Blanche whispered hoarsely once she was able. Then she cleared her throat as she looked at the minister. "Thanks for the offer, Reverend Ogelsby. Maybe I'll take you up on it. There are a few things about your God I wouldn't mind having answers to."

"He isn't just my God, Miss Loraine. He's the one true God, the only God. I'll look forward to answering your questions, if I'm able." With that, he walked toward the group that was standing closest to the mine entrance, an assembly made up of the wives and children of those trapped below.

For days, the town of Whistle Creek held its collective breath. Rescuers worked around the clock, digging and chipping away at the rubble of rock and timber.

By the second day, Edith had taken to her bed in a state of mourning. John Tyrell was nowhere to be found, and everyone agreed the only explanation was that he'd been in the mine when the cave-in occurred. Edith was inconsolable, convinced that her Johnny was lost forever.

By the third day, the attitude of those waiting for news changed noticeably toward Mary. While Blanche's presence was never entirely accepted—she had been an outcast for too many years—Mary was another matter. It was the sheriff who'd made the difference. Whenever the opportunity arose, Carson explained the exact nature of Mary's job at the saloon, making it sound more respectable than the townsfolk had imagined. He also made it a point to explain that Mary had lost her husband in a mining accident, thus putting her on more even ground with the other wives.

Of course, Mary didn't know she had the sheriff to thank for the warming attitude toward her. She only knew the women spoke to her more freely and without so much censure in their eyes, and she was grateful for it.

Sheriff Barclay himself rarely spoke to Mary in those long days of waiting, but she was always aware of him. He helped organize the shifts of volunteers. He rounded up more equipment. He consoled the families. Mary could see how much others respected him, how much they listened to him, and for some unexplainable reason, she was warmed by the knowledge.

It was on the fourth day of the agonizing wait that Mary met Fenella Russell. Twelve-year-old Nellie, as the girl was called, was the only child of Dunmore Russell, a Scotsman who had worked at the Lucky Lady for the past seven years. Dunmore was among those trapped by the cave-in. Nellie's mother had died many years before, and so Nellie waited alone for news of her father. Seeing that the child needed something to occupy her time and her mind, Mary asked her to watch after Keary and Baba.

The ploy worked the majority of the time. Baba didn't need watching, of course, but the active toddler kept Nellie constantly on the go, too busy to fret. Mary was glad. She remembered well what it was like to lose her parents. She knew the pain the girl was suffering. She hoped and prayed that Mr. Russell would be spared, just as she hoped and prayed for John Tyrell and all those other men.

The fifth day dawned with the first clear skies they had seen since Sunday. Steam rose from the rain-dampened earth as warming rays of morning kissed the ground. Perhaps it was only because of the sunshine, but there was an air of anticipation that spread through those camped near the mine entrance. And at noon, the words they had all been awaiting arrived.

"They've broken through! They've found survivors!"

Mary held Nellie in her arms as the child cried in heartbroken sobs. Mary cried, too. Only one man had perished in the cave-in, and that man was Dunmore Russell. Nellie was left alone in the world at the age of twelve.

A short while before, Mary had overheard Reverend Ogelsby say something about an orphanage in a town to the west of Whistle Creek. The very notion caused her heart to break. Nellie in an orphanage? She couldn't wish that on any child. Especially not Nellie, whom she'd already learned to care for.

"Would you like to come home with me, Nellie?" she asked gently as she smoothed the girl's scraggly hair back from her face. "Keary has taken to you, as have I. You'd be welcome altogether. And Baba likes you, too."

Nellie looked up with huge, sad eyes. Her nose was running, and her dirty, freckled cheeks were wet with tears. "Can I really? Can I really come stay with you?"

"Sure and I couldn't be wanting anything more."

The girl pressed her face against Mary's chest again. "Why'd he have to die?"

"I don't know, love. I don't know."

Holding Nellie tightly, Mary looked around. Women and children were hugging their husbands and fathers, smiling and laughing and rejoicing. The gloomy, fearful atmosphere from the last few days had changed dramatically to one of celebration. Only here, beside Blanche Loraine's tent, was there sorrow.

She saw Carson striding toward them, and her arms tightened around Nellie. Before he reached them, she said, "You'll not be taking Nellie to an orphanage, Sheriff Barclay. She'll be coming to live with me and Keary." She lifted her chin stubbornly, daring him to challenge her decision. "'Tis settled, and I'll hear nothing more about it."

His expression didn't reveal what he thought of her announcement. He simply stared at her for a few moments, then asked, "Are you sure that's what you want?"

"Didn't I say so?"

"Nellie?" He touched her shoulder. "Is that what you want, too?"

The girl nodded without looking at him.

"You're sure there's no other family we can contact? No aunts or uncles or grandparents?"

Nellie started to sob again.

Carson's gaze returned to Mary. She saw then that he was saddened, too. That he wished he could stop the child's pain and make it all come out right again. He had a tender heart, this man of the law. It seemed a strange contradiction for one who was so able with a gun.

"I'll help break camp," he told Mary, "and then I'll see you all back to town."

"We'll be getting her things together."

He nodded, then moved off.

"Nellie, would you show me where you live? We'll need to get your clothes."

The girl sniffed as she pulled from Mary's embrace. "I'll take you."

Blanche volunteered to keep an eye on Keary, who was napping soundly in the carriage. Then Mary and Nellie, with Baba at their heels, set off toward the small shacks that lined the foot of the mountain on the opposite side of the Lucky Lady compound.

The Russell shack, a single room with a potbelly stove, two cots, and an unsteady table with two chairs, was tidy and uncluttered. Mary discovered there was little for Nellie to retrieve. Most items inside the shack belonged to the mining company. There were only a few articles of clothing, the well-worn family Bible, brought to America from Scotland a generation before, and a fading photograph of her mother and father on their wedding day. Nellie was able to carry it all herself.

Mary fought the thickness in her throat and the welling of tears in her eyes. It was like seeing herself again after her ma died. She remembered the mean, dark tenant's hut with its thatched roof where Maeve Malone had breathed her last. She could see her own threadbare clothes and dirty bare feet. Mary had been fourteen at the time, tiny and skinny and raggedy. She hadn't been alone in the world like Nellie. She'd had her brothers and her da. But she'd felt alone, all the same.

"I'm thinking you'll like our house," she said, forcing a smile as they left the shack and walked toward the carriage. "Keary and I moved into it a week ago just, and 'tis a fine home for us."

Nellie's only reply was a loud sniff.

"Well, now. I guess you'll be seeing for yourself soon enough." She patted Nellie's shoulder, letting her hand linger in a gesture of comfort.

The road back to Whistle Creek narrowed as it left the Lucky Lady Mine, passing through a canyon with high, rocky walls. Carson drew in on the reins and pulled his horse back behind the Loraine carriage.

John Tyrell sat beside Blanche in the rear seat. He was dirty and hungry, but he was alive. In fact, some of the miners had called him a hero, saying it was his quick thinking that had saved many of them from dying along with Dunmore Russell. When they'd praised John, Carson had seen something new in the younger man's face—hope, pride, a sense of renewed worth—and he believed John was going to be okay from here on out. Those things didn't take away the disfiguring scars from his face or give him back the use of his arm, but they restored something of greater value. Add to that Edith's love...

Yes, he reckoned John would be okay.

Carson's gaze shifted to Mary. She sat in the front seat, driving the horses, Nellie and Keary beside her. She'd worked tirelessly over the past few days. She'd camped out at the mine as if she had a loved one trapped below. She'd been a constant source of comfort to those around her. He knew because he'd found himself observing her whenever possible, taking comfort himself in her presence.

He wondered if Mary had loved her husband with the same sort of passion as Edith apparently loved John. He wondered if

Mary had waited for days by the mine in West Virginia. He wondered if she'd wept inconsolably when she'd learned her husband wouldn't return to her and her child. He wondered if she would ever be willing to love again.

It was a crazy thing to wonder. Especially since it had nothing to do with him.

He would do well to remember it.

Eleven

Whatever was I thinking? Mary wondered as she cut the mutton into fairly large pieces.

Why had she invited the sheriff to supper again? The disaster at the mine had saved her from honoring her first invitation, but then she'd issued another. Yesterday, when Carson brought her a rooster and six laying hens, the request had just slipped out, as natural as you please, and there'd been no way she could take the words back.

There was no mistaking it. She'd gone daft. Completely and utterly daft!

Mary began to peel and slice the potatoes and onions for the Irish stew, her thoughts churning.

She was becoming much too dependent upon Carson. She was certain she should refuse all the kind things he did for them. First it was the use of this cabin, then it was the stacks of firewood he'd chopped. And in the week since the miners were rescued, he'd done even more. He'd brought supplies from Chuck's Mercantile, saying it was because Mary had taken Nellie in and would need the extra food, and then he'd repaired the outhouse and patched a spot in the roof. Next he'd put up a chicken coop, and now he'd supplied the chickens, too. Carson had never said anything untoward to Mary, never indicated he wanted anything—respectable or otherwise—in repayment. He always waved off her thanks, saying he would do this for anybody.

She wasn't convinced that was entirely the truth.

Perhaps Mary didn't listen to her better judgment because it was so obvious Keary was smitten with Carson. Or maybe it was because the man seemed to be just as smitten with the little boy.

Or maybe it was because Mary herself. . .

But she wouldn't even consider that!

With the back of her wrist, she swept wisps of hair from her forehead. Then she put a layer of potatoes in the pot, followed by a sprinkling of parsley and thyme. She covered the potatoes with sliced meat and onions and seasoned it with salt and pepper. Then she repeated each step, topping it all with a layer of potatoes. She poured a measure of water over the meat and vegetables before covering the pot and setting it on the stove to simmer gently.

Faith, but she hoped Carson was fond of Irish stew and potato-apple dumplings.

Baba's barking and Nellie's laughter filtered through Mary's troubled thoughts and drew her toward the open doorway. The August sun glared down on the meadow from a cloudless blue sky. It would be more than an hour before it dipped behind the mountains to the west and gave them respite from the heat of the day. Mary was surprised to find the air was nearly as hot and still outside as it had been inside the cabin. She shaded her eyes with one hand as her gaze sought and found the children.

Nellie sat on the ground, her back leaning against a tree. She held Keary in her arms and pointed at Baba, who was trying to catch a butterfly. In her futile pursuit of the insect, the galloping dog barked and jumped and tumbled, ears flapping like hairy flags in a strong wind. Mary laughed aloud at the sight.

Baba's chase was interrupted by the sound. Looking, Baba saw her mistress and bounded over in her direction. The dog plopped down in front of Mary, tongue hanging out one side of her mouth. Mary would have sworn Baba was grinning.

"Ah, you're a corker, you are," Mary said as she stroked the dog's head. "A real corker."

Baba barked in agreement.

Glancing up again, Mary saw Nellie and Keary walking toward the cabin, Keary's little legs moving as fast as he could make them go. A feeling of pure, unadulterated joy shot through her.

How had it happened, all of this? She had a home of her own and work she enjoyed because it challenged her mind. She had a healthy son. She had friends in Blanche and Edith and John. She had Nellie, who was both someone she could help and someone who could help her. She had one of the ugliest dogs in the world, who loved them all. She had chickens in the coop and food in the larder. She had lovely clothes, like nothing she'd owned in her entire life. She had no right to any of it, and still it had come her way.

Tomorrow would bring problems, to be sure. And yet, even knowing there would be more worries, she felt oddly secure. There was a rightness about the here and now, a joy in simply being alive.

How had it all happened?

As if in answer to her question—or perhaps, as one more example of the blessings she enjoyed—Carson appeared on his dun gelding, looking dashing in his black Stetson, a white shirt with a string tie around the collar, and black trousers and suit coat. He didn't normally wear such fancy clothes, and so she knew he had dressed up for this supper with her.

Her heart flip-flopped, then began to race. He was early. He wasn't supposed to come until six o'clock. Mary wasn't cleaned up. Her hair was a shambles, and she probably had flour on her cheeks. Her dress was soiled from her cooking and cleaning, and the stew wouldn't be ready for another two hours.

"Nellie," she said quickly, "be keeping an eye on Keary and welcome the sheriff while I put myself to rights. Tell him I'll be out directly." Then she stepped back and swung the door closed.

Faith and begorra!

She was so nervous she could scarcely make her fingers unbutton her bodice. There was no call for her to be feeling this way, but there it was. She did feel it. All aflutter. Excited and nervous. The way she used to feel when Seamus...

Her careening emotions were stopped by the cold dash of reality. Carson was nothing like Seamus, and she was no longer the foolish girl who had fallen for an Irishman's blarney. Besides, something told her Carson would be far more dangerous to her heart than Seamus had ever been.

She sank onto her bed and closed her eyes as she faced another truth.

She was guilty of a grievous crime, whether the law found her or not. Even if she let herself fall in love with Carson, nothing could come of it. The fear of discovery would always stand between them. He was too good. He deserved better than that from her. If Mary were to give her heart again, it would have to be with complete honesty. She could never be honest with Carson.

"Then I shall be making him me friend," she whispered. "'Tis possible between a man and a woman and would be enough." She stood and hastily began to change her clothes. "'Tis friends we shall be, then."

By the time she was dressed and her hair once again pinned in place, Mary had convinced herself there was nothing to worry about. She was convinced she felt nothing more for Carson than friendship and appreciation for all he'd done to help her. She was convinced of it right up until the moment she opened her cabin door and saw him holding her giggling son high above his head.

Then her heart called her the liar that she was.

———

From the corner of his eye, Carson saw the door open. He lowered Keary, holding the toddler against his chest, and turned toward the house.

He'd thought Mary beautiful the first time he'd seen her. He thought her even more so today. She was wearing a blue gown the color of camas flowers. Her cheeks were flushed a becoming pink. She had captured her long, thick hair in a bun, but wisps curled at her nape and near her temples. She looked deceptively fragile.

"Sure and you're too early for supper, Sheriff Barclay."

"I know. I thought I might chop some more wood for you."

Her gaze slipped down and up the length of him. "In your fine clothes, will you now? I'm thinking not. 'Tis too much you've done for us already. How will I ever be repaying you?"

He thought to tell her she could give him a kiss. He'd been thinking about that a lot lately. And maybe he would have asked for that kiss if Keary hadn't suddenly squawked a demand to be put down.

Just as well, Carson thought as he lowered the boy to the ground.

Keary hurried toward Baba, Nellie obediently following after him. When Keary reached the dog, he buried his face in the animal's coarse coat and hugged her around the neck, then took off in a jerky run, giggling as Baba followed.

"That's the ugliest dog I've ever seen," Carson said with a shake of his head. Then his gaze returned to Mary.

"'Tis the truth." Her smile was repeated in her eyes. "But we none of us have much to say about that. We are born to look the way we'll look."

He couldn't stop himself from saying, "And you, Mrs. Malone, were born to look particularly beautiful."

She blushed and glanced away, turning her eyes toward her son. "'Tis kind of you to say so, Sheriff."

"Not kind. Just the truth."

"'Tis the dress Miss Blanche gave to me." She ran the palms of her hands over the skirt, and he saw they were trembling.

Was it possible she felt the same nervous excitement when they were together as he did?

He removed his Stetson, then took a step toward her. "It isn't the dress, though it's pretty enough. It's you, ma'am. Just you."

Her gaze swung back to him. "I'm thinking 'twould be better if you weren't saying such things."

He reckoned she was right. It would be better. But the cold hard fact was, he wanted to say them. He needed to say them. He was feeling things he'd never felt before, things he'd never expected to feel, and he wanted to explore them.

Lord, I don't know much about loving a woman. I don't know the right things to say or do. But I keep on thinkin' this is where you want me, so if it isn't, you'd better show me quick.

The Kenrick mansion on Madison Avenue, built twenty years before and paid for out of the vast fortunes of Pendergast Industries, was a model of good taste. The grand dining room was no exception. Hundreds of electric lights glowed brightly from crystal chandeliers. Gilded mirrors lined two walls. A third wall was solid glass, looking out onto a private garden of sculptured hedges and colorful flowers.

That evening, as Portia Pendergast Kenrick looked down the long table set with fine china and beautiful silver, her thirty guests seated in a carefully selected order along both sides, she thought how very content she had been in this house. She and Winston owned other residences, of course, but it was this house she had always preferred. Invitations to Portia Kenrick's supper parties were eagerly sought after. It was a well-known fact in New York society that one wasn't anyone unless one had been a guest in the Kenricks' Madison Avenue home.

At the far end of the table sat Portia's husband. Even without her glasses, which vanity precluded her from wearing when entertaining, she could see that Winston was flirting with the women on either side of him. In fact, if Portia wasn't mistaken—and she wasn't—she believed the woman on his right, Amelia Pedersen, was his most current lover. She wondered if Mr. Pedersen had also guessed of the clandestine visits these two participated in.

But it wasn't Winston's latest conquest that caused Portia's brow to furrow in thought. It had more to do with her husband's ever-increasing obsession with finding Mary Malone and the silver cigar box the foolish girl had taken. Winston's behavior was quite out of character. It was far more than mere anger that Mary had struck him—undoubtedly well deserved, if Portia knew her husband, and she did. No, there was an underlying sense of panic in his actions, in his words. And that was very unlike Winston.

Why would he be afraid? What would give him cause to want to find that silly cigar box so desperately? Oh, it was valuable, but only relatively so. It could be replaced with a quick order to the silversmith, and Winston knew it. The excuse of sentimentality he continued to use didn't ring true. So why?

138

There was much more to this matter than Winston wanted Portia to know. Which, of course, was precisely why Portia was so determined to discover the truth.

It was also why she was paying Tibble Knox—paying quite handsomely, she might add—to report to her before he reported anything to her husband. Tomorrow the gnomelike detective would tell Winston he had located Mrs. Inga Bridger in Uppsala, Iowa, and it was Mrs. Bridger who might hold the key to finding Mary. Portia knew Winston would insist on accompanying Mr. Knox to Uppsala to meet with Mrs. Bridger. What he didn't know was that Portia was going to insist on going with them as well. She could already imagine his reaction.

She smiled at her guests as she motioned for the serving to begin. Then her gaze returned to the far end of the table and to her husband.

Yes, she could imagine what Winston's reaction would be.

Her smile broadened as she engaged in a bit of conversation with the gentleman on her left.

⁓

Shadows were growing long in the protected valley as Mary and the others sat down to supper. Carson had carried the table and chairs out of the cabin and set them beneath the spreading branches of an ancient Rocky Mountain maple, and it was there they dined on the thick and creamy stew, brown soda bread, and the old-country pudding, made with a potato paste filled with apples, cloves, and sugar, and topped with butter.

Baba positioned herself between Nellie and Keary, having quickly learned this was the place where she would benefit the most. Keary always threw food on the floor when he was no longer hungry, and Nellie couldn't resist slipping a bite to the dog every now and then.

Mary turned a tolerantly blind eye on the shenanigans. The Whartons, the Wellingtons, and the Kenricks would never have allowed pets in their fancy dining rooms. But Mary didn't care. Come to think of it, none of her former employers would have allowed children in their fancy dining rooms either.

What mattered to Mary were the smiles on Keary's and Nellie's faces. Especially Nellie's. The girl was always willing to help, and she adored Keary, had become almost a second mother to him. But she was often teary-eyed, and sometimes she had nightmares. Today was the first day since she'd come to stay with Mary that Nellie had truly smiled and enjoyed herself, earlier when Baba had been chasing the butterfly and now as they sat around the table.

"How come you're not a miner?" Nellie asked Carson all of a sudden.

He leaned toward the girl and, in a stage whisper, said, "Because I'm scared to death of the mines." Then he smiled, the look assuring them all that he was teasing. As he straightened, he asked, "Would you like to hear how they found the silver in these parts?"

Nellie nodded.

"Seems old Noah Kellogg and a few friends of his were prospecting up in this district when Kellogg's jackass wandered away. So Kellogg and the others went after it. They found all sorts of traces of that jackass, wads of its hair where it had scraped against timber and such, so it wasn't hard to follow. Tracks plain as day. Well, when they finally caught up, there it was, standing on the side of a hill, staring off across the canyon, its eyes fixed on something and its ears set forward. When those men got to that jackass, it didn't run off again. Just kept staring across the canyon at what turned out to be an ore chute that was reflecting the sun's rays like a mirror. The sheer glitter had that pack animal mesmerized, so they say. Made Kellogg a mighty rich man." He grinned at Mary. "I keep setting that horse of mine loose in the hills, but he never has found me a vein of galena. Guess I'll have to keep sheriffin' for a living."

Mesmerized. That was a good word to describe the way Mary felt beneath the blue of his gaze. Mesmerized. Scarcely able to breathe.

"Is that story true," Nellie asked, "or are you just spinning yarn?"

Carson glanced at the girl. He drew an X over his chest. "Cross my heart." Then he winked at her and said, "'Course, even plumbers and housewives know full well that silver and lead lose their brightness when exposed to the air. Turns a drab gray like most of the other rock around here. So I expect most of the tale is pure moonshine. But it does make for good story-telling."

Nellie scowled. "If I told a whopper like that, my father would've tanned my hide for lying." Her eyes immediately welled with tears. She hopped up from her chair and raced off, disappearing around the side of the house.

Carson started to rise. "What did I say? I–"

"No," Mary said quickly. "Stay here. She's just needing some time to herself. Let her be."

He looked at her. "But what did I–"

"'Twas nothing you did or said, Sheriff. 'Tis only when she remembers her da. Then the crying comes on her. I'm thinking it will pass soon enough. Time'll do what words cannot." She stood even as he sat. "You just be staying there while I pour the coffee."

"If you're sure." He sounded unconvinced.

"Aye, I am that." She offered a gentle smile. "I'll be but a moment." She turned and walked toward the house.

The rooftop of the cabin was splashed in gold as the last rays of sunshine reached into the valley. In a moment, evening would arrive. Dusk was mere minutes away. It would soon be time for Carson to leave, to ride back to town before darkness fell. Mary knew she should hurry and send him on his way. But she was reluctant to have him go. She'd enjoyed this meal more than she wanted to admit.

Perhaps because, in admitting so, she would realize exactly what it was she could never have.

Twelve

Carson dreamed of Mary in a blue gown, her wild mass of hair falling free. She was running through a meadow of wildflowers, and her laughter drifted to him on a breeze. He ran after her, stretching out his arm to touch her. But try as he might, he couldn't catch her. He ran and ran and ran, but she was always out of reach.

Always just out of reach.

Hot coffee splashed over the rim of the cup and onto Carson's left hand, scalding him.

"Blast!"

The tin cup clattered to the floor, splattering coffee in a wide swath. Quickly, Carson returned the pot to the stove. He shook his hand, as if trying to throw off the pain. Then he grabbed a towel and mopped up the mess he'd made, muttering all the while.

It was the fault of that dream. He couldn't get it out of his head. He couldn't think straight, couldn't even pour himself a cup of coffee because of it. Even now, if he closed his eyes, he would see her, running through that flowering meadow, looking beautiful and wild and free.

Maybe his dream was trying to tell him something. That he was supposed to catch her? That he would never catch her?

Only he didn't put much stock in dreams. At least not his own. God hadn't created him to be a dreamer of dreams like Joseph of the Old Testament. No, indeed. Carson was a practical man, the sort who lived by rules and hard facts and reality. It's why he was good at his job.

And yet...

Before he'd left the cabin last night, he'd invited Mary and the children to have supper with him in town this evening. He couldn't cook, but Zeb Brewer over at the Whistler Café could. He was aware that taking Mary to supper would cause talk, if there wasn't plenty of it already. In all the years he'd been sheriff of Whistle Creek, Carson had never paid court to a lady. He'd never been interested before now.

That was no surprise, of course. There weren't many single females in these parts. Having supper with Mary and her little brood would be grist for the gossip mill.

Suddenly it occurred to him that he didn't care what the gossips said.

He sat back on his heels, his hands braced against his thighs, while he mulled over this unexpected discovery.

It was true. He really didn't care what folks said or thought. He wanted to be with Mary Malone. The more often, the better. He wanted to know everything about her, what caused her to laugh, what caused her to cry. He wanted to run his fingers through her thick cascade of ebony hair. He wanted to listen to her sweet Irish brogue and breathe in the soft scent of lilacs that always lingered near her. He wanted to see the twinkle in her wide brown eyes when she looked after Keary.

Oh, the little colleen had gotten under his skin something fierce. He didn't know if what he felt was love, but it had to be something close to it.

He shook his head slowly. There was no denying it any longer. Carson was thinking along the lines of matrimony.

Marriage. Carson Barclay was actually considering marriage. A home, family, roots, obligations. He waited to feel a sudden chill, a return to old truths about the untrustworthiness of most women, old beliefs about lawmen never marrying. They didn't come. Instead, he felt a lightness of heart such as he'd never felt before.

I don't suppose this surprises you, Lord, but it sure surprises me.

Smiling, he stood, tossed the towel into a box near the stove, then grabbed his hat and left the office. He whistled softly as he strode along the sidewalk toward the café. He hoped Zeb would be amenable to cooking up something special tonight.

A woman ought to have a special supper on the night she received a proposal of marriage.

Mary hurried along the trail toward home. She was feeling somewhat anxious. For the first time, she'd left Keary behind that morning while she'd gone into work at the saloon. She knew Nellie was a responsible sort. She'd observed how well the girl took care of Keary. Still, Mary had found the hours agonizingly long and would be glad to get home and see for herself that both children were all right.

Then, of course, there was the added anxiety about tonight. It seemed she was doomed to ignore common sense. Otherwise, why would she have accepted Carson's invitation to take supper with him in town? Why would she be anxious about what dress to wear and how to fix her hair and whether or not Keary would be on his best behavior?

"Mrs. Malone!" an unfamiliar male voice hailed from behind her. "Wait!"

She stopped and turned. She recognized the mine owner as he rode toward her.

"Good day, Mrs. Malone." Bryan Halligan grinned as he drew near.

"Good day to you, Mr. Halligan," she answered, hoping her intuitive dislike for the man didn't show in her tone of voice.

"I'm honored that you remember me, ma'am." His grin broadened. "And I'm glad I caught you before you made it all the way home. I just missed finding you at the Painted Queen."

His words caused her to tense. "You were looking for me, sir?"

"I was, indeed." He dismounted, then faced her again. "I've been up at the Lucky Lady Mine, overseeing the investigation into that unfortunate collapse of the tunnel"—his gaze flicked over her appraisingly—"and I found myself hungry for some delightful female companionship. I was hoping you might consent to have supper with me."

As was true the first time she'd met this man, Mary found herself reminded of Winston Kenrick, and a chill shivered up her spine. Instinctively, she took a step backward. "I cannot, Mr. Halligan, but 'twas nice of you to ask."

One corner of his mouth twitched before Halligan said, "Please reconsider, my dear Mrs. Malone."

There was something menacing in his eyes, a look that once again reminded Mary of her former employer.

"Sure and 'tis not possible, sir." She wanted to light out for home, but she hated the idea of him following her there. She hated the idea of him knowing where she lived—which he apparently did.

"I won't be in Whistle Creek long. My work at the mine is nearly finished."

"Then I hope you'll be having a safe journey back to Spokane." She started to turn away.

He laid his hand on her arm, not grasping, yet somehow holding her there. "Mrs. Malone, it would be a mistake to make an enemy of me." He spoke softly, but it didn't disguise the threat in his words. "Now, agree to have supper with me. You'll be glad you did."

Her temper flared hot. "I'll have you taking your hand off o' me." She tried to jerk away.

"Just who do you think you are?" His grip tightened.

"I'm thinking I'm Mary Emeline Malone," she answered through gritted teeth. And then she kicked him in the shin as hard as she could.

Halligan yelped in surprise. He released his hold on her arm and stumbled back a step.

Mary's instincts shouted at her to run, but she stubbornly held her ground. She was tired of running scared.

"I'll not be bullied by the likes o' you, Mr. Halligan. You're not me master. I'm a free woman, I am, and I'll not be having supper with you tonight or any other night. Will you be understanding that plain enough now?"

Halligan's eyes narrowed. "You'll be sorry you did that."

She gave her head a tiny toss in reply, a show of bravado she wasn't feeling on the inside. "I'm thinking you're wrong."

For a breathless moment, he continued to scowl at her. Then, abruptly, he turned, remounted his horse, and rode away.

The fury drained from Mary in an instant, leaving her shaken and weak in the knees. *Control your temper, Mary girl,* her da had told her, but she'd never learned to follow his advice. If she had, she wouldn't be living in Idaho, hiding from the law.

Carson stepped into the darkened church. "Christy?" he called softly. "You in here?"

A shadow toward the front of the building moved. A moment later, it became the clear shape of a man walking toward him.

"What's this all about?" Carson asked once he could see the mine manager clearly. "Why'd you send a note for me to meet with you here? You could've come to my office."

"Halligan's somewhere in town," Jeff Christy answered, "and I didn't want him to see us talking."

"Why not?"

Jeff jerked his head toward the nearest pew, and the two of them sat down.

"What's up?" Carson prodded when the other man still didn't answer his previous questions.

"Sheriff, I think Halligan's going to blame that collapse in tunnel nineteen on the miners. The ones who have vocally supported the union in the past. He's going to make it look like the cave-in was intentional rather than an accident, like those men were trying to cause trouble."

"Why?"

Jeff raked the fingers of both hands through his hair while he stared at the floor. "He wants to force the miners to go on strike."

"Strike? But why—"

"So he can bring in scab labor for a pittance of what he pays these men. You know how cheap new immigrants will work. Especially the ones who don't speak English. That, in turn, will drive down wages."

"Is Halligan crazy? Doesn't he remember what happened in this district six years ago?"

Jeff nodded slowly. "He thinks they'll give in, accept the lower wages he wants to pay before the strike stretches out too long or real rioting begins. And if it does, he's confident the governor will step in like he did before. In the meantime, he can get rid of those union organizers."

"Halligan's an idiot."

"Look, Sheriff, I don't have any proof of this. It's just a gut feeling." He paused, then added, "But if I'm right, this whole town could explode."

"I know."

"I've got a lot of friends working in the mine. I don't want to see any of them hurt, maybe killed. Losing Dunmore was bad enough."

Carson frowned thoughtfully. "You don't think Halligan was behind the cave-in, do you, Christy?"

There was a pregnant pause before the manager answered, "There's no evidence that says he was. It still looks to me like an accident."

"Hmm."

Jeff Christy rose from the pew. "I've got to get back to the Lucky Lady. Do what you can, Sheriff."

"Yeah."

Carson waited while the other man slipped out the back door of the church, forcing himself to sit still until enough time had passed for Jeff to be long gone from town. In the meantime, he searched his mind for a solution to the problem.

He didn't like Bryan Halligan. Never had. He was the sort of man who cared little for human life—except for his own, of course. And he made no bones about thinking all underground workers made too much money at three dollars a day, especially since anything they made cut into his own personal profits.

But would Halligan really try to cause a strike?

Last time there was trouble in the Coeur d'Alene district, the strikebreakers had come under attack. One man had been killed and many more injured in an explosion caused by an ore car filled with a hundred pounds of dynamite. Part of a stamp mill had been demolished. The governor had called up six companies of the National Guard, and President Harrison had sent twenty companies of United States infantry. Six hundred miners and their supporters had been imprisoned for several weeks without trial or hearing.

It was hard for Carson to believe anyone would want to intentionally cause something like that again. But if anyone would, Halligan was the man.

Carson left the church, still mulling over the situation. Out of habit, he followed his circuitous route around town, taking Church Street to the depot, then heading east along Lucky Street toward River Street and the rear entrance of the Painted Queen.

He supposed it wouldn't hurt to stop at the saloon. It was possible he might overhear something that could be of use to him. If Jeff suspected Halligan of trying to place the blame of the cave-in on the miners, he supposed others might be thinking the same thing.

He came to an abrupt stop when he saw Halligan himself riding out of the draw that led to Carson's cabin—the cabin where Mary and the children were now staying. Reflexively, his fingers tapped against the gun strapped to his thigh.

What reason, except to see Mary, would take Halligan up that trail? he wondered.

The answer was, None.

He started walking again, quickening his pace so he would arrive at River Street about the same time Halligan rode over the bridge crossing the Coeur d'Alene.

"Hello, Halligan."

"Sheriff."

"I heard you'd been out at the mine."

"Yes." Halligan reined in.

"Have you discovered what caused it? The accident, I mean." He'd chosen his words purposefully, and now he waited to see what the mine owner's reaction would be.

Halligan shook his head. His expression remained neutral. "Nothing yet."

"Too bad."

"Don't worry. We'll find the cause."

Carson was getting nowhere fast. He decided to change course. "I see you were up to my old place. I didn't know you and Mrs. Malone were friends." He couldn't keep the edge out of his voice, no matter how hard he tried.

"I wouldn't say friends exactly." Halligan leaned down and rubbed his shin with his fingertips before dismounting. When he faced the sheriff again, he said, "I hope you're keeping your eyes and ears open for troublemakers. Like I told you before, I'm sure something is afoot with the miners. I think that cave-in's just the beginning." He headed for the center of town, leading his horse behind him.

Carson didn't fall into step beside Halligan as was surely expected. He simply stood and watched the other man walk down River Street, then turn west on Main, disappearing behind the barbershop and bathhouse.

Jeff was right. Carson had no doubts left. Halligan meant to put the blame on the miners. He meant to cause trouble at the Lucky Lady and in Whistle Creek, not avoid it.

But what had Halligan wanted with Mary? He turned his gaze up the draw. For some reason that question concerned him more than the possibility of riots and strikes.

It shouldn't, but it did.

So for the second time in as many days, Carson rode to his cabin several hours before he was expected.

———

"Oh, you poor thing," Mary whispered when she saw the gelding. She completely forgot the reprimand she'd been forming in her head, about Nellie and Keary wandering so far from the cabin.

"I told you," Nellie said. "How long you think he's been there?"

"Sure and I wouldn't be knowing."

The swaybacked pinto stood with his left foreleg lifted off the ground, the knee swollen more than twice its normal size. The knotted end of a frayed rope was snagged in a fallen tree, keeping him from lifting his head above knee level. His black-and-white coat was crisscrossed with tiny cuts and scratches, probably from the branches and thick underbrush of the mountain trails that had brought him to this place, but it looked to Mary as if a whip had caused the welts on his rump.

"Poor laddie," she crooned as she took a step toward him, half expecting him to try to bolt.

But when she looked into the horse's eyes, she knew that was a needless worry. This animal hadn't the strength to run. Mary wasn't sure he would survive another hour.

"Well, boyo, 'tis a fine mess you've got yourself into altogether. Let's be seeing if we can get you free." She circled behind him, then leaned down and freed the snared lead rope.

The horse nickered softly. It sounded a bit like gratitude.

"How're we gonna get him home?" Nellie inquired.

Mary could only shake her head. She knew little about horses. She was able to drive a buggy but had never felt a great deal of confidence when holding the reins. Her da had been too poor to own much in the way of livestock. A few chickens and a goat for milking. Certainly never a horse.

Cautiously, she touched the swollen knee. The horse gave a sort of grunt but didn't strike out at her. She decided to probe a little more, and when she was finished, she was fairly convinced nothing was broken.

"'Tis a bad sprain, I'm thinking," she told Nellie as she straightened. "If we go slow down the trail, we could get him to the house and see that he's fed and watered. Will you be leading the way with Keary?"

"Sure."

"Well, then." Mary took hold of the rope as she stepped in front of the animal. Then she stared him straight in the eyes. "'Tis some walking you'll have to do, if you've a mind to go home with us."

As if he understood, the horse gingerly set the hoof of his injured leg on the ground and limped forward.

Nellie grinned. "Look at him, Keary! He's coming with us."

Keary squealed merrily.

They followed a well-worn deer track down the mountain. It was narrow and slippery with tiny rocks and shale. The going was slow. Mary's skirt got snagged once, suffering a small tear before she had it freed, but other than that, they all managed to reach the meadow without mishap.

"Sure and we're here," Mary said as she patted the horse's neck.

The sound of thundering hooves alerted her to the presence of another. She turned in time to see Carson slide his steed to an abrupt halt.

"Where have you been?" He vaulted to the ground, his gaze sweeping from her to Nellie and Keary, then back again.

Mary was too surprised by his sudden appearance to be insulted by his demanding tone of voice. "Nellie found this poor horse up the mountain."

"And you went up there without the rifle I gave you?"

"The rifle?"

"What if there'd been a cougar or a bear? You shouldn't be traipsing around in the forest without protection."

Her anger came as swift as ever. "I'll be going where I like, when I like, and 'tis not you who'll be telling me otherwise, Sheriff Barclay."

He stepped forward, towering over her, his blue eyes glowering as he stared down. His hands gripped her shoulders, firm but not painfully so. "Don't you know how worried I was when I couldn't find you?"

"Sure and you've no cause to worry about me." She tried to jerk away.

His fingers tightened. The kiss came as suddenly as her anger, but was more unexpected. It was over just as quickly.

She should slap him, she thought as he backed away. She should tell him he'd had no right to do that. She should tell him she wanted nothing to do with him. Not now. Not ever.

But her treasonous heart wouldn't listen to the wise counsel of her mind. Not while her lips tingled from the pressure of his. Not while she could feel the racing of her pulse.

"I'm sorry," he said—but he didn't sound so. He still sounded angry. "I shouldn't have yelled at you. But when I didn't find you here..." His words trailed into silence.

This could not happen, this attraction that crackled between them. She could not allow it to happen. It was dangerous for her, and it was unfair to him. She needed to stop it now, before it was too late. Before he learned the truth about her. Before she told him any more lies.

—

Carson wanted nothing so much as to pull Mary back into his embrace and kiss her again. Slowly this time. As brief as it had been, that first kiss had shaken him to the bottom of his soul. Now he wanted to savor the taste of her soft lips against his. He wanted to test the emotional upheaval in his heart and see if it was real.

"Sure and you must not do that again," Mary said softly, confusion in her wide, brown eyes.

"I didn't mean—"

Nellie's giggle interrupted him.

Mary blushed. "I'm thinking it would be better if we didn't go to supper with you, Sheriff Barclay." She stepped around him, still leading that limping rack of bones she called a horse.

"Mary, wait." He touched her shoulder, then pulled back his hand. "I'll say it again. I'm sorry. I lost my head. I was afraid something had happened to you and the children."

She glanced at him.

"Please, have supper with me."

Nellie chimed in, "Please, Mary."

Carson offered an apologetic grin. "I promise to be on my best behavior."

Mary shook her head slowly. Then she looked at Nellie. "Take Keary to the house."

"But—"

"Now, Nellie." Her tone brooked no argument.

"Oh, all right. But I don't see why."

Mary waited until Nellie obeyed before she turned and met Carson's gaze again. "'Twould be a mistake for you to think there is more than friendship between us, Sheriff Barclay."

He would have been disappointed, except he could see that she was wrestling with her own feelings. He was certain she felt something more than friendship for him. He wasn't giving up yet.

"Mary—"

"No." She raised her hand to stop his words. "'Tis on me own I wish to be. Just me and me son."

"And Nellie and Baba and now this miserable pinto." He smiled again, appealing to her sense of humor. "After all these other strays, outcasts, and orphans, won't you take pity on me, too?"

"You're no outcast," she argued, "and you're too old to be an orphan."

His smile vanished. "But I am alone, Mary."

She caught her breath.

He couldn't help it. He reached out and drew her to him, holding her close. "Don't you see there's something special happening between us?" he asked, his voice low and husky. "I've never felt anything like this. Have you?"

"No," she whispered, shaking her head, her gaze never leaving his. "No."

"It is more than friendship." He brushed his lips against her cheek. "Admit it. It is more."

She closed her eyes, and he felt a quiver run through her. "'Twould be a terrible mistake to admit such a thing."

"Why?" He kissed her forehead.

"I cannot say."

"Why?"

Her reply was so soft, he could scarcely hear her. "Do not ask me, Carson."

Perhaps it was because she'd used his Christian name. Perhaps it was the catch in her voice. Or perhaps it was the note of quiet desperation he'd heard therein. Whatever the reason, Carson understood he had pressed her too far.

"All right, Mary, I won't ask." He rested his cheek against the top of her head. "But it doesn't change what I feel, and it won't change what I want. Remember that, will you?"

"Aye, I'll remember."

~Thirteen

Monday, 15 August 1898
Whistle Creek, Idaho

Dear Inga,

It was good to receive your most recent letter and to learn your wonderful news. I know how much you have hoped and prayed for a baby of your own, and God has heard your prayers.

Today I am driving over to a neighboring town and the mine there where I will inquire about Quaid. It is becoming more imperative that I find my brother, for I am unsure how long I will be able to remain in Whistle Creek. I am thinking it is not good for us to stay much longer. The sheriff's interest in me is one I cannot return.

When I was little, my da was forced from job to job, and he took his family with him. I do not know how many places we lived through the years, but there were many. I used to wish for one home where I could live forever, like the titled families who owned the lands he worked. And to be honest altogether, I would love to stay in this little cottage in the mountains. It is perfect—or as near to perfect as I have ever known.

But to stay would be unfair to the kindest man it has been my good fortune to meet. Aye, it is true. Carson

Barclay is a wonder of a man, handsome and tall, strong and kind and honest. The sheriff is a man of integrity, he is. I am believing he means to propose marriage, but I cannot accept. I cannot tell you why anymore than I can tell him why. So I know it would be better if I should take myself from this place and soon.

My Keary turned a year old last week. He no longer walks with unsure steps. He runs instead. He jabbers constantly, though he makes no sense as yet. He is such a handsome lad, and he holds my heart in his wee hands. There is not anything I would not do to protect him and keep him from harm. Now that you will soon have a child of your own, I know you must be understanding how I feel.

I must close this letter and be about my day's work. I pray that all goes well with you throughout your confinement. Do write again soon, and give my love to your parents and sisters.

With affection always,
Mary Emeline Malone

A seemingly endless fit of coughing left Blanche wilted and longing for the simple luxury of one deep breath of air. *Why was it,* she wondered as she leaned against the pillows at her back, her eyes closed, *that folks seldom knew what really mattered until it was too late?*

"Should I send someone for the doctor, Miss Blanche?"

She opened her eyes. "No, Martin," she answered hoarsely. "We haven't finished our business."

The lawyer shook his head, but he didn't argue with her. Instead, he flipped another page of the thick document, then handed it to her. "There is the new paragraph regarding the Painted Queen Saloon. You already know how I feel about this change you've made."

"Yes, I know." She frowned as she carefully read everything through. It wasn't that she didn't trust Martin Burke. She did. But Blanche had learned long ago that it was she and she alone who had to take responsibility for her business and her own well-being. Sometimes the learning had come hard, but she had learned.

Martin leaned forward. "At least allow me to find out a little more about Mrs. Malone. I could send out a few inquiries. You say you met her in New York. Why not—"

"No!" She gave the man a cross look, then resumed reading.

The lawyer bounced his heels off the floor while restlessly tapping his fingertips against his knees. Blanche had to concentrate hard to ignore the irritating movements, but finally she was convinced everything was exactly as she wanted it.

"Give me a pen, Martin, and bring in the witnesses. I'm ready to sign."

"I still think you're making a mistake, Miss Blanche. This place could bring a small fortune if you were to sell—"

"Martin."

He sighed, defeated. "All right. I'll do as you ask."

"Thank you." She smiled wearily. The business of dying, she was finding out, wasn't any less complicated than the business of living.

A short while later, with her revised will signed and duly witnessed, Blanche bid her lawyer a good afternoon and watched as he took his leave. Then Greta brought her a fresh pot of tea.

"Tea," Blanche muttered as the cook poured the fragrant brew into a cup. "Who'd've thought I'd take up drinking tea instead of brandy?"

Greta clucked her tongue.

Blanche turned her gaze out the window toward the thickly treed mountains beyond. Her eyes filled with tears, much to her irritation. It seemed she was becoming a sentimental fool in her last days.

"No place else like here," Greta said.

Blanche didn't try to respond. There was nothing to say. After all, she agreed. There wasn't any place like her glorious Silver Valley. This was home.

In silent understanding, Greta patted Blanche's shoulder before quietly departing.

Alone again, Blanche tossed off the light coverings on her bed and sat up, then lowered her feet to the floor. With great effort, she stood and made her way across the bedroom to the window. Each breath came with difficulty, and she concentrated hard not to give in to another coughing spell.

At the window, she leaned her forehead against the glass and stared out at the sunny afternoon. Below her lay the town of Whistle Creek. The dusty streets were quiet, usual for a Monday afternoon. She wondered how many of her neighbors had heard that the infamous madam was dying.

And dying soon, she thought as she listened to her own belabored breathing. Very soon.

She sighed and closed her eyes. She supposed it was time for that little chat with the good Reverend Mordecai Ogelsby.

———

Carson tugged on his hat brim, the better to shade his eyes. The air was still and hot and the sky blindingly clear, but a sixth sense told him they were ripe for a thunderstorm come evening. Not a welcome possibility with things as dry as they'd been. It only took one lightning strike to start a raging forest fire.

And they had trouble enough without adding Mother Nature into the mix, he thought with a frown.

"Halligan's gonna do it, ain't he?" John asked. "He's gonna pin the blame on me."

The two men were riding west toward Osburn. Carson had heard a rumor that Halligan had a man bringing in cheap labor for the Lucky Lady, just in case there was a strike. He wanted to see for himself if it was true.

Just in case.

"Yeah, I think that's what he's planning to do."

The younger man shook his head. "You know it ain't true, Sheriff Barclay. I didn't go into the mine to cause trouble, and I'm sure a lot smarter than to blow up a tunnel with me in it. What happened to me"—he pointed at his scarred cheek—"was an accident. But if I was settin' something on purpose, I'd know exactly what I was doin', and I wouldn't get caught neither."

Carson believed him, but it didn't matter what he believed. Besides, Halligan wasn't after the truth. By picking John Tyrell to take the fall, Halligan had chosen well. Accuse the hero of the cave-in of wrongdoing, and he would have the trouble he was after.

"We've got to make the men see reason, John. If they'll hold onto their tempers—"

"Sheriff, it ain't just me. If Halligan fires those other men, the ones tryin' to organize the union, you know what'll happen."

Frustration made Carson grind his teeth. There should be something he could do, but he felt helpless to stop what was coming. When trouble flared, Halligan was going to demand protection, and it would be Carson's job to provide it. The National Guard would probably come in. Scab labor would work the mine. Good men would be out of work. Families would be thrown out of their homes, and innocent people could get hurt if violence became part of the package. In the end, the miners who kept their jobs would go back to work for a reduced wage, and Halligan would take his and his partners' increased profits back to Spokane to enjoy.

The two men rode on in silence for the better part of half an hour. The whole time, Carson searched his mind for a solution, for some way to stop the trouble before it began. But every idea that came to him was quickly discarded. It seemed to him that Halligan held all the cards.

They were almost to Osburn before John spoke again. "I asked Edith to marry me."

"What?" Carson reined in abruptly.

John grinned. "You heard right. My brother's givin' me a small section of land to build a house on. Miss Blanche says I can keep on at the saloon, and if I get tired of that, Wade says I can work the farm with him."

"You sure you're not rushing into things, John? You're just beginning to get your feet under you."

"You mean I haven't been sober all that long, and you're wondering if I'm gonna stay that way."

Carson shrugged.

"Or maybe you're wondering if Edith's gonna want to be a farmer's wife."

"Would she?"

John took quick offense at the comment, and his voice revealed it. "She hasn't always kept company in a saloon. Edith grew up on a farm over in Montana. She knows what the life is like, and she knows she loves me, too."

"Look, I didn't mean—"

John waved his hand, dismissing whatever Carson had been about to say. "No, it's okay. I shouldn't've got mad so fast. Edith ain't no innocent girl. That's true enough. But she's got her a good heart, and she loves me just like I am. I reckon that's all I need to know."

"Then I'm glad for you, John. I mean it. I'm happy for you both."

The younger man grinned. "Thanks. Now how about you?"

"Me?" Carson clucked to his horse and moved out.

John quickly caught up. "You think everybody in town hasn't noticed you've got eyes for Miz Malone? When're you gonna ask her to marry you?"

He shot the fellow a look that clearly said, Lay off. He hadn't talked to Mary since the night he'd kissed her. She'd been avoiding him and doing a great job of it.

But he'd sworn to himself that he would be patient. Holding her in his arms as he had that night, feeling her heart-beat next to his, he'd known he would have to move slowly if he was to win her. He'd sensed then that she was more fragile and jittery than he'd thought her at first. So if it was time and space she needed, he was determined to give it to her.

He just hadn't known it would be this blasted hard.

—

It was nearly six o'clock by the time the rented horse and buggy carried Mary along the road back toward Whistle Creek. Much later than she'd intended to return from Wallace, but she was too excited to care.

Today she had found a man who once worked with Quaid. True, it had been two years ago, but the man had known her brother. He was pretty sure Quaid was still in Idaho. He'd even promised to ask around for her, see if anyone knew of Quaid's current whereabouts.

Sure and it would be perfect altogether if she were to find Quaid now. She would leave Whistle Creek. She would go to live with her brother. She would be safe from the law.

And Carson Barclay would be safe from her.

Her heart skittered, and her emotions plummeted, her joy and excitement immediately forgotten.

It was a terrible thing, the way she had lost her heart to the sheriff, and there was no denying it, not even to herself. It was bad enough that she had weakened in her resolve never to play the fool for a man again. It was worse that it had happened with this particular man.

Carson was going to ask her to marry him. She sensed it. He'd made it clear in a dozen different ways. But no matter how much she cared for him—or precisely because of how much she cared for him—she would have to refuse. She couldn't marry the sheriff. Even if the truth about New York and Winston Kenrick never came out, she couldn't live that particular lie. As Carson's wife, always fearing the day of discovery would be a hundred times worse than anything she lived now.

She closed her eyes, giving the horse his head, and remembered the way Carson had kissed her. The brief touch of his lips upon hers shouldn't have affected her so greatly. It had been over in an instant.

No, it hadn't been over in an instant.

It still wasn't over.

She drew a shaky breath, recalling the way Carson had held her close, the brush of his lips against her cheek and forehead, the gentleness in his voice.

"You thought you loved Seamus once," she scolded herself.

But her argument didn't work. She knew Carson was different. She knew he was exactly the sort of man she had dreamed of when she was a young girl in service. Seamus had lied to get her into his bed. Carson would never do such a thing. He was good and kind and just, and when he went to church, he did it without a heavy burden of guilt.

Mary opened her eyes and stared up at the darkening sky. "Why now?" she demanded. "Why did I find him after it was too late, after me sins were too great to be forgiven?"

As if in reply, the wind rose, drowning out the clip-clop of the horse's hooves and the music of the river.

You could tell him what you've done.

Before the thought had scarcely registered, Mary rejected it. She couldn't tell him. Carson would be honor-bound to turn her over to the authorities back east, and then what would happen to Keary? It was the same fear, the same question, the same quandary, she'd always had. Nothing had changed. There were good people in Whistle Creek who might take him in and raise him, but no one could love her son the way she did. No, she could never tell the truth. She would have to live with her crime until her dying day.

And that would mean living without Carson.

"I'll be finding Quaid," she whispered to herself. "I'll be finding me brother and we'll all be going away from here, and I'll forget Sheriff Barclay altogether." She was silent for a long time before adding, "And 'tis a fine liar you've become, Mary Emeline Malone, if you'd be believing that 'tis true. A fine liar."

The storm swept up the valley with a sudden vengeance that surprised even the old-timers. There was little warning. First there were a few clouds on the western horizon, and then came the battering wind, with gusts strong enough to knock a man right off his horse.

Carson listened to the walls of his office creak and moan and was thankful he and John had made it back from Osburn before the storm hit. He hoped Mary and the kids were okay.

He rose from the chair behind his desk and walked to the window, gazing out at a huge cloud of dust rolling down Main Street like a giant tumbleweed, driven by the furious wind. The sky had grown as black as midnight in a matter of moments, and the clouds looked ready to drop a deluge of rain on the small town. At least there hadn't been any lightning thus far.

Maybe this storm would cool things off, and he didn't mean just the weather.

He turned from the window, his thoughts straying to what he'd learned in Osburn. Halligan had gathered himself quite the little workforce. Right now they were standing around in the saloon, swilling beer and whiskey. But eventually...

Beside him, the door flew open, crashing against the wall. A strong gust of wind sent the papers on his desk flying like a dervish.

"Sorry!" John shouted as he grabbed the door and pushed it closed again.

Carson raised an eyebrow, then strode across his office to retrieve the strewn papers.

"I thought you ought to know. Miz Malone ain't back yet, and Edith's getting worried."

Carson stopped abruptly, then turned toward John. "What did you say? Back from where?"

"From Wallace."

"What was she doing over there?"

John shook his head. "Edith didn't say. Mary left Keary and Nellie with her and rented Stover's buggy. She told Edith she'd be back before dark."

Carson muttered beneath his breath. Fool woman. What business did she have over in Wallace? Especially on a day like this. He could've told her it was going to storm. Besides, he'd warned her these mountains were full of disreputable men, and she shouldn't be traipsing around by herself. Why hadn't she listened to him?

"I'll go find her," he grumbled, jamming his hat on his head.

"I'm comin', too."

Carson nodded, then pulled on his slicker, although he doubted it would help much, from the look of the storm clouds. He figured they'd all be half-drowned before they got back to town.

—

Blinded by swirling dust, pebbles, and dried pine needles, Mary drew back on the reins, stopping the buggy in the middle of the narrow road. She couldn't expect the horse to continue in this. They had to find shelter of some sort. At the very least, she needed to turn the animal's back to the wind until the worst was over.

She climbed down from her seat and felt her way forward, holding onto the harness as she went. Just as she reached the horse's head, a blast of wind knocked Mary a step backward. Her skirt flew up, slapping and snapping like a flag. Above the noise of the storm, she heard the horse whinny in alarm. It reared, striking out with its hooves. Mary took another quick step back—

And felt the earth give way beneath her feet.

—

Carson's heart nearly stopped when he saw the Stover rig come flying along the road without a driver. He didn't try to stop the runaway horse. He figured it would reach Whistle Creek on its own.

"Come on!" he shouted at John, then dug his heels into Cinnabar's ribs and set off at a gallop. It didn't take him long to realize he would miss any sign of Mary if he didn't slow down, even though taking his time was the last thing he wanted to do.

As he reined in, he glanced over his shoulder at John. The younger man simply nodded in understanding. Then John guided his horse to the mountain side of the road, his gaze sweeping the underbrush amidst the trees. Carson turned his mount toward the side of the road that overlooked the turbulent white water.

The wind at his back continued to stir whirlwinds of dirt, making it difficult to see clearly. He almost wished it would go ahead and rain. Maybe then...

He stopped abruptly. A sixth sense told him something was not as it should be. It took him a few moments to realize ground at the edge of the road had fallen away, crumbling down the steep slope to the river.

"Mary!" he shouted, his hands cupped near his mouth. "Mary, can you hear me?"

The wind grabbed his words and carried them off before even he could hear them.

He dismounted and carefully approached the edge. "Mary?"

He tried telling himself there was no reason to believe she had fallen. She could be anywhere. She might be perfectly all right, standing under a tree farther up the road. The horse might even have run away from Wallace. Mary could be stranded but safe.

Then he saw her, clinging precariously to a jagged outcropping of rocks, her legs and skirt immersed in the churning, foaming river.

"John, she's here!" Carson cried as he grabbed his lariat from his saddle.

Quickly, he made a loop and dropped it over the saddle horn. He cinched the other end around his waist. By the time he was ready to start his descent, John was there, too. The younger man took Cinnabar by the reins.

"Pull us up when I give the signal," Carson shouted over the wind.

John nodded that he understood.

The moment Carson stepped over the edge, more earth came loose. Pebbles and dirt showered Mary below.

"Hang on," he called, hoping she could hear him.

She didn't move.

Several anxious moments passed before Carson reached Mary's side. Her bonnet, if she'd worn one, was missing. Her head was turned toward him, her right cheek pressed against a cold, damp rock. Her hair, wet from the constant spray off the river, was plastered against her left cheek. Her eyes were closed. The knuckles of her right hand were white from her tight grip on the stones, but her left arm and hand were limp at her side. She was shivering uncontrollably.

"Mary, I'm here."

Just as the words came out of his mouth, jagged lightning brightened the stormy sky, followed by a loud crash of thunder.

Carson saw Mary's whole body tense, but she didn't open her eyes. He looked upward; he could barely see John. Then he glanced at the lariat tied around his waist. He sure hoped the knot would hold, because he was going to have to let go.

He took a quick gulp of air, then released the rope and reached for Mary, gripping her firmly by the upper arms. Only then did she open her eyes. They were glazed with fear and pain.

"I've got you, Mary," he said loudly. "Let go of the rock. Take hold of me."

She didn't budge.

"You can trust me, Mary. Let go."

Another flash of lightning.

Another boom of thunder.

Mary loosened her death grip on the rocks, and he pulled her into his embrace. She wrapped her right arm around his neck and held on tightly.

"Are you hurt?" he demanded, but he knew the answer already.

She nodded mutely.

His right arm tightened around her as he gripped the rope with his left hand. "Pull us up, John," he shouted. Then to Mary he said, "Don't worry. I'll get you home."

She laid her head against his shoulder and closed her eyes again.

If it had been up to Carson, he would have kept her there the rest of their lives.

— Fourteen

"Sure and there's nothing much wrong with me, Dr. Ingall," Mary said as the physician gently manipulated her right knee. She tried and failed to hide the flinch of pain.

"Hmm," was his reply.

"I cannot be lying in bed when there's so much work to be done," she persisted. "I've been down too long already. Miss Blanche will be needing me to look after her ledgers, and Edith is planning her wedding, and—"

"Mrs. Malone, if you put weight on that leg before it's ready, you could do permanent injury to the knee." He pointed to her left arm. "And I don't want to see you out of that sling for another week."

Mary released a deep sigh.

With a shake of his head, Jakob Ingall straightened. "Sheriff Barclay warned me you'd be a stubborn patient."

"He did, did he? And I'd like to know what he—"

The doctor chuckled as he touched her shoulder. "Don't go having a conniption. He only said it out of concern for you, Mrs. Malone."

She sighed again, her burst of temper gone. She knew Carson cared. He cared too much.

And so did she.

Dr. Ingall closed his black leather bag. "Nellie Russell seems to be thriving here. It's a kind thing you've done, giving her a home with you."

"She's a sweet girl altogether. I'd not want her anywhere else."

The doctor headed toward the cabin door.

"Dr. Ingall?"

He stopped and looked back at her.

"How is Miss Blanche? Edith will only say I'm not to worry meself."

For a moment she thought the man would shield her from the truth. But finally he said, "I don't believe she has much longer, Mrs. Malone. Perhaps a few weeks. Perhaps less."

"She's been very kind to me," Mary whispered, her throat tight. "She had no reason to be. I was no one to her." She shook her head. "I know what she is and all, but there's good in her, too."

Jakob Ingall nodded again, then exited through the open cabin door. It wasn't long after he left before Nellie and Keary appeared in the same doorway.

"How are ya, Mary?" the girl asked.

"Well enough and tired of all the fussing."

"Sheriff Barclay said he's bringing us supper from town. Can we eat outside again?"

Mary's heart did its familiar little flutter in response to Carson's name. "Aye," she answered softly. "We can eat outside again."

Keary pulled free from Nellie's hold on his hand and ran across the room to climb onto the bed with his mother. Mary smiled as she helped him up and snuggled him in the crook of her right arm. He jabbered something nonsensical.

"The sheriff said I could try riding Cloud pretty soon," Nellie commented, referring to the horse they'd found the previous week. "He says I'm light enough, I can't do Cloud no harm. I think his leg's doing better than yours."

Mary raised an eyebrow.

The girl laughed. "Well, it's true."

"Is it now?"

"Can I leave Keary here while I go brush Cloud? I'd like him to look good when the sheriff comes."

"Aye."

"Thanks, Mary." She vanished in a heartbeat.

Mary stared at the empty doorway. She was gladdened by Nellie's high spirits, but she knew the mood could shift suddenly, as it often did, leaving the child in tears. Carson did much to help, she admitted reluctantly. He never failed to say something to Nellie that made her smile or laugh. He had an uncanny way with children.

"Why does he have to be so perfect altogether?" she asked her son softly. "And why is it I have to. . ." She hesitated, knowing everything would be changed once she confessed her feelings, even only to herself. But there was no denying the truth any longer. "Why is it I have to love him when there's no hope for the two of us?"

Keary shook his head, as if he'd understood.

Mary smiled, but there was no happiness in it. Loving Carson Barclay would only bring her more heartache. How had she let it happen? How had she let him become such an important part of her life?

She remembered the moment he'd rescued her from the edge of the river. *You can trust me, Mary.*

Could she? Could she trust him? She wanted to. With everything within her, she wanted to trust him. How could she? Or rather, how could she allow him to trust her, after all she'd done? He was a good and honest man. And she? She was an unmarried mother with a past full of mistakes and a string of lies too many to count. He represented the long arm of the law. She was in hiding from the law. What possible future could they have?

She heard Nellie shout a greeting, and Mary knew the man of her thoughts had arrived. Her pulse quickened as she sat up straighter. Keary wiggled, trying to get down, having heard Carson's reply to Nellie. In a flash, he slipped from her one-handed grip and off the bed and rushed toward the door.

Just as Keary reached it, Carson stepped into view. He scooped the toddler up, tossing him high and catching him, eliciting a squeal of joy from the boy.

"Where are you off to, Keary Malone?" Carson's gaze met with Mary's, and she momentarily lost the ability to breathe. "And how are you, Mary?"

"I'm fine altogether," she answered, the words barely audible. She took a quick breath, then said, "The doctor was just here."

"I know. I ran into him on the trail. He says you're not fine altogether, and you're to stay off of that leg. That's just what you're going to do."

"Well, if you know so much, Carson Barclay, why would you be bothering to ask me?"

"Have I made you mad at me again, Mary?" he asked with a teasing grin.

She started to nod, then shook her head. She didn't know what she felt at the moment. Everything within her was at odds.

Carson's grin widened. "I'll be right back." Then he disappeared from view, Keary still in his arms.

Mary let her head fall against the pillows behind her. She recalled the terror she'd felt when she'd been clinging to those jagged rocks, trying not to be swept away in the river. She was a poor swimmer. She would have drowned if she'd lost her hold and gone into the water, and that was precisely how she felt now. Like she was drowning. Like she was helpless against the swift current that was carrying her away.

Carson returned, pausing a second time in the doorway. This time, instead of holding her son, his hands held a large bouquet of purple, yellow, and white wildflowers. "I thought these might brighten the place a bit."

"Aye," she whispered, "they will that."

He stepped toward her. "Mary..."

"There'd be a jar in the cupboard. You should be putting them in water."

He arrived at her bedside and went down on one knee. He placed the flowers on the floor near his boot, then removed his hat and set it next to the flowers. "Mary, I have something I want to say. I've been wanting to say it for quite a while now." He took hold of her hand as he spoke.

As she looked into the blue of his eyes, Mary felt that drowning sensation again. She had a nearly irresistible urge to touch the tiny scar in his left eyebrow, to run her fingers through his golden brown hair, to feel the afternoon shadow of his beard on his jaw.

"I've never done anything like this before," he said as his fingers tightened around hers. "I never wanted to."

"Carson, don't."

He ignored her protest. "I don't know any fancy words, so I'll just come right out and say it. You know I love you, Mary Malone. Last week, when I realized I could have lost you, I knew I couldn't wait any longer. I want to marry you. Say yes, Mary. Say you'll marry me."

"Oh, Carson."

There were no words to describe what she felt, hearing his simple declaration of love. It was like the heavens opened up and poured joy directly into her heart. Only the joy was brief, for he offered her something she could never accept.

"I think you love me, too, Mary."

She shook her head. "I can't."

He smiled, and his eyes teased her. "Yes, you can. I'm not entirely unlovable, am I?"

"Oh, Carson," she repeated. Then to herself, *I didn't mean I couldn't love you.*

"Marry me." He drew closer. "Marry me soon."

He kissed her then, his mouth tender upon hers.

Her heart skipped, stumbled, raced. It seemed that she had been resisting this moment and longing for this moment from the first time she'd laid eyes on him. She wanted all the things a woman would have with a man like Carson. Peace and contentment. Safety and comfort. And love. So much love.

Things she didn't deserve.

She pulled her right hand free from his, then placed it on his chest and pushed him away. She stared into his watchful eyes, saw the love, knew he could see hers, too.

"I can't marry you," she said hoarsely.

"Why not?"

Mary closed her eyes. Another sigh escaped her lips. "There are things you don't know about me. If you did, you would not be saying you love me."

"Try me." He captured her hand again.

She shook her head.

His grip tightened. "Look at me, Mary." His voice was soft but firm.

She thought if she ignored him, he would eventually give up. He didn't. The seconds flowed into minutes, and he didn't move, didn't release her hand. He just waited. Finally, she had to look at him as he'd demanded.

"You do not know who I really am," she told him. "I am not good like you."

"Is that what this is about?" He kissed her again, this time with tenderness. Then he stood and walked over to the doorway where he stared outside at the golden afternoon. "I guess you don't know much about me either."

I'd be knowing I love you, Carson. I love you and I shouldn't.

⸺

Carson had never liked remembering the past, let alone talking about it. As he stared outside, memories flitted through his head, things he'd rather leave forgotten. But if it meant persuading Mary to be his wife, he'd recall every sordid detail of his life and recount them for her. Now that he'd discovered love, he wasn't about to let it slip away from him. He wasn't going to let her slip away.

"There wasn't much good about my childhood," he said honestly. "I grew up in a place a lot like the Painted Queen. My . . . mother"—even after all these years, he couldn't keep the bitter edge from that word—"owned it. That's why I hated having you and Keary at the saloon. Because I know what it's like for a boy to grow up in a place like that, living around women like . . . my mother."

He didn't tell her he'd once thought she might be like Aldora or how mistaken he'd been. Never had he known two women more dissimilar than Aldora and Mary.

"I took off on my own when I was thirteen. I had a real chip on my shoulder, too. By the time I was fifteen, I could play poker with the best of them, including dealing from the bottom of the deck. I could handle a gun as good as any man, and I wasn't afraid to aim and fire, even if it meant killing somebody.

I wandered from one small mining town to another, hating them all but not knowing anything else. When I could find work, I worked. When I couldn't, I stole. Usually I stole."

He glanced over his shoulder. Mary was watching him, listening.

"I wound up in Silver City when I was sixteen. It's about three, four hundred miles south of here. It was winter, and I was cold, hungry, and without money. So I decided to take a few things from the general store."

He remembered that large hand slapping down on his shoulder as he'd shoved a pair of gloves into the waistband of his trousers.

"I was caught stealing by Sheriff Hailey." He smiled to himself, recalling David's grim expression. "He could've just thrown me in jail and let me serve my time, but for some reason, he took an interest in me. I'll never know why. I had a foul mouth. I was dirty and scruffy, and I had an attitude that said to blazes with everyone. But for whatever reason, he decided I was worth saving."

He took a step toward the bed and Mary.

"In all my life, I'd never had anybody talk to me about God or sin or forgiveness. I'd never been inside a church, and I'd sure never read the Good Book. Couldn't hardly read at all, for that matter. But the Haileys, David and Claudia, they made sure I heard about God's love and what he sent his Son to do for me. They took me in, became my family, loved me. I did plenty of bad things when I was a kid that I can't ever change. That's something I just have to accept. But that's not who I am now, because God made me something different."

He wondered if she understood what he was telling her, then figured she didn't. He raked the fingers of one hand through his hair, frustrated by his seeming inability to express himself better.

"Mary, it doesn't matter to me who you were or what you did before you came here. I'm in love with you, for better or worse."

Silence followed. Carson waited and watched. He saw the different emotions flitting across Mary's face—fear, hope, frustration, longing, despair.

Despair most of all.

"'Tis no use, Carson. It wouldn't be right. 'Tis not the same what you did and…and what I've done."

He took another step toward her. "Try me."

Another lengthy silence filled the room.

"Mary, nothing you could tell me would make me stop loving you. Nothing."

"Not even if you were to know Keary's da's name was Maguire, not Malone?"

For a moment he didn't understand what she was saying. And then he did.

"Aye, 'tis true. We were never married, Seamus Maguire and me. 'Twas Miss Blanche who called me Mrs. Malone, but in truth, 'tis unmarried I am and unmarried I have always been."

Carson saw Mary steeling herself for his judgment and condemnation. A few short weeks ago, he would have judged and condemned her. But not now. Not when he loved her like he did. Loving her had changed him, softened his heart, maybe even shown him it was time he did some forgiving of his own.

"It doesn't matter," he said, hoping she could hear the earnestness in his voice. "I'll raise Keary as my own. I'll love him as my own. I'll be his dad."

She turned her face toward the wall. A sigh escaped her. "I'm thinking you should go, Carson."

"You're a stubborn woman, Mary Malone."

"Aye, that I am."

He sat on the edge of the bed, took her hand once more, forced her to look at him again. "I can be just as stubborn as you. I'm not going to give up. I'm not going to stop loving you. I'll just wear you down until you don't have a choice except to say yes. You'll see."

———

Winston drained the brandy snifter, then set it beside his dinner plate. It had been a disappointing day. They had returned from Uppsala to Des Moines after nightfall with nothing to show for their troubles. He was now intent on drowning his aggravation in alcohol.

He glared across the table at his wife, who was having an intense but muted discussion with Tibble Knox. Winston couldn't hear what they were saying, but he didn't care.

He glared at Portia, despising the sight of her. It didn't matter how elegantly she dressed, his wife would never be anything but the plain, plump daughter of an uneducated buffoon who'd gotten lucky and made a fortune. Winston had been shackled to her for twenty-four years. Far too long, in his estimation. He wanted out. He was desperate for a way out. But he couldn't go without money and plenty of it.

"What now, Knox?" he suddenly demanded, causing not only Portia and the detective to look his way but people at the surrounding tables in the hotel dining room as well.

"We could wait and return to the Bridger farm next week," Tibble answered him. "It's possible Mrs. Bridger might be able to tell us something her little sister couldn't. But I suspect it would be a waste of time. I don't think Miss Malone is in Iowa now nor that she came here after leaving New York."

"What makes you so sure?"

"Let's call it a hunch."

Winston grunted. "Like the one that brought us here?" he asked sarcastically.

"Hardly." The little man patted the corner of his mouth with a linen napkin. "I was able to gain some helpful information from Mrs. Bridger's sister." He grinned. "Including the whereabouts of Elizabeth Steele, Miss Malone's other shipboard friend. Mrs. Steele is living in Montana. I recommend that we go there next."

"It could be another wild-goose chase."

The detective appeared unruffled. "It could be. Might I suggest you and Mrs. Kenrick return to New York City while I do my job? Then you wouldn't be wasting your time if it turns out there is nothing to be learned from Mrs. Steele. I will gladly send you daily telegrams, if that's what you want."

"No, Mr. Knox," Portia said before Winston could speak. "I believe we shall continue on with you. I have never been out West. I should like to see it, regardless of whether or not we find Mary."

Winston filled his snifter with more brandy and took another deep swallow. In his heart he cursed women. All women. Especially two—Portia Pendergast Kenrick and Mary Malone.

His plan had been working well. Right up until that ill-fated moment in his study. He'd been so close to escaping the clutches of his wife. He'd been so close to secreting away a fortune for himself. But without those papers hidden in the secret compartment of the silver box, he was doomed. He'd be tied to Portia until the day he died.

What if Mary doesn't have it anymore?

As always, the thought made him shudder. It was possible Mary had sold the valuable box for cash to pay for her flight from New York. It was possible she had dropped it in a ditch somewhere, not wanting to keep the weapon she'd used against her employer.

But Mary was his only hope of recovering it, and so he was determined to find her. No matter what it took, he was going to find Mary Malone, and when he did, he was going to make her pay for all the trouble she'd caused him.

———

"Are you saying all I've got to do is ask, and God'll forgive me and let me into heaven?" Blanche peered at Mordecai Ogelsby. "What's the catch?"

"There's no catch, Miss Loraine."

"There's always a catch. You sure you don't want me to give every last cent to the church or something?"

He shook his head. "God's gift of grace is free."

"But what about the awful things I've done? A whole lifetime of things. Can't undo them, you know."

"Neither could the thief on the cross." Reverend Ogelsby leaned forward. "You're looking for excuses to run, but you're forgetting it was God himself who caused you to seek him and his forgiveness."

Blanche closed her eyes. This meeting wasn't going quite how she'd expected. She'd thought she would have the error of her ways exposed and castigated. She hadn't figured on being offered absolution. Did she even want forgiveness for the life she'd led?

A shiver passed through her. It seemed as if she were standing on a precipice, eternity yawning before her. A misstep and...

She opened her eyes. "I don't want to go to hell, Reverend. Deserve it, I surely do, but if God'll have me—"

"He will." Reverend Ogelsby took hold of her hands. "Pray with me, Miss Loraine."

Fifteen

Carson was as good as his word. He didn't give up. He kept on asking Mary to be his wife. Every time he saw her, he proposed again. And she was sorely tempted to accept. After all, she loved him, and he loved her. Why shouldn't she take hold of the happiness he offered?

Lying on her bed, waiting for her leg to heal, gave her a great deal of time to think about marrying him. She discovered countless reasons to agree, and she found just as many reasons to refuse. But it always came down to Winston Kenrick and that day in his study. She knew she could never marry Carson because of that one crucial moment in her past.

She tried telling herself that if the authorities hadn't found her after more than a month they weren't ever going to find her. She tried telling herself that the law didn't even suspect her, that they were looking for someone else entirely. She tried telling herself that if she didn't get caught it made it all right.

But it didn't.

Again, she considered telling Carson the whole truth. She wanted to believe he would understand, as he'd promised.

But would he?

She remembered how Carson had spoken so easily of God's forgiveness. But he'd been talking about boyhood mischief, not murder. Mary knew there was no forgiving that.

She'd heard it shouted from more than one pulpit. No, eternity would be a hot and horrible destination for Mary Emeline Malone.

So if she was to know any happiness, it would have to be here on earth.

It was a hot August Sunday afternoon. Carson came out to the cabin after church, once again bringing a bouquet of flowers. The first thing he did upon arrival was tell Mary he loved her. Then he gave her a kiss that left her breathless and gave Nellie the giggles.

"It's too hot to be stuck in here," he announced suddenly. He scooped Mary into his arms and headed outside, calling behind him, "Nellie, bring Keary. We're going into town."

He carried Mary to the buggy he'd driven out. Then he stood waiting for Nellie and Keary to catch up rather than setting Mary on the seat immediately.

"You can put me down," she told him, hoping he wouldn't. She loved the feel of his arms around her.

"Not yet." He gazed into her eyes. "Are you ready to change your mind, Mary Malone? Are you ready to marry me?"

"Sure and I've told you I can't."

"Sure and you have told me that," he said with a grin, mimicking her accent. "But 'tis unwilling I am to believe you, me darlin' girl."

"You'll be making fun of me now."

His smile faded. His voice softened. "Ah, Mary. Don't you know I'd never make fun of you? I love you too much."

Why not give your consent, Mary? a small voice whispered in her ear. *'Tis happy you'd be with him. 'Tis happy Keary would be, too.*

She closed her eyes as she laid her head against his shoulder. She knew the answer to her own question. She couldn't tell him the truth, and she couldn't marry him with such a lie—even a lie by silence—between them.

"What is it we'll be doing in town?"

"I thought you might like to see Miss Blanche. John says she's been asking for you."

Mary felt a catch in her heart. She was afraid she knew what that meant. Blanche must not have much longer to live. "Have you seen her?"

"Not recently."

"I'm wondering why it has to be this way," she whispered, more to herself than to Carson.

He didn't answer.

She lifted her head from his shoulder and met his gaze. "She has a good heart, no matter what else you might say about her."

"She brought you here." He brushed his lips across her forehead. "How can I have anything against her now?"

Carson had never spoken truer words. Mary had changed the way he felt about Blanche. Mary had changed the way he felt about lots of things.

Nellie and Keary arrived, and reluctantly, Carson set Mary on the buggy seat. Then he lifted Keary and placed him in his mother's arms while Nellie scrambled onto the rear seat.

As Carson stepped into the buggy and settled beside Mary, he considered the picture they made. They must look like a family.

His family.

By heaven, he wasn't going to let Mary Malone or her son or young Nellie get away from him. He was laying claim to his family. Whatever impediments kept Mary from agreeing to be his bride were going to be torn down. He didn't know how, but he did know it would happen. He was going to make it happen.

He slapped the reins against the horse's backside, and they set off toward Whistle Creek. The journey was made in silence, each of them lost in their own thoughts.

When the buggy arrived at the rear entrance of the Painted Queen, Carson glanced over his shoulder and said to Nellie, "Why don't you take Keary over to Chuck's Mercantile while Mary and I see Miss Blanche?" He reached into his pocket and pulled out a couple of coins. "Here. You can buy some peppermint sticks or licorice or whatever you like."

"Thanks, Sheriff Barclay!" the girl exclaimed.

"But you have to keep a close eye on Keary," Carson cautioned.

"I know. I always do. I'll make him hold my hand the whole time."

Carson hopped to the ground, then handed Keary to Nellie. He watched for a moment as the two of them started down the boardwalk, Keary's short legs churning to keep up with Nellie. When he glanced toward Mary, he found her watching the children, too, her expression pensive.

"A penny for your thoughts," he said.

Her gaze shifted to meet his. "I'm thinking 'tis blessed I am altogether, and I'd be greedy to be wanting more."

He decided against arguing with her, even though he understood what she was saying to him. "Come on. Let's get you inside." He lifted her once again into his arms, cradling her against his chest, and carried her toward the back entrance of the saloon.

———

Blanche heard the door open, heard the footsteps drawing close to her bed, wondered who had entered her bedroom this time.

"Miss Blanche? 'Tis Mary. I've come to see you."

She opened her eyes with effort. Everything was an effort for her now. But she smiled when she saw Mary in Carson's arms. "Hello, Mary," she whispered, her voice raspy. "How are you?"

"I'm fine altogether." Mary looked at Carson. "Set me down now."

He lowered her to the chair beside the bed. Then he glanced at Blanche. "I'll just step out into the hall. Leave the two of you alone for a while."

Thanks, Blanche mouthed.

Carson nodded.

When he was gone, Blanche reached for Mary's hand. "I don't have much time."

The younger woman shook her head. "Don't be saying that. 'Tis not true."

"Let me say my piece while I've got the breath to do so." She concentrated on not coughing. "The truth is the truth."

Tears glimmered in Mary's eyes. It surprised Blanche how it made her feel, seeing Mary cry for her. Blanche had never expected anyone to sorrow at her passing. She'd never expected anyone to miss her or care when she was gone. She'd lived a hard life. She'd sinned in countless ways. She'd mocked society and its rules. She'd never cared what others thought of her. Or, at least, she'd believed she didn't care. Until now.

"Mary, you've become my dearest friend."

"And you mine." Mary's fingers tightened around Blanche's hand.

"I know there's something troubling you, something you fear that drove you from New York."

Mary visibly paled.

"It doesn't matter to me one whit what it is that caused you to run. I've done it all myself anyway. But I want you to be safe and happy when I'm gone. You and your boy."

"I'm thinking we'll be fine, Miss Blanche."

"I think you will, too." She tried to smile even as she fought for more air in her lungs. "Especially knowing that the sheriff has taken such a shine to you."

The tears returned to Mary's eyes.

"It might help if you were to talk about it. It might free you from it."

Mary shook her head. "I can't."

"I'll take it to my grave, whatever it is."

The words only served to upset Mary more. Her tears fell, leaving damp tracks down her cheeks.

"Tell me, my dear girl."

"I. . .I killed a man."

Blanche nearly responded with a denial. It was too outrageous to believe. Mary? Gentle Mary?

"'Twas an accident. I wasn't meaning to kill him, but no one would be believing that."

Blanche waited patiently, certain Mary would continue now that she'd begun. She wasn't disappointed. Like a dam bursting, the words spilled out of Mary. She told Blanche about Seamus Maguire's betrayal. She told her about the hardship of her pregnancy, alone in New York City with only the kindness of strangers to help her through. She told Blanche about the hope that had come when she was employed by the wealthy Kenricks and the way Winston Kenrick had stalked her and the day he'd tried to force himself upon her. Mary told her about the moment she realized her employer was dead and her flight into hiding. And she told Blanche of her hope of finding her brother Quaid, who had once lived in Idaho.

When Mary was finished, she laid her forehead on the bed at Blanche's side. Her shoulders shook as she wept, but she made no sound.

Blanche stroked Mary's head with her free hand, wordlessly offering what comfort she could. She knew from experience that it wasn't words she needed so much as quiet acceptance. How many times had she heard similar stories? The details were different, of course, each story carrying its own tragedy, but the result was the same. A woman's life destroyed. A heart losing its ability to trust and to love. Children abandoned.

"Mary?"

The younger woman lifted her face toward Blanche.

"Promise me you'll stay in Whistle Creek. Don't run away again. Stay here. The sheriff won't let anything happen to you."

"If he was knowing the truth about me—"

"Carson won't let anything happen to you, Mary. I know it." She felt herself growing weaker and resented it. There was still so much to be said. She lifted her hand and touched Mary's cheek with her fingertips. "Don't shut up your heart. You'll only regret it when you're old and dying. Trust me. I know."

Blanche released a sigh as her hand dropped to the bed. She closed her eyes and listened to her own agonized breathing. Death had spread its shadow over her, but strangely, she wasn't afraid. Not after her talk with Reverend Ogelsby. She knew a peace in dying that she'd never known in living.

But there was still something she wanted to accomplish, and so she kept dragging air into her failing lungs, praying that her opportunity would come.

——

Carson wasn't sure why he returned to the Painted Queen after taking Mary and the children back to the cabin. It wasn't like he and Blanche had been friends. Still, he couldn't shake the feeling that he needed to talk to her one last time.

He arrived at the saloon during the quiet time of early evening, when the sun hovers in the western sky and the air is still and mild. Because it was Sunday, the streets were empty, most folks in their homes.

It was a teary-eyed Edith who led Carson into the bedroom.

When Blanche saw him, she whispered, "You came back.... I was hoping...you would."

Carson nodded, not sure what to say, not sure why he was there.

Blanche glanced at Edith, who understood and withdrew, closing the door behind her.

"Come." Blanche patted the bed at her side. "Sit down, Sheriff. There isn't...much time."

The sound of her belabored breathing caused his own lungs to ache.

"Do you...love Mary?"

"Yes."

"Look after...her."

"I will."

She closed her eyes, and for a moment, he wondered if she was gone.

Then she spoke again. "There is much...I'm not at liberty... to tell you.... But this much...I can.... Mary has...a brother."

"She has several brothers. She told me about them."

Blanche looked at him. "No, she has a...brother...in Idaho...in the mines.... She came here...to find him.... Help her...find him." She coughed faintly.

Carson could see she was fighting hard to say what she wanted to say.

"His name...is Quaid...Quaid Malone.... Don't...let her know...that I told you."

He nodded to indicate he'd heard.

Weakly, she lifted her hand and placed it on his arm. "Give her time.... She is...afraid."

"I know, but not why."

"I can't. . .tell you more." Breath rattled in her throat and lungs. "She must. . .tell you herself."

"But—"

Clawlike, her fingers tightened on his arm, and she raised her head. "Forgive me. . .the things I. . .done, Sheriff. I. . .didn't know any. . .better way." Then she fell back against the pillows.

He spoke without thinking. "I forgive you, Blanche."

Carson heard a whisper of air escape her lips, but there was no corresponding drawing in. Blanche Loraine was gone.

He hadn't expected to feel a lump in his throat. But then he would never have guessed her last words would be to ask his forgiveness. Maybe if someone had offered Blanche a hand in friendship years ago, things might have been different for her. That someone could have been him, he realized with a twinge of regret.

Maybe Mary was right not to tell him her secrets. Maybe he wasn't as fair and forgiving as he liked to think he was.

Carefully, he straightened the sheet over Blanche, then placed her hands, one on top of the other, on her abdomen. Finally he rose from his chair and walked to the door. When he opened it, he found Edith in the hallway. John was with her, his arm around her shoulders. She took one look at Carson's face and began to weep in earnest.

"I'll let Doc Ingall know," Carson told John.

His feet felt heavy as he descended the stairs and went out the back door. He paused on the boardwalk and drew in a deep breath, thankful that he could do so. Then he headed toward the doctor's home.

Blanche had asked him to take care of Mary. That's what he intended to do. But how was he to do it if she refused to marry him?

The answer was simple. She had a brother in America. In Idaho, if Blanche was to be believed. Now Mary's visits to the Lucky Lady and to Wallace made sense. She'd been searching for Quaid, a miner by trade. That was how Carson would begin to help her. He would locate her brother for her.

But there was more to be done than find Quaid Malone. Blanche had said so, and he knew it was true. Carson needed to discover what it was that Mary feared so much. It was more than just folks finding out she was an unmarried mother. That might have brought her censure, but by itself, it wasn't enough to quell Mary. She was more courageous than that. She'd proved it in countless ways since her arrival in Whistle Creek.

So what was it that at times caused the look of a hunted animal to come into her eyes? What was she so afraid of?

Carson knew he needed answers to those questions before he would ever convince Mary to become Mrs. Barclay.

~Sixteen

At the funeral, Carson stood with Mary and the children, offering support by his presence. The pastor, who had returned to Whistle Creek especially for this purpose, prayed for Blanche Loraine's immortal soul and spoke words of comfort for those who mourned her passing. There were not many. Edith, John, Mac, and a few others who had worked for Blanche at the Painted Queen. Some of the miners. A smattering of townsfolk.

Not many to show for the years she had lived in Whistle Creek, Mary thought as she watched the casket being lowered into the ground.

She missed Blanche more than she'd expected she would. Her heart ached with it. She had lost a friend, the person who, like the Good Samaritan of old, had reached out to a stranger and helped in a time of need. Now Mary was alone once again.

As if he understood what she was thinking, Carson's hand tightened on her elbow. She glanced up and found him observing her in that piercing manner of his.

You aren't alone, his eyes told her. *I'll take care of you and the children. Marry me.*

Aye, she could do that. It would be so easy. She loved him with her whole heart. Without a shred of doubt, she knew it would be a pleasure to live with him, to give birth to his babies and watch them grow. He would protect and cherish her. She had been on her own for many years. It would be grand altogether to rest in his arms.

But just as always, the wisp of hope was shattered by the image of Winston Kenrick, lying on the floor of his study, a crimson stain spreading across the carpet.

It would be better if she left Whistle Creek. Better for the sheriff whose wife, when he took one, needed to be above reproach. Better for Mary, too, because as it was, she was tortured by what she wanted and couldn't have.

When the brief service was over, Martin Burke approached Mary and Carson. "Miss Loraine's last will and testament will be read tomorrow afternoon in my office. She requested that you both be present. Shall we say two o'clock?"

Mary nodded.

"We'll be there," Carson replied.

We'll be there. He made it sound so simple. We. Carson and Mary. A couple. A family. Yes, it was indeed a cruel twist of fate, finding what she wanted and knowing she could never have it. If Carson were anything other than a lawman . . .

But he wasn't, she told herself with resignation, so there was no point dwelling on it. It would be much better if she ended any association between them, once and for all.

Carson's fingers tightened on her arm again. "I'll see you and the children home."

"No." She withdrew from his grasp. "I'm thinking 'twould be better if we went on our own."

"Mary—"

"Don't you be arguing with me, Sheriff Barclay. 'Tis how I'm wanting it."

He frowned. "You're a stubborn woman, Mary Malone."

"Aye." She lifted her son into her arms. "So you've told me before. More than once."

He stopped her with a gentle touch on her shoulder. "There's no need to—"

"I'll be leaving Whistle Creek soon," she interrupted as she looked into his eyes and felt her heart breaking. "I'm thinking 'twill be better that way altogether. I'll be thanking you for your kindness and the use of your house and all you've done for me and me children."

She glanced down at his fingers, still resting on her shoulder. After a long moment, his hand dropped away.

"Where will you go?"

"I wouldn't be knowing just yet."

"Why are you running away?" He paused a moment, then added, "From me."

She shook her head.

"Running never solved anything, Mary. I know from experience."

She believed him, but she also believed staying would be worse.

"Come, Nellie. 'Tis time we went home." *Before I start to cry.*

⸺

Carson watched the three of them go, Nellie carrying Keary, and he felt a wave of frustration wash over him. Why wouldn't she see reason? Dad-burned stubborn female! Things had been a whole lot simpler when he'd wanted nothing to do with women or marriage. He should have stuck to that way of thinking.

He spun on his heel and strode toward town. He walked with a purposeful stride and an air that said, Don't talk to me. Nobody did.

Didn't he have enough troubles right now? There were the scab workers Halligan had hired, loitering over in Osburn. There were the whispers of accusations against John and the other miners who'd been trapped in the tunnel. That was enough trouble for any sheriff without adding a woman to the mix. Whistle Creek and the Lucky Lady Mine were like tinderboxes, just waiting for something to ignite them so they could burst into flames. If not for Mary, Carson would have been concentrating on keeping the peace, making sure nobody struck that particular match. But because of her, he'd been picking wildflowers instead of doing his job.

He should have had more sense than to go soft for a woman. He'd seen few enough men made better by infatuation with a female. What man could ever figure what a woman was thinking, let alone what fool thing she might do? You couldn't trust them. They weren't logical. They didn't think and reason like men.

So let her go, he told himself. *I mistook what God wanted. So be it. Better I found out now.*

He hadn't been looking for love before Mary came to Whistle Creek, and he would get along just fine without it once she was gone. She could go find her brother without his help. He didn't owe Mary Emeline Malone a thing. Not one blasted thing!

By the time he stormed into his office and slammed the door behind him, Carson was in a fine fury. For a short while longer, he continued to silently rail against women in general and Mary in particular, and he almost believed the words he mentally spouted.

Almost.

Finally, he sank onto his chair, braced his elbows on the desk, and lowered his forehead onto the heels of his hands.

How had she done this to him? he wondered. How had that tiny slip of a woman created so much confusion in his mind in so short a period of time?

He leaned back in his chair and stared at the ceiling. Up until the last month or so, he'd never been given to much introspection, but now he saw with sudden clarity a few truths about himself. David Hailey had rescued him from a life of crime and helped him find peace with God, but Mary had awakened his heart. Claudia Hailey had removed much of the bitterness he'd harbored, but Mary had taught him by example what it meant to truly care about others.

God, have I been that self-righteous all along? I helped John, but it was to keep peace and order, not 'cause I cared so much about him. But Mary, she looked beyond the surface, didn't she? She really cared about Miss Blanche, even knowing what sort of woman she was.

He thought of Jesus, eating with the sinners and tax collectors, Jesus whose feet were washed in the tears of a harlot, and his heart broke with shame as he saw himself for the self-righteous pharisee he was. A pharisee so quick to judge others rather than looking at his own faults.

The office door opened, and Mac MacDonald, the card dealer at the Painted Queen, stepped inside. "You got a minute, Sheriff?"

"Sure." He took a deep breath to clear his head. "What do you need, Mac?"

"I'm leaving Whistle Creek later today."

"Sorry to hear that."

Mac shook his head, then shrugged. "It was time to move on. I never stayed so long in one place in my life as I have here. Only stayed because of Miss Blanche. Anyway, 'fore I go, I thought you should know something. I heard Halligan's gonna be back in town in a day or two. I don't know what he's plannin', but I don't expect it'll be anything good."

Carson nodded. This wasn't news to him.

"There's a chance he might bring the federal marshal with him. That's the rumor."

Carson raised an eyebrow. "For what reason?"

"Tyrell. He seems to have it in for the boy."

Again Carson nodded.

"It's easy enough to see why. The miners are calling Tyrell a hero. They blame the cave-in on unsafe conditions, and that's Halligan's fault. Tyrell's got the power right now to rally the miners behind the union supporters if he wants to. Halligan can't afford for that to happen."

"No," Carson agreed thoughtfully, "he can't."

"Well, that's all I come to say." Mac put on his hat. "Good luck, Sheriff."

"Thanks, Mac. I imagine I'll need it."

Actually Carson suspected the whole town was going to need it before this was over.

———

Portia was delighted with Bozeman, Montana. It was like stepping into a dime novel. The majority of men on the streets wore boots, wide-brimmed felt hats, and gun holsters strapped to their thighs. And the women! Well, they were certainly different from those back home.

Yes, the Wild West was everything Portia had hoped it would be and more. She imagined the ladies and gentlemen who attended her glittering soirees and supper parties would be scandalized to know just how much she was enjoying herself. Certainly her husband was not of the same mind. Winston was positively taciturn, if not downright morose.

It had taken some doing, but Portia had finally persuaded Winston to remain in Bozeman with her while Tibble Knox journeyed north to New Prospects. "If Miss Malone is there," she had told her husband the previous day, "Mr. Knox will return for us before confronting her. If she is not there, we will have saved ourselves the discomfort of a stagecoach ride."

In the meantime, Portia was able to entertain herself with a variety of pastimes, not the least of which was tonight's outrageous performance by a traveling theatrical troupe. Oh, yes. Her society friends would be scandalized, indeed.

Portia cast a sideways glance toward Winston. He was slumped in his box seat, his forehead creased in thought. She was certain he hadn't seen a minute of the comedy. Poor dear man. Whatever was the matter with him seemed to be growing worse by the day. His tension was palpable.

For an instant, she felt sorry for him. Her husband had hungered after many things in his life, things that remained beyond his grasp. His problem, of course, was that he thought the world and all that was in it was his due, simply because he was born a Kenrick. It had never occurred to him that he should have to work for the things he wanted or the things he already had.

When he looked at his wife, Portia knew, he saw someone of less value than he simply because she came from the working class. Her father hadn't inherited his money as a gentleman should but had earned it by the sweat of his brow. Winston had married Portia for her inheritance, had lived off her wealth, but he had resented her because of it.

She turned her attention back to the stage, but her thoughts soon wandered.

Portia had always considered herself a pragmatist. She had long ago accepted that she and her husband would never share love. She had put up with his affairs and dalliances, looking the other way rather than upsetting the applecart—as her grandmother would have said—with accusations and recriminations. Didn't it follow then that she was as much at fault for the state of her marriage as Winston?

The question left a bad taste in her mouth. The answer was no more comforting when it came to her.

Portia had settled for the type of marriage they shared because she'd thought Winston was right. She'd thought he was better than she. She'd thought the glittering life of proper society he'd offered was worth sacrificing herself to obtain.

She glanced at him again and knew a sudden sadness. What might her life have been like if she hadn't sold herself so cheaply?

———

"I need a favor, John."

"You know I'll do whatever I can for you, Sheriff."

Carson looked around the deserted saloon. The Painted Queen had been closed for several days, out of respect for Blanche Loraine. Still, he lowered his voice, in case someone was on the staircase or on the other side of the door. "Mary has a brother, and there's a good chance he's working in one of the mines in the panhandle."

"A brother?" The eyebrow on the unscarred side of John's face lifted. "So that's who she was lookin' for. Why didn't she say so before?"

"She still hasn't said anything. She doesn't know that I know."

John made no comment, but curiosity flickered in his eyes.

"Mary's been trying to locate her brother, but for whatever reason, she hasn't wanted to ask anybody's help. But I don't want her getting hurt again. I was hoping you might look for him."

"Why me?"

One thing Carson had learned about John Tyrell in recent weeks was that he was nobody's fool. Now that he'd stopped drowning himself in self-pity and booze, John had also proven he had a fair amount of pride in doing for himself. He wouldn't take it kindly were he to guess he was being sent out of town for his own protection. So Carson needed to choose his words carefully; he had to be convincing.

He glanced toward the doorway, then returned his gaze to John. "You were right about my feelings for Mary. She means a lot to me, and I don't want to lose her. But she's determined to leave Whistle Creek now that Miss Blanche is dead. I think it's got something to do with her brother, but I won't know until I can find him and talk to him myself. Only I can't leave town right now." He leaned forward. "I need somebody I can trust, John. I also need somebody that other miners will be willing to talk to. If I go asking questions, they'll be suspicious 'cause I'm the law. But not you. They'll talk to you 'cause you're one of them."

John nodded thoughtfully.

"His name's Quaid Malone."

"Malone?" There was no judgment in the younger man's voice, just a request for clarification.

Carson nodded. "Malone."

"What else do you know about him? How long's he been workin' the Idaho mines? What's he look like? Anything like that."

"I don't know much. I think he probably came to America back in about. . ." Carson's voice trailed into silence as he tried to remember what little Mary had revealed about her family.

Her brothers had gone their own way after their father died, she'd said. "Must be back about ninety or ninety-one," he finally concluded, "although I don't know that for a fact."

John leaned back in his chair. "How soon do you want me to go?"

"Today be too soon? I'll supply the horse and the money you'll need. If it takes you longer to find him and you run out of funds, I can always have it wired to you wherever you are."

John responded with a grin. "You do have it bad for her, don't you, Sheriff?"

"Yeah," he answered, a reluctant smile curving the corners of his mouth.

Why kid himself? He wanted to help and protect John, but this search for Quaid Malone was all about Mary. If she left Whistle Creek, Carson would be a lost man. He wanted her in his life. He wanted her and the children in his home. He wanted them to have more children, a house full of them. Two houses full of them, if that's what Mary wanted.

"Yeah, I've got it bad for her."

John's chair slid back from the poker table, and he rose to his feet. "Well then, I guess I'd best tell Edith I'll be gone for a while. I won't say why, just that I've got a job to do for you."

Carson stood, too, and offered his right hand. "Thanks, John. I appreciate this more than I can say."

"I'm glad to do it." John shook the proffered hand, no hint of a smile remaining on his face, his voice serious. "It's little enough I can do after what you did for me."

Carson wished he'd be able to convince Mary to stay as easily as he'd been able to convince John to go, but he figured the chances of that were about as good as Cinnabar's leading him to silver like Kellogg's jackass was supposed to have done.

Not very doggone likely.

~Seventeen

Wednesday, 24 August 1898
Whistle Creek, Idaho

My dear Beth,

My heart is filled with sadness as I write this letter. Dawn is just lightening the sky. The children still sleep innocently in their beds. Oh, how I wish I could sleep as they do, but it is not to be.

Yesterday, we buried my special friend, Miss Blanche Loraine. She departed this world on Sunday last, taken by the consumption that had eaten at her lungs for so long. It is only for myself that I mourn. To wish her back would be cruel, for I know at last she is no longer in pain. Her suffering was great in her final days.

The time has come for me to leave Whistle Creek. My work at the Painted Queen is done. The records are in order, and while others here hope to continue working for the new owner, whoever that may be, I have no wish to do so. I am thinking it was Miss Blanche who made the work so enjoyable to me and not the work itself.

So now I must be asking a favor of you, dearest Beth. I have only just discovered how near Whistle Creek is to New Prospects. If we would not be a burden to you and Mr. Steele, I would be asking if Keary, Nellie, and I might be staying for a week or two on your ranch, just until I can decide where I should go and what I should do.

It is a lot to ask, I know, but I do not know where else to turn. I do not seem to be any closer to finding Quaid's whereabouts, so I cannot depend upon family for assistance. And I cannot stay here. To do so would be a grave mistake.

I must confess to a wee bit of selfishness as well. I am eager to hold your babe in my arms and see for myself if she looks like your husband as you have claimed in your letters. Already your Regan is three months old, and if I do not come soon, she will be walking like Keary before I see her. I know you must find that hard to believe, but it is true. She will be running with Janie before you turn around.

But as much as I long to come, dearest Beth, you must be honest with me. If our coming will prove a hardship to you in any way, you must tell me so. Talk with your husband, and then send me word by telegraph. I will await your answer for the next two weeks. I do not feel I can wait any longer than that before I must go.

Your affectionate friend,
Mary Emeline Malone

The morning air was crisp. The smell of approaching autumn drifted on a breeze that whispered through the meadow grass and caused the branches of the pines and aspens on the hillside to wave gently. Puffs of clouds, pure white and dazzling, floated against an azure canopy. A bald eagle, his wings spread wide, rose elegantly, lifted by an unseen hand, soaring above the mountaintops. In the corral, Cloud snorted, then bobbed his big black-and-white head and pawed at the dirt with one hoof. Down near the creek, Baba chased a squirrel along the bank, barking noisily in her hopeless pursuit.

Mary stood in the open doorway of the cabin and stared at the familiar scene. A terrible homesickness welled up inside of her, and she hadn't even left yet. Instinctively she knew it would be much worse than when she'd departed Ireland. She also knew the reason it would be worse.

This time, she would be leaving Carson.

She closed her eyes and remembered the last time he'd kissed her. Even now, she could imagine his lips upon hers. She could still feel the tingling sensation that coursed through her in response. How wonderful it would be to share with him her most secret thoughts, to reveal her true self to him as she had to no other.

She imagined him speaking, heard his voice as clearly as if he were actually with her. *Mary, it doesn't matter to me who you were or what you did before you came here. I'm in love with you, for better or worse.*

She sighed as she opened her eyes, then turned and closed the door.

It would matter to him if he knew what she'd done. It would have to matter to him because he represented the law of this land. Mary had no choice but to leave. She was never to know what it would be like to be his wife. That was her punishment for killing a man—to be denied the love and happiness Carson offered her.

Mary gave her head a tiny shake. There was no point feeling sorry for herself. It wouldn't change anything. It wouldn't change anything at all.

"Nellie, we must be getting ourselves ready. We're going to town."

The girl looked up from the book she was reading to Keary. "Will we see the sheriff? Keary and I've made somethin' for him. It's just some pine cones and such nailed to a piece of wood, but I think he's gonna like it."

Mary felt the tightness in her heart. "Aye, we'll be seeing Sheriff Barclay at Mr. Burke's office later today, and I'm sure he'll like whatever you made. But first I must post a letter and then see to some final details at the saloon."

"Can I ride Cloud into town?"

Another image flashed in Mary's mind, this one of Carson leading the pinto while Nellie sat on the horse's bony back. Both Carson and Nellie had grinned broadly, as if they'd achieved something of enormous proportions. The memory was from only a few days before, but so much had happened since then, it seemed much longer.

Mary could hear the strain in her voice as she asked Nellie, "Did Sheriff Barclay say it would be all right to ride Cloud so far?"

"He didn't say I couldn't."

Mary raised an eyebrow.

The child lowered her eyes, and her shoulders sagged. "Well, I suppose he didn't say it'd be all right."

All this over leaving the horse behind for a few hours. What was going to happen when Mary told Nellie they were moving and couldn't take Cloud with them? And who would want the pitiful, swaybacked animal? What if he were to be mistreated again? What if...

But she couldn't think about that. It wasn't to be helped.

Mary's head started to ache, a persistent pressure near her temples. She pressed her fingertips against her forehead and closed her eyes for a moment. When she opened them, Nellie was watching her with a confused expression.

She forced a smile. "Well, I'm thinking we'd best be hurrying. There is much to do."

⚊

Carson stood on the sidewalk outside the mercantile, his shoulder braced against the building as he listened to the idle conversation of Dooby Jones, Chuck Adams, and Abe Stover. Abe's wolfhound lay sleeping beneath the bench upon which his master and Dooby sat. Occasionally the dog whimpered and his legs twitched, but he never opened his eyes. As they talked, Chuck washed the mercantile window, a useless war against dust and grime but one his wife insisted upon.

"Shore am glad t' see the weather coolin' off," Dooby said. "Been a hot summer."

"Yup," Abe agreed with a quick glance at the sky. "We could use some more rain, too. Forest seems mighty dry. Sure would hate to see any fires startin' up. I'm guessin' the first snows are still several weeks away."

Chuck dropped his soapy rag into the bucket, then placed his fingertips against the small of his back and arched backward. When he straightened, he said, "Abe, you'll be complaining that the snow came too soon once it starts. You always do."

"I ain't never complained about snow."

Dooby and Carson both laughed.

Chuck snorted. "You must think I'm the forgetful sort. There you sit, over at the Painted Queen, sipping your beer and wishin' summer'd come."

Dooby glanced at Carson. "Say, Sheriff. You heard what's gonna happen to the saloon now that Miss Blanche is gone?"

"Haven't heard."

"I reckon Burke knows," Abe interjected. "He's been her lawyer ever since he come to Whistle Creek."

"She have any family?" Chuck asked as he resumed his scrubbing duties.

Carson shook his head. "Not that I heard of."

"Wonder why she and Perkins never married?" Dooby said.

Chuck and Abe offered a few suggestions, from the sublime to the ridiculous.

Privately, Carson thought they had more important things to wonder about than the Painted Queen shutting its doors. Like what to do if the miners went on strike. Or worse, if there would be rioting. Now that's what made his blood run cold.

And speaking of blood running cold, he thought when he recognized Bryan Halligan riding in their direction.

Halligan drew his sleek black gelding to a halt in front of the mercantile. Touching the brim of his hat, he said, "Morning, gentlemen. Nice day, isn't it?"

"What brings you to Whistle Creek again so soon?" Carson tried to keep his voice neutral.

"Mine business." Halligan glanced away, looking toward the saloon. A smile curved the corners of his mouth. "And maybe something personal."

Carson followed the direction of Halligan's gaze just in time to see Mary and the children crossing Main Street. He wondered what had brought her to town so early. They weren't due at the lawyer's for several more hours.

He continued to watch as the threesome moved along the boardwalk to Whistle Creek's post office, then disappeared inside. When he turned, he saw that Halligan's gaze had followed them, too. He bristled, wanting nothing more than to inform Halligan that Mary was his.

Only she wasn't his. She'd made that clear enough.

His eyes narrowed. Maybe something personal, Halligan had said. Well, he'd be hanged before he'd let Halligan anywhere near Mary. Something personal, his aunt Gertrude!

And Mary was going to be his. He wasn't letting her leave Whistle Creek. He didn't care if he had to hog-tie her and lock her in his jail until she agreed to marry him. She loved him, and he wasn't going to lose her. Not to her own fears and not to another man.

Carson pushed off from the wall of the mercantile. "If you fellas will excuse me, I've got things to see to myself." He stepped off the sidewalk and headed across the street, ostensibly toward his office. His real destination was the post office.

"Sheriff," Halligan called after him, "could you wait a minute?"

Carson stopped and turned. Halligan nudged his gelding forward, and Carson waited in silence for the man to speak again.

"I was wondering if you could help me. I'm looking for John Tyrell."

Carson remembered what Mac MacDonald had told him. He cast a furtive glance up the street, wondering if the marshal was in town. Was that why Halligan was on horseback? He usually took the train from Spokane. Maybe he'd ridden in with the marshal.

"Haven't seen him today," he answered as he looked at Halligan once more. "What do you need him for? Maybe I can help."

"I have a few more questions for him. About that accident"—skepticism dripped from the word—"at the mine last month."

"I'm surprised you haven't wrapped up your investigation yet."

The mine owner's mouth flattened, and a tic appeared at the corner of his right eye. After a moment's pause, he said, "The miners haven't been cooperative, but I'll have the answers I want soon, Sheriff. I promise you."

The air was heavy with their mutual animosity.

Carson forced himself to relax. "You know, Halligan, now that I think on it, seems to me I heard John was called out of town on some sort of business. Don't know where he went or when he'll be back, though."

Halligan cursed. "You sure he's coming back? You sure he's not on the run?"

"I'm sure." Carson grinned. "He's getting married in a few weeks."

"Married?" Halligan's tone implied, Who'd have the cripple?

"Yeah, married." He itched to take a swing at Bryan Halligan. Just one good punch would improve Carson's mood immensely. "Got himself a real sweet girl, too. He'll be back. You can bet on it. By then we ought to know who's behind the trouble at the Lucky Lady. Shouldn't we?" He tugged on his hat brim, pulling it lower on his forehead. "See you around." He walked away before the other man could reply.

Simmering anger and a load of frustration made Carson's stride long and quick. For a lawman who preferred his town and his life to be peaceful, quiet, and orderly, he wasn't having much success at keeping things that way lately.

Mary smiled at the postmistress. "Thank you, Mrs. Finley. I am hoping you'll feel yourself again soon." She glanced over her shoulder at Nellie, who was attempting to keep Keary out of mischief.

"You're lucky to have that girl's help," Susan Finley commented. "I'm wore out just watching that boy of yours. My girls are near grown, and I've forgotten what it's like to have small ones underfoot."

"Nellie's been a blessing, to be sure. 'Tis sorry I am she lost her kin, but I'll never be sorry she's come to live with us. I love her like me own."

"You know, Mrs. Malone, the ladies of our church circle would be right pleased if you'd join us some time."

Mary turned toward the postmistress again.

She must have looked surprised, because Mrs. Finley quickly added, "We'd all like to get to know you better. You were a godsend when the accident happened at the mine. We all heard about it in town. Then you took that little girl in. Such a Christian thing to do."

Mary knew it was by way of an apology, and she was touched. Only it came too late. Here she was, fixing to leave Whistle Creek just as others were starting to accept her into their midst.

For a moment, she entertained the fantasy. Mary Barclay, wife of the sheriff, pillar of the community. She envisioned herself in a gracious home, surrounded by well-behaved, well-dressed children, all of them with their father's golden-brown hair and stunning blue eyes.

"Keary!" Nellie cried, shattering the daydream. "Come back here!"

Mary whirled around in time to see Keary dart out the door. "Keary!" She hurried after him, knowing how quickly he could move. If he should run into the street when a horse or wagon was coming—

She stopped on the sidewalk, arrested by the sight before her.

It wasn't the first time she'd found her son in Carson's arms. In that moment, it seemed as if Keary was always running toward trouble, and the sheriff always managed to be there to stop him.

"What's the matter with you?" Carson snapped at her. "What if he'd run out in front of a wagon or something?"

Mary drew back, surprised by the anger in his voice. "He slipped away from Nellie, and I—"

"That girl's not his mother. You are. I may not always be around to rescue him when you're not paying attention."

As was too often the case, her temper flared. "And are you thinking I don't know that altogether?" She stepped forward and held out her arms. "I'll be thanking you to give me boy to me now. Sure and I wouldn't be troubling you any further."

He ignored her outstretched arms, looking behind her. "Nellie, come here."

The girl hurried forward as commanded, her face pale and her eyes wide.

"Carson Barclay," Mary warned, "don't you dare frighten her."

He still paid her no attention. "Here," he said to Nellie. "Take Keary to the Painted Queen. Shut yourselves in Miss Blanche's office and don't you move until Mary or I come for you. You hear?"

Nellie nodded.

Carson set Keary on his feet and passed his hand into Nellie's.

Before Mary could react or try to stop what he'd put in motion, Carson grabbed her hand, spun on his heel, and pulled her along with him as he headed for the sheriff's office. She was breathing hard by the time they reached their destination.

Carson opened the door, then put her in front of him and gave her a gentle push inside. Once he was inside, too, he closed the door firmly behind him.

Mary turned, sputtering like a wet hen. "Now see here—"

She was in his arms before she knew what was happening. His lips captured hers, ending her objections. Her anger melted beneath the onslaught to her senses. This was a different type of kiss from those they had shared before. There was no tender persuasion here. This was fierce.

Mary had no sense of time or space. She didn't know if it was minutes or hours before he ceased his wondrous assault. When he withdrew slightly, she knew she would have fallen were it not for the door at her back and the arms that held her still.

"I'm sorry I yelled at you," he said, his voice husky. "I didn't mean to take out my frustration on you or Nellie. You know I wouldn't hurt any of you for anything. Don't you?"

She nodded, mesmerized by the intense look in his eyes.

"Now, let's get something else straight between us, Mary Emeline Malone. I've always hated disorder in my town. I've worked hard to keep things nice and peaceful since I was elected sheriff. I'm trying hard to keep it that way right now, but there's unrest brewing. Plenty of it. I can feel it, and I can smell it. I'd like to be able to count on just one thing."

Despite herself, she whispered, "And what would that be, I'd be asking?"

"You." His lips brushed hers as he spoke, as faint as the touch of butterfly wings.

She closed her eyes. "Me?"

"Yes, you." He kissed her again, slow and deep. When he was through, he asked, "Now, are we finished arguing about this? Are you going to agree to marry me?"

"Carson, you wouldn't be understanding. I can't. You don't know—"

"Hmm." He cut her off with more kisses. He raised his hands to cradle her face, spread his fingers through her hair, dislodged her bonnet.

I'll be leaving Whistle Creek, Carson Barclay. I cannot marry you. It would be wrong for me to do so, and if you knew the truth, you'd think it wrong, too. So I'll be going away from here and from you. It'll be better altogether. You'll see.

"Marry me, Mary Malone," he whispered near her right ear.

"I cannot."

"Marry me," he whispered again, this time near her left ear.

"Oh, Carson, you—"

"Marry me. I need you, Mary. I need to love you. I need you to love me."

There was a reason she had to refuse him. What was it?

"I've been patient. I've tried to give you plenty of time." His mouth was near her ear as he whispered the words. "I don't want to wait any longer."

She knew there was a reason she must refuse him.

"I've been a loner all my life, Mary. I don't want to be alone any more."

Sure, and I don't want to be alone meself.

"Marry me."

She sighed. She hadn't the strength to resist him. It was useless to try, loving him as she did.

"Marry me."

A heartbeat more of hesitation, and then, "Aye."

He drew back mere inches, stared down at her. "What? What did you say?"

Her heart quickened as she met his gaze, her capitulation complete. "I said, aye. I'll marry you." She swallowed hard, then added, "And I'm hoping you'll never regret it, Carson Barclay."

He let out a whoop of joy, then effortlessly lifted her and whirled her around the room. When he set her feet on the floor, he kissed her again.

"I love you, Mary," he whispered when their lips parted at last, "and I'll never regret it. Never."

⁓

"She's in a town called Whistle Creek," the detective reported. "It's across the border in Idaho. Maybe three hundred, maybe three hundred and fifty miles from here. The railroad's got a regular run up there, although it's not the most direct route. Still, it would be faster than hiring a rig and going over the mountains."

Winston was on his feet, pacing, his heart pumping. "At last."

"When can we leave, Mr. Knox?" Portia asked in her usual calm and cool manner.

"We'll take the next train to Pendleton, Oregon, spend a night there, and then head north. We'll be in Whistle Creek by Friday afternoon."

Winston stared out the window of their hotel room. By Friday afternoon, he thought. By Friday they would find her. He clenched his hands at his side. He was going to make her pay for the trouble she'd caused.

"What is Mary doing there?" his wife inquired of Tibble Knox.

Winston glanced over his shoulder.

The detective consulted his notepad, then answered Portia, "It seems she is working at a saloon."

Winston called Mary a foul name beneath his breath.

Portia sent him a censuring glance. "Vulgarity is unnecessary, dearest."

He swallowed an angry retort. As soon as he got those papers he'd hidden away, he would be free of Portia. He wouldn't have to listen to his wife or look at her a moment longer. All he needed were those papers, and then he would be free.

And heaven help Mary Malone if he didn't find them.

~Eighteen

Mary stared at Martin Burke, unable to speak.

"Well," the attorney said as he closed the file, "except for a generous bequest to the orphanage in Wallace and another to the Whistle Creek Methodist Church, that's everything." He removed his spectacles and pinched the bridge of his nose between thumb and index finger, muttering, "Though what I ever did to make her leave that spoiled dog to me..." He let the words trail off as he glanced toward Nugget, asleep in his soft bed in the corner of the office.

Carson cleared his throat. "Why did she single us out, Martin?"

"Because she liked both of you. A great deal, obviously."

"But to leave me the Painted Queen..." Mary shook her head.

The attorney frowned. "I'll be honest with you, Mrs. Malone. I tried to talk Miss Blanche out of that particular addition to her will, but she was determined. She told me she trusted you to do what was best for all concerned."

"But what if I don't want to own a saloon?"

"It's yours to do with as you please. And, as I said, she trusted you to do what's right."

It was too much to comprehend. The direction of Mary's life had changed in a matter of hours. First she had agreed to marry Carson, a man she loved with her entire heart and soul. Now she found herself the owner of the Painted Queen Saloon and a wealthy woman in the bargain.

She could see that Carson was just as overwhelmed by what Blanche Loraine had left him—a large section of land, complete with a lake, plus a healthy number of shares in the Lucky Lady Mine. Even Mary, who had kept Blanche's books, hadn't known the complete extent of the woman's holdings.

Carson rose from his chair and offered his hand to the lawyer. "Well, we thank you, Martin. I guess it'll take a while for it to sink in." The two men shook hands, then Carson turned toward Mary. "I think we should talk about this." He helped her rise with a gentle hold on her arm.

After a soft farewell to Martin Burke, Mary allowed Carson to steer her out of the office. Neither of them said a word as they crossed Main Street, then followed the sidewalk through the center of town.

It didn't seem possible, any of it. Less than two months ago, Mary had been working as a maid, making barely enough to support herself and her son. She'd been alone and friendless in an uncaring city. She remembered the day that had sent her fleeing from New York. She remembered that moment on the train when she'd met Blanche.

"I'm thinking I won't ever believe it," she said as they entered the sheriff's office. She turned toward Carson. "Sure and I still can't think why she would leave the Painted Queen to me."

He shook his head. "I'm pretty surprised myself." He removed his Stetson, then raked his fingers through his hair. "What will you do with it?"

"Sure and I don't know."

"You don't mean to keep it, do you?" He sounded both surprised and worried.

Oh, her temper was a cursed thing. There was no denying it. "I've no wish to run a bawdy house, Sheriff Barclay. But I'll not fancy you thinking you can tell me what to do, now that we're to be married. I'll be no mousy wife you can order about as you please, and you'd best be knowing it before it's too late."

He stared at her for a moment, then surprised her by laughing aloud. When he was able, he said, "If that was the sort of wife I wanted, I'd never have fallen in love with you, Mary." His eyes twinkled with amusement. "You're the most stubborn, hardheaded woman I've ever met." The way he said them, the words sounded strangely like a compliment.

Despite herself, she smiled back at him.

"Let me try again." He stepped toward her, took hold of her upper arms, and drew her close. Looking down into her eyes, he said, "Mary dearest, I think you should close the Painted Queen. But I'm willing to trust God to show you what's the right thing to do."

It was late by the time Mary got both the children to sleep. She knew she should crawl into bed herself, but she was too keyed up. So much had happened that day. She still couldn't take it all in.

She grabbed a shawl and threw it over her shoulders, then stepped outside into the blanket of night, closing the door behind her. She was quickly enveloped by silence. Though the air was cool, there was no wind tonight. Stars twinkled gaily in the heavens. There was no moon to dull their brightness, and they reminded her of jewels spread across a black cloth.

Mary took a deep breath, letting the night air fill her lungs. After releasing it, she walked toward the corral. Baba joined her, following at her heels. Cloud lifted his head and snorted, then crossed to where she stood.

"'Tis married I'm to be," she told the horse as she stroked his muzzle. "Would ya fancy that."

Cloud's ears flicked forward.

"And the Painted Queen is mine. But what am I to be doing with it?"

She hadn't needed Carson to tell her that owning a saloon wasn't in her future. But what about the women who lived and worked there? What would happen to them if she suddenly closed the Painted Queen? Some of them had chosen the only life open to them, apart from starvation. They'd been pushed to the edge, surviving the only way they thought they could. It might have happened to Mary, if circumstances had been different.

What would she have done in order to keep Keary from going hungry?

"Faith, I've done much worse than work in a bawdy house," she whispered as a shiver raced through her.

She shook her head, driving off the unpleasant image. She wouldn't entertain thoughts of the past tonight of all nights. She had too much to be happy about. She wasn't going to let her past spoil her joy.

She set her thoughts on Carson. She remembered the first time she'd seen him, the day she stepped off the train. Oh, how he'd frightened her, the tall handsome man with a badge and a gun. Now he was to be her husband.

She placed her forearms on the top rail of the corral, then rested her chin on her right wrist and closed her eyes.

Her husband. Carson Barclay, her husband.

A deep sigh escaped her.

"Lovely," a male voice said out of the darkness.

Baba growled as Mary whirled around, a gasp of surprise on her lips.

"What do you want?" she asked breathlessly as her gaze found the man on horseback, his silhouette a shade darker than the night around him.

"I came to see you, Mrs. Malone."

She recognized his voice then. Bryan Halligan. She glanced toward the house, wondering how quickly she could run to it.

Halligan dismounted.

Baba growled, more menacing this time.

"Call off your dog. I'm here to talk."

"At this hour?"

He chuckled. It was an unpleasant sound. "I admit it is a bit late. But I only just heard the news about Blanche Loraine's will, and I wanted to discuss it with you."

"And what business would that be of yours, Mr. Halligan?" She moved away from the corral, taking a couple of steps toward the house, then stopped, hoping he wouldn't notice.

He noticed. He moved in the same direction. "I'd like to make you an offer for the Painted Queen."

"An offer?" It wasn't what she'd expected him to say.

"I'd like to buy it from you. I'm willing to pay a good price, and you'd be free to do what you want. Besides, you don't know anything about running a saloon in a mining town. Keeping the accounts for Miss Blanche was one thing. Keeping those soiled doves. . ." He had the audacity to laugh softly. "Well, that's another matter."

Mind your tongue, Mary, she seemed to hear her da caution as her temper sparked, but as usual, she didn't heed the voice from her past. "There's nothing that I'd be selling to the likes o' you," she snapped, her contempt obvious, "and now I'd have you leave me place."

"But you haven't heard my offer."

"Sure and I have no intention of listening to anything you have to say, Mr. Halligan. I'm thinking you're a hateful man, with no good intent for anyone but yourself. I'll thank you to be going now."

He chuckled again. "All right. If you don't want to talk business, maybe we should consider something more pleasurable to us both."

His comment deserved no answer. She marched toward the house, her head held high in a show of disdain.

Suddenly, Halligan had her by the shoulders and spun her around. When Baba moved in with an ominous growl, Halligan served the dog a vicious kick in the ribs, sending her flying into the darkness.

"Baba!" Mary cried.

"I'm losing my sense of humor." Halligan gave Mary's shoulder a hard shake.

Before she could respond, before her temper cooled and fear could replace it, she felt something rush past her. Then Halligan grunted and fell backward to the ground.

"You leave Mary be!"

For a moment, Mary didn't believe what she'd heard. "Nellie?"

Nellie's and Halligan's shadows rolled away from her.

"Nellie!"

By the time Mary moved forward, Halligan had gained the upper hand. He dragged Nellie up by her hair. Profanity issued from him in a scalding stream of words, barely heard above Nellie's shrieks. Even in the darkness, Mary could see him give another violent yank on her hair.

"Stop! You're hurting her," Mary screamed.

"I'll do more than hurt her."

Nellie tried to kick him.

He slapped her with his free hand.

Just as Nellie had done moments before, Mary threw herself at him. And just as Nellie had done, she caught him unaware and knocked him off his feet. With a thud, they hit the ground. Mary was prepared for a struggle, but there was none. Halligan stopped fighting. Apparently, he'd had enough.

She jumped to her feet and reached for Nellie. "Are you hurt?" She cradled the girl's head between her hands.

"No," Nellie whimpered. "I'm okay."

Mary glanced over her shoulder. Halligan still hadn't moved. She felt a tiny shiver of alarm. "Go in the house, Nellie."

"Not without you."

"You'll be doing as I say."

"No! I'm stayin' with you. You might need me."

Mary thought to argue, then decided against it. It might be better not to be alone. "Then stand over by the house." She gave Nellie a little push to send her on her way.

Taking a deep breath, she turned again. She saw Baba, obviously not seriously harmed by the kick, standing over Halligan, sniffing at the man's still body. Unnaturally still, it seemed to Mary.

Could it have happened again? Just as she'd dared hope for happiness, could it have happened again?

She stepped toward Halligan, her thoughts swirling. She seemed to be in two places at once—in a book-lined study in New York City and in an open meadow in the mountains of Idaho. She could see two men, both of them lying deathly still because of something she'd done. Because of her temper. She'd escaped her guilt the first time. But now...

Halligan moaned.

Baba growled.

Mary gasped, surprised, then thankful, and then angry all over again.

She whirled about and raced into the cabin, where she grabbed the rifle Carson had provided. She was breathing hard by the time she returned to stand in the light spilling through the doorway.

"I'm thinking you should leave now, Mr. Halligan," she called to him as he staggered to his feet. "And I'll thank you never to return."

He cursed. "You'll regret this."

Sure and I already regret it.

She couldn't marry Carson without telling him the truth. The past would come back to haunt her if she didn't. She would find no peace, no real happiness, not as long as she let the lie remain. No, she either had to refuse to marry Carson or she had to tell him the truth.

She lifted the rifle to her shoulder and aimed it at Halligan. "Leave," she ordered in a voice devoid of emotion. "Just leave."

She didn't lower the rifle until he'd mounted his horse and ridden away. Even then she stood staring into the night. Her heart ached. She felt lost and confused.

Finally, she forced herself to draw a steady breath. "Come, Baba," she called to the still-wary dog. Then she placed a hand on Nellie's shoulder and guided the girl inside.

Bright and early the next morning, Carson rode out to the property Blanche had left to him. As he sat astride Cinnabar, staring at the crystal-clear lake, morning sunlight glittering over the surface of the water, he felt an overwhelming sense of gratitude to his Maker.

He couldn't imagine what he'd done to deserve such perfect happiness. Mary would soon be his wife. He would have a son in Keary and a daughter in Nellie, and hopefully, there would be more children in his future. He had good friends he could trust. He had the newly inherited interest in the Lucky Lady that made him a man of some means. And now he owned this beautiful section of land, where he would build Mary the finest house she could ever wish for.

Of course, he knew he'd never done anything to deserve it. But miraculously, it was his, and he was thankful for it.

He knew it was too late in the year to start building. The first snowfall was no more than a month away. Winters came early in these parts and lasted long, but those winter months would give him plenty of time to design exactly what he wanted Mary to have.

The house would be two stories with an attic and a porch that wrapped around two sides. He would paint it white with green shutters at the windows. The front would face the lake and the sunrise. Mary could sit on the porch in the morning and see the golden light flickering on the water, just as he was doing now.

He grinned at the image in his head. He'd never been much for daydreaming, but he'd discovered there was pleasure to be found in it.

He straightened in the saddle and turned his dun gelding toward the road. He wanted to see Mary. He wanted to hold her in his arms and kiss her as he had yesterday. They hadn't set a wedding date yet. Today he was going to convince her it should be soon. Real soon. Maybe next week.

He nudged Cinnabar into a lope, eager to see his bride-to-be. It seemed in that moment that nothing could go wrong ever again. His life was perfect and seemed destined to stay so.

Fifteen minutes later, just as the east end of Whistle Creek came into sight, he found out how wrong he was.

～Nineteen

The miners poured into Whistle Creek, their voices raised in anger. Dozens of them. Well over a hundred, it looked like. Some carried guns or rifles. Others toted tools of their trade. A few of them rode horses or mules. Most were on foot. There were even wives and children in their midst.

"Where's Halligan?" someone shouted. Others picked up the cry. "Where's Halligan? We want Halligan."

A knot formed in Carson's belly as he approached the front wave of the mob. He drew Cinnabar to a halt, bumped his hat brim with his knuckle, tipping it back on his head, then leaned his forearm on the saddle horn in a deceptively relaxed pose. His eyes focused on Pete Edwards, the apparent leader of the group.

The surge of miners slowly came to a stop. Silence spread from the front of the mob to the back. All eyes were fastened on the sheriff.

"What's going on, Edwards?" Carson asked the leader.

"Halligan's fired Grigg and the others that were trapped with Russell and Tyrell."

The announcement didn't come as a surprise. Carson had been expecting it for some time now.

"He's cut our wages, too," someone else interjected.

Carson felt the knot in his gut twist. "That's rough, fellas," he said evenly, keeping his gaze on Edwards, "but that's no reason to come swarming into Whistle Creek, making it unsafe for folks to walk down the street."

"We come to find Halligan. We want to talk to him."

Carson shook his head, then shrugged. "Why didn't you talk to him at the mine?"

Edwards spit into the dust. "Because the coward had Christy do his dirty work for him. That's why."

Well, Carson thought, at least they weren't blaming Jeff Christy for the bad news. And nobody had mentioned the scabs waiting over in Osburn. Maybe they didn't know about them yet.

"We heard Halligan's in the saloon."

Carson straightened in the saddle and once more swept the mob with his gaze. "I'm not having any trouble here," he told the men, raising his voice so he could be heard at the back of the crowd. "Go on back to your homes. If you want a meeting with Halligan, send a representative or two. There's no need for all of you to be here." His gaze swung back to Pete Edwards. "And there's no call for guns, either."

"You sidin' with Halligan, Sheriff?"

A murmur of discontent rose and fell.

Carson's eyes narrowed. "I'm siding with the law. And those who break it will have to answer to me. That goes for Halligan, and it goes for all of you. Is that clear?"

There was more grumbling, but Carson saw men beginning to turn and walk away. He waited, unmoving. He saw the angry glances exchanged amongst those closest to him, and he knew he'd won only a momentary victory. One thing he'd learned over the years: Trouble rode a fast horse. It would be back, and he would have to face it down again.

When the last of the mob began to drift away in small clusters, Carson turned Cinnabar toward the Painted Queen. He found Bryan Halligan sitting at Mac MacDonald's old table, nursing a whiskey. He was alone.

Carson pulled out a chair opposite the mine owner, turned the chair around, then straddled the seat. "You surprised me, Halligan. I expected you to cut wages after you had to call in the National Guard."

Halligan scowled at him as he rubbed the back of his head, wincing as if something hurt.

"When're you bringing in the scab labor? They must be costing you a pretty penny to keep over in Osburn."

"Shut up, Barclay." Halligan took another gulp of liquor.

"I don't see what you have to gain from all this."

"And I don't see that it's any of your business."

Carson leaned forward, pressing his chest against the back of the chair. "It becomes my business when it causes trouble in Whistle Creek."

Halligan was silent for a moment, then said with a smirk, "Maybe all you care about is the value of those shares you inherited from Miss Blanche."

Carson didn't figure the comment was worth a reply.

"What did you do to earn them, Barclay? Cut Miss Blanche a deal? Maybe the good folks of Whistle Creek should know you've been on the take."

Carson tamped down his inner fury. He'd learned long ago that a cooler head prevailed in situations like this.

Halligan sloshed more whiskey into his empty glass and abruptly changed the subject. "I want you to arrest John Tyrell."

"On what charges?"

"Destruction of property, to start with."

Carson didn't have to ask what Halligan meant. He had a good idea where this was going. But he asked anyway. "What property is that?"

"You know very well what property." Halligan drained half his glass of its amber contents. "Mine property. He was the cause of that cave-in at the Lucky Lady. He took dynamite into the tunnel and tried to blow up the entire section. Only he got trapped by accident. Him and the others."

"What reason would he have to blow up the mine?"

"Because he's a bitter drunk. Because he's a cripple and he blames the mining company for it. Because he's a fool." Halligan's voice rose a notch in volume with every sentence. "How should I know what's going on in his head? Are you going to do your job, or do I have to call in the federal marshal to do it for you?"

There was more behind Halligan's words and actions than simply trying to reduce wages and make a larger profit for himself and the other owners. But for the life of him, Carson couldn't figure out what. It didn't make sense. What Halligan was doing would cost the owners far more in the long run than what they would save in reduced wages.

"Well?" Halligan demanded. "What are you going to do?"

Carson rose to his feet. "You bring me some proof of your suspicions, and I'll arrest him. But not until then."

Halligan hopped up, knocking his chair over backward in his haste. "The word of Bryan Halligan is all the proof you need."

Tension knotted the muscles in Carson's neck. "Maybe in Spokane that's how it works, but not here. I don't arrest somebody without just cause. In Whistle Creek, a man is innocent until proven guilty."

"You won't arrest him because he's your friend."

"You're right. John Tyrell is my friend. But I'll arrest him if there's reason to. I've arrested him before. You bring me evidence of his involvement, and I'll put him in jail until a trial can be arranged." He rested his knuckles on the tabletop. "In the meantime, you watch what you do and what you say. I'm the law in Whistle Creek, and don't you forget it. You hear me, Halligan?"

The other man's face turned bright red.

Carson paused a heartbeat, then spun about and left.

———

Mary had wrestled with her decision throughout the previous night, sleeping little. She'd silently debated with herself all morning as well. She knew she had only two choices: Tell Carson about Winston Kenrick, or refuse to marry him and leave town as she'd originally planned. One or the other.

But which was she to choose? Which would be the better thing to do? For Carson, for the children, for herself.

She loved Carson. She longed to spend the rest of her life with him. Keary loved him, too, and she knew Carson would make a grand father for her son.

But what would he do if she told him about her reason for fleeing New York City? She'd realized, sometime during her many hours of contemplation, that it wasn't jail she feared most. It was causing Carson to go against his ideals, to compromise his own integrity. She feared that more than a prison cell.

If she left suddenly, disappeared into the western wilderness, what would that do to him? Would he search for her? Would he learn to hate her?

And, as always, there were the children to consider. Who would care for them? Would they forget her if she was taken away? Worse, would they learn to despise her?

Mary had a hundred questions and no answers. She'd found no way to predict the future. She knew she would have to make her choice, and soon.

In the midst of her confusion, she cursed Bryan Halligan. Not for his assault last night but for forcing her into this untenable position. For making her face what she'd managed to avoid since accepting Carson's proposal of marriage.

It was now after lunch, and Mary felt no closer to a decision than she'd been last night. Keary was down for his nap, and Nellie was quietly working on some embroidery, something Edith had taught her how to do.

"Sure and I think I'll be taking a walk," Mary told the girl, trying her best to sound casual. "Will you keep an eye on Keary while I'm gone?"

"'Course."

Mary felt a welling up of anxiety, a fear of what the future might bring. "You're a good lass, Fenella Russell," she said huskily, her voice filled with emotion. "I don't know what I'd ever do without you. I'm glad altogether that you've come to live with us. You're like me very own daughter, and that's the truth of it."

The sudden outburst caused Nellie to glance up from her sewing, her eyes wide with surprise.

"I. . .I thought you should know the way of it." Mary forced a smile, then hurried outside.

But her escape into the mountains in search of answers was thwarted. As she stepped into the summer sunlight, she saw Carson, riding toward the house. What was she to say to him? Was now the time?

Then she noticed his strained expression, and she forgot her own dilemma. "Carson? What's wrong?"

He didn't answer. He simply dismounted, then took her in his arms and held her close.

She could feel the steady beat of his heart. His breath was warm on her scalp as he pressed his cheek against her hair. His strong hands spread wide across her back.

"Carson?" she whispered after a lengthy silence. She drew back but didn't leave the circle of his arms as she looked at him. "Tell me what's troubling you."

He shook his head slowly, his gaze locked with hers. "Halligan."

Her heart jumped. Did Carson know what had happened here last night?

He kissed her forehead, then whispered, "The whole town's coming apart at the seams." He kissed the tip of her nose. "I needed to hold you before it does." He kissed her on the lips. "I love you, Mary."

She couldn't leave him. She knew in that moment that leaving was not an option. She would have to tell him the truth. Maybe he wouldn't want her any longer. But whatever happened, it would be up to him, for Mary could never walk away of her own volition.

The words she'd never allowed herself to speak aloud slipped quietly into the open. "And 'tis you I love, Carson."

He stilled, staring down at her once more, his gaze searching, hungry. "Say it again," he gently demanded.

"I love you." Oddly enough, instead of feeling more vulnerable because of her admission, she was strengthened by it. Her fears about the future retreated.

Carson's voice was husky as he drew her close again. "You'll never know how I've longed to hear you say that."

"There's more I need to be telling you, Carson. Much more."

He didn't seem to hear her. "Will you marry me next week when Reverend Ogelsby is in town?" He kissed her again, long and deep, a kiss that left them both in want of oxygen.

When their mouths parted, Mary put her hands against his chest and gently pushed herself away from him. "'Tis talking we must be doing first, Carson Barclay. There's something important I must tell you."

He grinned and the tension left his face for the first time since he'd arrived. "I don't feel like talking, Mary. I feel like kissing some more."

"Faith and begorra," she muttered but was unable to keep from returning his smile. Would one more day matter so much? Tomorrow would be soon enough to tell what had to be told.

The moment of peace was shattered by a distant boom that caused the air around them to vibrate. In unison, they broke apart and turned their eyes toward Whistle Creek. A few heartbeats later, an enormous black cloud rose above the hilltops.

"It's started." Carson spun toward his horse. He swung into the saddle, then looked at Mary. "Whatever happens, you and the children stay here. Understood? Don't leave the cabin. I promise I'll come back as soon as I can. Just stay here until I do."

—

The black smoke from the burning storage shed—a cavernous building belonging to the Lucky Lady Mine—could be seen for miles. It rose swiftly, a belching dark cloud staining the clear blue of the sky. Ash and embers drifted down on the town. Men and women rushed to dampen rooftops to prevent the fire from spreading.

Carson joined the townsfolk in their battle against the raging blaze. Everyone was aware of the danger. Many a city and town had been destroyed by fire. The people who made their homes here, who had their businesses here, stood to lose everything they'd worked so hard to build unless they could contain the flames.

Luckily, the storage shed was located near the railroad tracks. There were no other buildings nearby, and the river formed a natural barrier between the fire and the parched summer forest. Chances were good they could stop it from spreading.

As Carson flung buckets full of water on the fire, he swore to himself that he'd find out who'd caused the explosion that started the blaze. All indications pointed to the miners, especially after this morning's angry demonstration, but a sixth sense told him that was too obvious. He suspected this was another part of Halligan's plan. But a plan for what? What did he stand to gain from destroying his own property?

"Look out!" someone shouted.

Carson jumped aside just in time to avoid being struck by a falling timber. Drawing a steadying breath, he decided he'd better concentrate on the fire first and solve the matter of who started it later.

⎯

Evening settled over the mountain meadow like a soft gray blanket. The children were fast asleep in their bed, but Mary remained at the window, watching. Carson had promised to return, and so she waited.

The moment she spied him, riding toward the cabin, she raced outside. There was nothing shy or reticent about the way she approached him. She'd been worried sick, and she needed to reassure herself that he was all right.

As soon as she reached his horse, she laid a hand on Carson's thigh. Even in the twilight, she could see the smudges of soot on his face, the weary sag of his shoulders. "Is the news so terrible altogether?"

"Could've been worse." He dismounted, then turned toward her. "The only thing lost was the mining company's storage building down by the tracks. It burned to the ground, but we saved everything around it."

"I'm glad you came back. I've been worrying for the sight of you."

"I should be investigating what started the fire." He reached out, tucked a loose strand of her hair behind her ear. "But I wanted to see you."

He sounded more than tired. He sounded defeated, and that was unlike the Carson Barclay she knew. Mary stepped close, wrapping her arms around his chest.

"I smell smoky," he objected, but even as he spoke, he hugged her to him. Tight, with a grip that said he didn't want to ever let go. "I saw what happened in this valley the last time the miners went on strike. There were riots. People died. Others were arrested. Buildings were blown up. I don't want to see that happen in Whistle Creek. I just don't know how to stop it. I should be able to stop it, but I can't figure out how."

"You're too tired to think straight," she replied as she eased back and met his gaze. "Come and sit down. There's a pitcher of lemonade in the springhouse. I'll get some for you."

He nodded, and she took his hand and led him to the bench outside the front door of the cabin. With a wave of her hand, she commanded him to sit. Once he'd done so, she hurried inside for a glass. A quick glance reassured her the children hadn't stirred.

After going to the springhouse for the lemonade, she returned to where she'd left Carson. She found him leaning against the cabin wall, his head back, his eyes closed. She paused, uncertain if she should disturb him or let him rest.

"I'm not asleep," he said softly, without opening his eyes.

"'Tis sleeping you should be, I'm thinking."

He patted the bench. "Come sit beside me, Mary."

She did so.

He put his right arm around her shoulders, then pulled her close to his side. "I wonder if it wouldn't be better for you and the children to leave Whistle Creek for a while."

"Are you expecting it to be as bad as all that, then?"

Instead of answering, he leaned his cheek against the top of her head, and his grip on her upper right arm tightened.

It was strange, she thought. Not so very long ago, she'd been wanting to leave Whistle Creek. She'd been wanting to take herself and the children away from here. She'd been willing to go into hiding. She'd even thought it would be best for Carson if she were to do so.

But now it was the last thing on earth she wanted to do. Leaving him would be the same as ripping out her heart. She couldn't go away from this place, away from him. She wanted to remain here, in his arms, forever.

"I'm thinking we'll stay," she said at last, "if 'tis all the same to you. I'd not be drawing a peaceful breath were I to put any distance between us, Carson." Her throat was thick with emotion, and she felt the sting of tears behind her eyes.

Carson straightened, took the glass of lemonade from her hand, and set it on the ground. Then he gently pulled her across his lap. The embrace seemed natural, comfortable, as if they'd been doing it for years. She looked into his eyes, and even though she couldn't see him well in the gloaming, her heart quickened.

"I never expected to find you, Mary."

She swallowed the lump in her throat.

"I wish this wasn't happening now. Halligan and the miners, I mean. I want to be thinking of you. Just you."

"Aye," she whispered, wishing the same.

"I don't know a lot of flowery words. The kind a man ought to sweet-talk his lady with. Poetry and such. I wish I did.

You deserve them, Mary. I never knew anyone who deserved them more than you do."

Slowly, he lowered his head toward hers until their lips met. The kiss was tender, slow, sweeter than any words could have been. It made Mary's head spin, her heart flutter.

"I wish Reverend Ogelsby was going to be here tomorrow," he said, his voice a husky whisper.

She swallowed, unable to speak, wishing the same.

"I'd better go."

She wished he could stay.

"I'd best go now," he half groaned, half growled.

"Not yet."

He silenced her with another kiss, a brief, quick, frustrated kiss that spoke volumes.

What if she lost him forever? What if, after she made her confession and he knew the whole truth, he didn't want her anymore?

"Stay awhile," she whispered.

More than seeing his gaze, she felt it. "Don't tempt me, Mary. I'm not feeling very strong right now."

"But—"

"Shh." He brushed his lips over hers. "You deserve everything wonderful and perfect."

She felt a warmth in her heart. He didn't need flowery words or poetry to tell her she was cherished, to tell her that he valued her. The knowledge made her feel both glorious and unworthy. No matter what tomorrow might bring, she would remember this moment forever.

~Twenty

Sweat trickled down Carson's back as he rode toward Whistle Creek beneath the hot afternoon sun. He'd spent hours at the Lucky Lady, talking to the striking miners, hoping he could get some answers before it was too late—if it wasn't too late already. Once again, he'd come away empty-handed.

"What would you have done, David?" he muttered aloud.

A better job of things, he answered himself. David Hailey would have found answers by this time. Carson was sure of it.

"You'd better find out who started that fire," Halligan had shouted as he'd stood before Carson's desk earlier in the day. "You make some arrests. Do your job. Or, so help me, I'll do it for you. I know you're turning a blind eye to what's going on. I know you favor the miners."

Carson was glad he hadn't made any accusations of his own. He still thought Halligan might have set the fire, but he didn't want the man to know of his suspicions. Not until he had proof.

Only he wasn't sure he'd have the time he needed to get his proof. The mood at the Lucky Lady was ugly. If the miners weren't behind the fire yesterday, they'd probably be behind the next incident. And there would be another incident, as surely as the sun would rise again tomorrow morning. It was only a matter of time.

He felt the blistering sun beating on his back and cursed the lingering heat wave. Tempers were shorter in weather like this. Including his.

—

As the train whistle sounded its mournful cry, Portia stared out the window, watching the passing countryside. She found the scenery breathtaking. The mountains rose like pyramids, covered in green blankets of pine and fir. The sky overhead was a blinding blue. The river ran clear and smooth at times; at others, the rapids made it froth like the mouth of a mad dog. Towns were few and far between, and those were small, made up of a saloon or two, a dry goods store or a mercantile, a smithy, and, if the town was fortunate, a doctor's office. There was seldom much else, other than a few homes.

What would it be like to live in such a place? Portia had found herself wondering with each stop. She'd looked at the men and women getting off the train in these "jerkwater towns"—as Winston called them—and she'd wished she could go with them. She knew their lives must be hard. She could see that by their faces. To live in country like this, to fight the elements day in and day out, couldn't be easy. But she wished to experience it for herself.

It came as an enormous surprise to discover she didn't want to go back to New York City once they found Mary. She didn't want to return to her beautiful home on Madison Avenue. From the time she was a little girl, Portia had been given everything her heart desired by the father who doted on her. Merlin Pendergast had done his best to lay the world at Portia's feet, including finding her the sort of husband who could give her what he couldn't—the right name. Marrying Winston had introduced her to the society she'd thought she craved. But money and position hadn't given her real happiness. Certainly her marriage hadn't given her any. She'd thought the price was worth it. She'd been mistaken.

"Whistle Creek, next stop," the conductor called, interrupting her musings.

"About time," Winston grumbled.

Portia turned toward her husband. Briefly, their gazes met. His eyes were full of anger and bitterness, and so much more. Loathing, perhaps. For her. She wondered what he saw in her eyes.

She wasn't going back to New York, she knew in that instant. It wasn't too late to find a shred of the happiness she'd missed. She couldn't change the past, but she could change her future. It was time she became responsible for her own happiness. She intended to start taking that responsibility now.

"Mr. Kenrick . . . ," Tibble Knox began. Winston and Portia glanced in his direction. "I suggest you and your wife check into the hotel while I learn Miss Malone's whereabouts."

"I'm going with you," Winston shot back quickly.

"But—"

"I'm going with you."

Portia looked out the window once again, thinking, *Mary came out here, all alone and penniless. If she could do it, so can I.*

⸺

When the knock sounded on Blanche's office door, Mary closed the ledger and called, "Enter."

"You wanted to see me?" Edith asked as she stepped through the doorway, a smile brightening her pretty face.

"Aye, that I did. Will you be closing the door behind you, please?"

Edith's smile vanished. "You sound serious."

"'Tis a matter of importance I wish to be discussing with you."

"Is it Johnny?" the girl asked, a note of panic in her voice. "Has something happened to him?"

Mary shook her head. "No, 'tis not your Johnny. 'Tis yourself this concerns."

"Me?" Edith sat down in the chair opposite the desk. "Have I done something wrong?"

Mary laughed softly. "I'm thinking I've alarmed you needlessly. I'm sorry for that altogether. 'Tis your help I want. Nothing more." She held up her hand, stopping the girl from speaking. "Hear me out."

Edith nodded.

"When I came to Whistle Creek, it was because Miss Blanche offered help to a stranger. I had nowhere to go, and I had little enough money to see me through. I wouldn't be knowing why she helped me. I'm thinking she didn't know either. It just happened."

"She helped me, too."

"Aye, I remember you telling me how it was." Mary rose from her chair and went to the window. "Most of the women who work here have similar stories to ours. No money and nowhere to go. 'Tis what's made them desperate enough to live like this. 'Tis what could happen to any woman." She paused, her thoughts wandering for a moment, reliving snippets from her past. Finally, she turned to look at Edith again. "I wouldn't be knowing for certain why Miss Blanche left the Painted Queen to me, but she must have known I wouldn't leave it as it is."

"What do you mean?"

"'Tis a safe haven I want to provide. A place for a woman to go when she's got nothing else. And her children, too, if she's got any."

"I reckon that's right nice of you, Mary, but—"

"And I want you to run the place."

"Me?"

"Aye. Because you understand what it's like." She lowered her voice. "And so do I. I was never married to Keary's da. I was thinking we were to be married when I joined him in America, but he married someone else before I came here. I don't believe he ever meant to marry me. He died without knowing he'd sired a son and left him without a name."

"Oh, Mary," Edith whispered. "I'm right sorry."

Mary realized there were tears in her eyes. She impatiently flicked them away. "'Tis not Seamus Maguire I cry for. 'Tis me own guilt and shame for the choices I made. 'Tis knowing what happens to many girls who make the same foolish mistakes. 'Tis knowing how hard it is to set things right again when there's so many who're wanting to keep you down once you're there."

Edith nodded.

"At first I was thinking of selling the Painted Queen." She returned to her desk as she spoke. "Then last night the answer came to me altogether. We'll make it a home for women in need. A safe haven, like I said. Maybe a way to turn lives in another direction. I'm thinking the reverend might take an interest in helping with the spiritual needs, same way he did with Miss Blanche."

"I wouldn't know the first thing about runnin' such a place as you're talking about. And I'd have to talk to Johnny first, before I could give you an answer."

"I was thinking I'd make him me business partner."

"A partner?"

"Aye, the both of you."

It was Edith's turn to rise, Edith's turn to walk to the window and stare outside. Softly, she said, "I never expected nothing like this to happen. Finding Johnny, that was enough for me.

More than I deserved." Her voice fell so low, Mary had to strain to hear. "Johnny doesn't seem to mind. What I've been, I mean. He says it don't matter. That I'm special. He says I ain't gettin' no bargain in him. But I sure wish I could go to him, all clean-like instead of like I am. If there'd been some other way..." Her voice drifted into silence.

"So you'll do it? You'll help me?"

Edith turned. She stared at Mary for a long time before nodding. "Yeah, I reckon I will. Johnny'll want to, too. You see if he don't." She crossed back to her chair. "What about the girls who're here now? What are you gonna do about them?"

"They'll be offered a place to stay as long as they want it. But they won't be allowed to entertain men. If that's what they want, they'll have to move on. For those willing to learn, we can teach skills so they can get jobs. Real jobs. Like teaching or dressmaking. Or they could learn to be cooks. Greta could help us with that."

Edith laughed aloud. "Greta? Not willingly, I wager."

"Aye, she will. You'll see."

For the next hour, the two young women enthusiastically discussed all the possibilities and made a host of plans for changes to the property. Mary wanted to fence in the property at the back and make a play area for children. Edith suggested enlarging the kitchen and dining areas. She also thought they should turn a large room on the main floor—once used for private high-stakes gambling parties—into a sewing room because of the daylight that came in through the westside windows.

They were still bubbling over with ideas when Shirley, one of the Painted Queen "girls," opened the office door. "There's a couple of men out front asking for you, Miz Malone."

"What do they want?" Mary asked, hating to be disturbed while the ideas were still flowing.

"Don't know. Just wanted to talk to the owner. In private, they said."

Mary supposed she shouldn't be surprised. Word that she had inherited the Painted Queen would have carried quickly through Whistle Creek and on to neighboring towns. These men were probably whiskey salesmen or some such, hoping to get the saloon's business. They were bound to be disappointed when they learned of the changes in store.

"I suppose I must be seeing them." She glanced at Edith. "We'll talk more later."

Shirley asked, "You want I should send 'em back?"

"Aye. And thank you, Shirley."

"No trouble, Miz Malone."

Edith rose from her chair and started to leave.

"Edith," Mary said, stopping her departure. "When I'm finished with these salesmen, I'm thinking I should have a talk with everyone who works at the Painted Queen. They should be told what I'm planning. They must all be wondering what I'm going to do."

Edith nodded. "I'll see to it." She smiled. "Don't you worry none either. It's all gonna work out fine. It's a real good thing you're doing. A real good thing."

⸺

Carson slammed the cell door closed. "Cool off, Edwards," he told the older man, "and then we'll talk." He glanced toward Thomas Crane, who was now sitting on a cot in the cell opposite Pete Edwards. Thomas was gently touching his split lower lip, then glancing at the blood on his fingertips. "I'm going to want to talk to you, too, Crane."

The two men had been brawling in the middle of Church Street, just as the three-fifteen was letting off passengers.

Carson had hauled both men off to jail, not asking who or what had caused the fight between the two miners.

As he walked into his office, Carson used his foot to shut the door that separated the office from the jail cells. He raked the fingers of both hands through his hair and muttered to himself. It was time he admitted he needed help. He couldn't handle this situation alone.

He stepped outside and stood on the sidewalk, glancing up and down Main Street. The afternoon sun continued to bake the town, blistering the paint on storefront signs. Horses stood at hitching rails, their heads hung low, their tails switching slowly. Abe Stover's dog had crawled beneath the raised boardwalk in front of the mercantile, seeking shade.

All was peaceful.

Before he sent a wire to Boise, Carson decided quickly, he'd call in a favor from Sheriff Parks down in Latah County. Maybe with a few deputies and a bit of luck, he could hold trouble at bay awhile longer. Maybe even long enough to get the answers he needed.

He looked toward the Painted Queen and wondered if it was full of miners. Friends of Edwards and Crane. If so, it probably wouldn't matter if he had fifty deputies to help him.

All was peaceful—but only temporarily. It could burst apart at any time.

His pride was causing him to use poor judgment, he thought grimly. He should have sent for help long before now. He didn't have time to waste, looking for clues all by himself. If the anticipated trouble erupted, Mary and the children—his family—could get hurt. He wasn't about to risk that.

He turned, reached through the doorway to grab his hat off the peg, then headed toward the telegraph office, his decision made.

When she heard the footsteps in the hallway, Mary rose from her chair and stood behind her desk, trying to look sure of herself, trying to look like the business owner she was. But when the taller of the two men stepped into her office, she lost the ability to breathe, to think, let alone to pretend a confidence she didn't feel.

"Hello, Mary," Winston said, a cruel smile curving his mouth. "I guess you didn't expect to see me."

She grabbed for the desk, hoping to keep herself from falling. It couldn't be him. She'd killed him. He was dead. Faith and begorra! Was this his ghost, come to haunt her?

He turned to the man behind him. "Wait for me out in the hall, Knox. I want to talk to Miss Malone in private." When the door was firmly closed, he looked at Mary once again. "I asked to see the owner. I didn't expect to find you here."

"I...I'm the owner," she answered without thinking—and immediately wished she hadn't.

"Indeed?" He smiled again. "Then you have done quite well for yourself in a short time." His gaze moved slowly over her. "Running a saloon seems to agree with you, Mary."

She ignored his derogatory tone. "I was thinking you were—" She stopped abruptly, not wanting to say the word aloud.

"Dead," he finished for her. "No doubt, you wished it so." He touched the back of his head, as if to remind her what she'd done.

"No." She sat down, her legs no longer able to support her. "I was only wanting you to stop."

His smile turned menacing. "Too good for me but not for this?" He waved his hand, then took two steps toward her. "I should—" He swallowed his angry words, but his hard gaze never left her.

She watched him control his rage, saw the cool, aristocratic mask slip into place. She wondered what he intended to do with her now. Many times she had imagined the authorities finding her, taking her back to New York to stand trial for murder. But never in her wildest dreams had she thought she would be facing Winston Kenrick himself.

For a moment, she felt relief. All these weeks, she'd thought she was guilty of murder. But she wasn't. He was alive. She hadn't killed him. She wouldn't have to confess to Carson that she was a murderer. She could marry him with a clean conscience. She could go to church again without guilt, knowing that God himself heard her prayers.

"You did try to kill me, Mary," Winston said, as if reading her thoughts. "You could hang for that alone."

A chill gripped her heart. "'Twas only because you were forcing yourself on me against me will."

"Who would believe that?"

"But 'tis true."

He chuckled softly as he settled into the chair opposite her. "Are you naive enough to believe the truth matters? What matters is who I am and who you are. That's all that matters. Fair or not, that's the way it is in this world, my dear girl."

*Carson...Keary...Nellie...*She felt her heart breaking as their names whispered in her head. *Carson...Keary...Nellie...*

Winston cleared his throat. "But I'm willing to forget what happened if you return what you stole from me."

It took a moment for his words to seep through her grief. When they did, she was confused. "What I stole?"

"The silver cigar box," he snapped, anger once again in his voice. "The one you struck me with. You took it when you ran, and I want it back."

She shook her head, not because she was denying she'd taken the box but because she was trying to remember what she'd done with it.

Misunderstanding her gesture, Winston leaped to his feet and leaned across the desk, grabbing her chin with one hand and squeezing tight. His face was mottled with fury. "What did you do with the box, Mary? Tell me." He squeezed harder. "Return it to me or, so help me, you'll regret it."

"I don't know where it is!" she cried out, fearing he would break her jaw in his iron grasp.

"What did you do with it? Did you sell it? Did you throw it away? You fool!"

"No. I had it when we got here. I...I put it out of sight so I wouldn't be remembering...so I wouldn't be thinking on what happened that day. I...I just wouldn't be knowing where I put it."

Winston released his grip and straightened. His cool facade slid into place, and he was once again the calm, controlled gentleman. "I suggest you find it, Mary, and quickly. We've taken rooms at the boardinghouse, since there is no hotel in this miserable town. You bring me that box by tomorrow morning, or I'll have you arrested for attempted murder." With those words, he turned and walked out of the office.

Mary stared at the closed door, her heart hammering, her mind racing.

Where had she put the box?

Her future depended upon finding it.

Twenty-one

By Saturday afternoon, the Whistle Creek jail cells were bursting at the seams, filled with grumbling, angry miners. Carson no sooner slammed the door behind one prisoner than someone sent news of another altercation. Matters had worsened after the arrival of scab labor on Friday's train. Most of those men were holding court in the Painted Queen, waiting for their orders from Halligan.

In anticipation of even more trouble, Carson deputized Wade Tyrell, Abe Stover, and Dooby Jones—and then he prayed that the help he'd sent for would arrive soon.

Carson sank down onto the chair behind his desk and closed his eyes, hoping to find a moment of peace. Then he heard footsteps running along the boardwalk. He groaned softly, knowing his respite was over before it began.

"Sheriff Barclay!"

He was on his feet in a flash. "Nellie?"

"Sheriff Barclay, you'd better come quick. It's Mary."

Long strides carried him across his office. "What happened? Is she hurt?"

"No, but she's acting real queer-like. She was up all night, searching through her trunk and the cupboards and Keary's toys. Opening things again and again. She brought us into town before the sun was hardly up, and now she's doing the same over at the saloon. She's got me scared. And Edith, too."

Nellie ran to keep up with Carson as he hurried toward the Painted Queen.

He didn't know what to make of the girl's words. It didn't sound like Mary. Maybe Nellie was reading more into whatever she was doing. Tensions were high. Even a child was sure to feel it.

Once inside the saloon, he paused. He looked behind him at Nellie. "Where is she?"

"Upstairs," she answered, jumping in front of him to lead the way.

Before they reached the bedroom, Carson heard furniture being moved across the floor. Then he heard Mary's voice, soft and mumbling, the words indistinguishable.

He paused in the doorway and looked in. Mary was jerking open the drawers of a bureau, her hands searching the empty cavity she found within. There was a wild, desperate look about her. Even at her most skittish, he'd never seen her like this.

His gaze flicked toward a corner of the room where Edith stood, holding Keary in her arms. She met his gaze and gave her head a tiny shake, the gesture stating her helplessness.

He looked at Mary again, then said her name softly.

She gasped and jumped away from the doorway.

"Mary, what's wrong?"

She shook her head. Then her frantic gaze began to rove around the room, as if she'd forgotten he was there. "I can't find it. 'Tis gone. I can't find it."

"Can't find what?"

"'Twas here. Edith thought it a jewelry box." She turned her back toward him. "Sure and I put it away so I wouldn't be seeing it, and now 'tis gone."

Carson was growing alarmed. All this over a jewelry box? He looked at Edith again, and again she shook her head.

Mary spun around. Tears filled her beautiful brown eyes. "Don't you see, Carson? I've lost it. I've looked everywhere. 'Tis gone, and now—" She choked on a sob.

In three quick strides, Carson was in the bedroom and gathering her into his embrace. "Whatever it is, we'll replace it, Mary. I promise." He kissed the top of her head. "I promise."

"You wouldn't be understanding," she replied as she pressed her face against his chest. "'Tis too late."

No, he didn't understand, but all he wanted at the moment was to stop her tears, to have her know he would do anything for her. "Shh." He stroked her back. "Shh. It'll be okay. I'll buy you a new jewelry box. An even prettier one. Shh. It'll be okay. I promise."

She drew in a ragged breath, then let it out as she whispered, "No."

He heard Edith moving across the room, heard her softly say, "Come along, Nellie. We'll leave the two of 'em be." Then the door closed.

Carson and Mary stood in the center of a room in shambles. He kept her in his tight embrace, his cheek pressed against the top of her head. Neither of them spoke or made a sound, but Carson knew she was crying from the way her body occasionally shuddered.

His heart ached for her, and he wished he could do something to stop her tears, to take away the desperation. He was a man of action, had always been a man of action. He hated this sense of helplessness. He wanted to fix whatever was wrong. But how could he fix it if he didn't know what it was?

He didn't look up when he heard the door open, assuming Edith had returned for some reason.

"My, my," a man said. "What have we here?"

Mary stiffened in his arms.

"Sheriff Barclay, I presume."

Carson glanced toward the stranger. From his silk top hat to his single-breasted gray walking suit to the shine on his leather-soled shoes, the fellow's attire proclaimed he was a man of means. So did his demeanor.

"You are Sheriff Barclay, are you not?"

"I am." His arms tightened on Mary when she started to pull away. "Who're you?"

The man smiled, but there was nothing friendly about it. "My name is Winston Kenrick." His gaze shifted from Carson to Mary. "I'm here to demand the arrest of Mary Malone."

"On what charge?"

"Attempted murder and theft."

It took the last remnants of Mary's strength to pull free of Carson's embrace, to raise her head and look into his eyes. She saw the surprise and the questions in their blue depths.

"Well?" Winston continued.

"What proof do you have?" Carson asked, his gaze still locked with Mary's. "When and where was this supposed to have happened?"

"I have all the proof you'll need over at the boardinghouse. There are statements from my physician and from several of my house servants. Mary fled New York because she tried to kill me. She was a maid in my house. She attacked me in my study. Ask her to deny it."

"Mary?" Carson queried softly.

"I wasn't trying to kill him," she whispered, barely able to speak.

"There!" Winston crowed. "That's all the proof you need to lock her up. She's as good as admitted it. Now ask her what she did with my property."

Carson shot the other man an angry glance, then looked at Mary again. "Tell me what happened."

"Just because the two of you are engaged doesn't mean you can ignore—"

"Shut up, Mr. Kenrick," Carson growled.

Mary knew what her former employer would do. If Carson didn't arrest her, Winston Kenrick would destroy him. He had the money. He had the influence with powerful people. She knew he wouldn't hesitate to use everything at his disposal against Carson.

"Sure and I'm thinking you should take me to jail," she said, blinking to clear her eyes of unwelcome tears.

"Mary—"

"I'll be asking Edith to see after the children. I'd be obliged if you'd look in on them now and again."

Carson grasped her by the upper arms and drew her toward him. His voice was low and stern when he spoke. "This isn't over. Martin Burke will represent you. We'll clear this matter up. You'll be all right."

She nodded, though in her heart, she believed him wrong. She was guilty enough. And even if the law didn't hang her, she could never marry Carson. Not after everyone heard what she'd done—and she knew they would hear. There was no keeping her sins secret now.

Carson understood Kenrick's not-so-veiled threats, but he didn't arrest Mary because of them. He took her into custody because he knew it was the only way he could get to the bottom of things.

Since the jail cells were full, Carson took her to his room above the sheriff's office. There wasn't much to it—a narrow cot where he slept, the small stove where he occasionally cooked something to eat, the table with one chair scooted beneath it, the pegs in the wall that held his clothes and his spare Stetson, the two curtainless windows, one looking out on Main Street, the other facing River Street. Still, it was better than a room made with steel bars, so he was thankful for it.

"Sit down," he gently commanded as he closed the door behind them. When she didn't move, he stepped past her and pulled out the chair from the table. "Sit down, Mary. Please."

She did so without meeting his gaze. She sat stiffly, her back ramrod-straight, her gaze fastened on the closed door.

Carson hunkered down beside her and placed a hand on her thigh. "Mary, look at me."

It took a few moments, but eventually she did as he asked.

"Now," he continued, soft and gentle, "tell me what happened with Kenrick. Tell me everything, Mary, so I can help you."

She gave him a sad smile. "I'm thinking you can't help me. 'Tis the truth Master Kenrick told you. I hit him and left him for dead. I was not trying to kill him, mind you, but that's what I thought I'd done all the same."

Carson took hold of her right hand. It was cold as ice. "Start at the beginning, Mary."

She ducked her head. "Then I'd have to go all the way back to Ireland."

He nodded, hoping to encourage her.

Tears welled in her eyes. "I've not been altogether honest with you, Carson," she whispered, and he could hear the pain in her confession. "I've wanted to be, but..." She let her words drift into silence.

"I love you. Nothing you say is going to change that."

He could tell she was struggling to believe him, wanting to but afraid to.

After a long while, she began to speak in a soft voice. "The Malones were poor, me da a tenant farmer like I told you before. But me ma was determined to raise us to be clean and upright. We were in church every Sunday. Ma wanted to make sure we wouldn't be tempted into sin." A sad smile flickered at the corners of her mouth. "'Twas difficult for her, her children being as they were. Headstrong and stubborn, the whole lot of us. Always at odds with the world and with each other. Worry made her old before her time. When she passed on, the light went out o' me da's heart. He wasn't ever the same again."

Carson wished he could take her into his arms and comfort her, but he knew he had to wait until her story was told.

"I went into service for the Whartons at their estate near Belfast when I was fifteen. 'Twas the first time I saw for meself how different from the Malones the rich lived. I had me own room on the third floor. 'Twas no bigger than one o' your cells below us, but I had it all to meself and I thought it was heaven on earth. I'm thinking it was then I started to want more than I should." She paused, then whispered, "Rising above me station in life, as me ma would've said."

Carson brushed a loose strand of her hair from her face, looping it behind her ear. She didn't seem to notice the gesture.

"After me da died, Padriac married a girl from Scotland and moved to the Lowlands. Three of me brothers went to England to work in the coal mines. Me brother Quaid came to America." She glanced up, then dropped her gaze quickly.

"I know about Quaid. I know you've been searching for him since you came to Whistle Creek. Blanche told me before she died."

Again she looked at him. "'Tis sorry I am I never told you meself."

He shook his head slowly, telling her with his eyes that it didn't matter.

After a lengthy silence, she continued her tale. "I was all alone in the world after that. Even when I'd been away in service, I'd always known me da and brothers were in our village.

Now they were all gone, and I was lonely without them. 'Twas the next year I met Seamus Maguire." She drew a deep breath, then let it out. "Ah, he was a handsome bloke, he was. His hair was auburn, and he had a smile that bewitched the girls from Donegal to Cork. I was no different from the others. For two years, I hoped he would notice me, but 'twas Brenna, the downstairs maid, he took a fancy to. It wasn't until the Whartons went back to England and took along both of us, Seamus and me, that he gave me a turn."

Mary rose abruptly from the chair and walked to the window. Carson stood but didn't follow her. He could tell it was difficult for her, talking about Maguire, and despite knowing she loved him now, Carson felt the thin blade of jealousy slice through his heart.

"Seamus didn't stay in service to the Whartons once we were in England. He was off to make his fortune, he told me. I thought that was the last I'd be seeing of Seamus Maguire, and it would've been better altogether if it had been. 'Twas more than a year later, after I'd left the Whartons and taken a position with the Wellingtons, that he returned to Buckinghamshire. He came to work as a groomsman for the earl, but he was already planning on leaving for America, just as soon as he'd set aside the cost of his passage from his wages."

Mary turned around. He saw her stiffen her spine, recognized the proud lift of her chin.

"Sure and I'll never understand how it was I let him take me to his bed without me being his wife. He had a glib tongue and a magic smile, he did. I believed with all me heart that he loved me and would marry me, just as he'd promised. Only he said we couldn't until I joined him in America. He made it sound like it was best to wait for marriage but not for bedding, and I was fool enough to believe him. No." She shook her head. "'Tis not true. I only wanted to believe him. I knew 'twas wrong."

"You were young and in love."

"Aye, 'tis the excuse I gave meself." She sighed. "When I realized he'd left me with a wee one, I came to join him as quick as I could. 'Twas full of hope and dreams I was when the ship landed, certain I could set things to rights. I had no way of knowing Seamus was dead." She took a ragged breath. "Or that he'd married someone else not more than a month after he'd left me behind."

If Seamus Maguire hadn't already been dead, Carson would have hunted him down and paid him back for the hurt he'd caused Mary. Carson knew, without hearing the rest of her story, that Mary had faced everything with characteristic courage and determination. She might have made mistakes, but he knew she wasn't guilty of any crimes worth imprisonment.

Carson strode across the room, took Mary by the hand, and led her back to the chair. With a gentle pressure on her shoulders, he forced her to sit once again.

"You don't have to tell me any more. It doesn't matter."

"No," she answered, her voice stronger. "'Tis time you know. 'Tis what sent me here." She met his gaze through a glitter of tears.

After an extended silence, she continued to tell him what had caused her to run from New York City.

—

"The sheriff took Mary to jail?" Portia watched her husband pace the width of their rented room.

"Yes, and by thunder, that's where she'll stay." His face was red with fury. "She refuses to give me the box. I told her I'd forget what happened if she just returned it."

"Perhaps Mary doesn't have it."

He whirled toward her. "Oh, she has it, all right. She has it."

If Portia had ever doubted there was more to Winston's obsession about that box than met the eye, it would have been dispelled by his behavior. He looked ready to kill.

"I don't trust that sheriff." He resumed his pacing. "Did I tell you he's engaged to Mary? The little Irish witch has cast a spell over him. For all I know, he'll turn her loose in the middle of the night. He might help her escape."

Portia feigned disinterest. "I'm sure that won't happen, dear. Mr. Knox will keep an eye on things." She rose from her chair. "Well, I suppose we shall be stuck here until Mary's trial. I believe I shall have a look at the shops and discover what I might do to occupy my time until it is over." She walked to the bureau. Gazing into the mirror, she settled her hat over her hair and secured it with two hat pins. When she finished, she turned toward Winston. "Would you care to join me?"

"No," he snapped irritably.

She'd known he wouldn't. She hadn't wanted him to. "Do try not to work yourself into too much of a lather, Winston. I'm sure this will all be over in short order and we can return to New York." She smiled sweetly. "I'll buy you a new box to replace the lost one."

Of course, Winston didn't suspect she had no intention of returning to New York, let alone buying him anything, but now was not the time to say so. She would wait until this matter of Mary was settled. She wanted to know why Winston had been so determined to find her. Portia's instincts told her it was important, that the truth affected her as much as Mary.

Carrying her parasol to shade her from the harsh sun, Portia strolled along the sidewalk. She pretended to be oblivious to the tension all around her, but she wasn't. She took note of the small gatherings of men, grumbling angry-faced men who were everywhere she looked—outside the café and the mercantile, in the shade at the side of the livery stables, and more noticeably, inside the Painted Queen. It seemed apparent that Mary's sheriff had more than enough trouble on his plate without Winston's adding to it.

Pausing on the boardwalk, she peeked inside the saloon. An enormous mirror backed the bar. The air was smoky, and voices were loud.

The Painted Queen. What an appropriate name.

Portia smiled as she considered what it would be like to own such a place. She could just imagine the expressions of her society friends back East. They would be aghast at the very idea of Portia Pendergast Kenrick, saloon keeper.

Then again, perhaps they wouldn't be. Most thought her beneath them, the upstart daughter of a working-class businessman. They weren't really her friends. They were people who wanted to be seen with Portia because of her money and because she was Winston's wife, not because they liked her. She had always known that.

Suddenly, she laughed aloud. The sense of freedom she felt was utterly amazing. She didn't need those men and women. She could do as she pleased. There were so many possibilities available to her. She only had to decide what she wanted to do, and she could do it.

Several people inside the saloon glanced up at the sound of her laughter. Portia waved at them, still chuckling, then turned and walked across the street. It was time, she decided, to meet Sheriff Barclay. Perhaps between them, they might find the answers they needed to set both Mary and Portia free.

Mary's throat ached by the time she ended her story. "And I wouldn't be knowing what happened with it after that," she said in a hoarse whisper, referring to the silver box.

It took more courage than she had left to look at Carson. So she continued to stare at her clenched hands and his hand lying on top of them. She had told him everything. She'd held nothing back, even though her heart was breaking from the telling. He would know now, as did she, that their union was forever doomed. There would be no wedding. She would never bear his name or his children.

After some time, Carson said, "It was self-defense, Mary. You were trying to protect yourself. Once we show that, you'll be free."

She blinked away tears. "Are you telling me you're believing that?" She smiled, loving him even more. She met his gaze. "Me, an Irish immigrant, and himself, a man whose supper guests include every judge and magistrate in New York City, I'll wager. They would not be believing the likes o' me, Sheriff Barclay, and well you know it."

He cocked his head to one side. "So are you going to give up? Are you going to let him take you away from Keary and Nellie?" He paused, then added, "And me?"

A spark of anger made her sit straighter. "And what is it you'd have me do, I'd be asking? I'm guilty as sin of hitting him, no matter what the reason. And I did take the box, may it ever be cursed."

"Yes." His expression turned thoughtful as he rose and began to pace. "Have you stopped to wonder why Kenrick would follow you all the way across the country to get it back? I haven't seen it, but it can't be worth that much to a man of his means. He's probably spent far more than its value in his search to find you." He rubbed his chin. "Is he the sort of man who would follow you for revenge?"

Mary frowned. She hadn't considered the why of it. "Aye, he might," she answered at long last.

Carson stopped pacing and turned toward her. "I'm not going to lock that door, Mary. I'm going to trust you to stay put. I'll tell Edith she can bring the children to see you whenever you want." He stepped toward her. "Stay angry, darling. Keep fighting. I'm not going to let Kenrick or anyone else take you away from me."

He'd never called her darling before, and she found it much to her liking. For just that moment, she forgot she was his prisoner. She forgot that her former employer was determined to see her hang. She forgot that the life she wanted had slipped out of her reach the moment Winston Kenrick arrived in Whistle Creek.

Unable to stop herself, Mary stood and moved into Carson's arms. He drew her to him, close enough that she could feel his heart beating. She let her head drop back, and their lips met in a long, bittersweet kiss.

Aye, she would stay angry, if it was what he wanted. There would be time enough for sorrow after she was forced to tell Carson good-bye forever.

—

A few minutes later, Carson left Mary in his one-room apartment. He couldn't help her if he stayed there and did nothing.

As he descended the narrow stairway, he said a quick prayer for her safety. Nothing in this world mattered as much to him as Mary, and he knew it would take a miracle for him to be able to protect her. She was right about the likelihood of a judge or jury believing her, the Irish housemaid, over a man like Winston Kenrick. It would take more than her word to free her.

He stopped suddenly. A woman—a stranger—was waiting in his office, seated near his desk. She looked up when she heard his footsteps. Her gaze was forthright and unwavering. Although not what one would call a handsome woman, she had a pleasantly shaped mouth and intelligent eyes.

After a moment of frank appraisal on both their parts, she said, "Sheriff Barclay?"

"Yes, ma'am. What can I do for you?"

"I'm Portia Kenrick."

His mouth pressed into a thin line, and he knew his gaze had hardened.

She inclined her head to one side, as if acknowledging his feelings. "I am not the enemy, Mr. Barclay. In fact, I hope to be a friend."

"A friend?" He stepped to his desk but didn't sit down. "And why is that?"

Her voice was determined, almost grim. "Because I am convinced Mary Malone is guilty of nothing except trying to escape my husband's unwelcome advances. And because I believe that box he is so determined to retrieve will give us the answers we both want."

Her words perfectly echoed Carson's beliefs, but he was still wary. He wasn't about to trust her too soon, despite his gut feeling that told him he could.

"Sheriff, it's apparent you have trouble on your hands in this town and probably have little time to search for something as insignificant as a silver cigar box. I'd like to offer the services of the private detective I hired, the man who brought us here. Mr. Knox is at the boardinghouse now. I'll pay his expenses, but he'll be instructed to do whatever you tell him."

"Why're you doing this?"

"Although not a fashionable thing to do, I made it a point to know all my servants." Portia stood. "I liked Mary, Sheriff Barclay. I would not have Winston ruin her chance for happiness." Her eyes narrowed slightly. "My husband and I have been married many years. I know him well. There is a reason for what he's doing that goes beyond revenge. I suspect I need to know his reason as much as you and Mary do." She held out a gloved hand.

Carson stared at the proffered hand for a long moment, then took hold of it. "I could use your detective's help, Mrs. Kenrick. I'm not going to let Mary be taken away."

"No," she said with a wry smile, "I don't think you will, Sheriff Barclay."

Twenty-two

Monday, 29 August 1898
Whistle Creek, Idaho

My dear Inga,

Much has been happening since my last letter. The secret I have kept from you and Beth and everyone I know has come to light, and I find myself in trouble with the law. My reason for leaving New York City so suddenly was because I struck my employer and thought him dead. It is with relief that I have lately learned the man lives, but now he has had me arrested for attempted murder.

The matter is made more awful altogether because I recently accepted a proposal of marriage from Sheriff Barclay. Now Carson has been forced to imprison me, and we will never be able to marry because of what I've done. I mourn what will never be. The joy of being Carson's wife is lost to me forever.

I cannot say that my imprisonment has been a terrible hardship, because Carson has placed me in his room above the jail cells, them being full of miners, for there is trouble at the Lucky Lady Mine. The room is sparsely furnished, but it has windows and plenty of sunshine and fresh air.

The children are staying with my friend, Edith, and have been to see me twice each day. Keary is too young to know there is anything wrong, but Nellie understands and is frightened. I know Carson has done his best to reassure her, as he does with me. Neither of us are fooled.

I am finding that inactivity is the worst part of my captivity. I wish I could make quilts like you or do embroidery work as Edith does, if only to keep my hands busy. I have tried keeping a journal, but there is nothing to write about except the past, and I would rather not think of it now. Baba, our dog, has come to stay with me, and she is some comfort. I find myself talking to her. If I was to be heard, folks might think me daft, and it is enough trouble I am in without that.

> Your friend,
> Mary

Bryan Halligan had heard about Mary Malone's arrest two days before, and the news made him smile. As far as he was concerned, she was getting exactly what she deserved. She'd spurned his offer to buy the Painted Queen, just as she'd spurned his amorous advances. He didn't take kindly to either rejection.

But his satisfaction over Mary's circumstances didn't last long. He forgot her completely when he received a telegram from his business partners. Michael King and Stephen Smothers were coming to Whistle Creek at the end of the week. They wanted to see for themselves what had caused the loss of revenue from the Lucky Lady Mine.

A fine sweat broke out on Halligan's forehead as he reread the telegram. He wasn't ready for this. Things weren't going as smoothly as he'd planned. That blasted sheriff kept getting in his way. No matter how angry the miners, most of them listened to Carson Barclay. Sure, the sheriff had arrested some of the most disruptive men, but real rioting had been averted.

Halligan lifted his gaze from the missive in his hand to look at the two burly men—his bodyguards—seated at the next table. The Whistler Café was quiet at this midmorning hour on a Monday, but Halligan was still glad these men were nearby. No one would bother him with them around.

At the same time, his bodyguards made it difficult to go about his necessary business. He couldn't risk their finding out what he'd been doing. If they were to inform Michael or Stephen...

Halligan shuddered at the mere thought of it. His business associates would show no mercy if they knew the truth. But he was determined to get them to sell out to him. He would be the sole owner of that mine, and one day, he would be the wealthiest man in Spokane. He didn't care what he had to do to make it happen.

He glanced at the telegram again. Perhaps another "accident" at the mine was in order. Nothing that would seriously damage silver production, of course; he had no wish to buy a worthless mine. But if another explosion and cave-in, for instance, were to happen when his partners were in Whistle Creek, they could see for themselves what he had been up against. They would finally support the cut in wages he'd insisted upon. They might even agree with his decision to hire scab labor, something they'd opposed in the past. They would certainly concur with the firing of all union supporters.

But mostly, they might decide the gain from the mine wasn't worth the trouble that came with it. They might finally agree to sell him their share of the business.

Yes, it was time for another accident at the Lucky Lady.

The second-story room was hot, the air oppressive despite the open windows. Mary lay on the cot, her eyes closed, her thoughts drifting in a state of half sleep.

She imagined Carson, sitting in the shade of a tall tree near his cabin. The creek gurgled and splashed nearby. Carson leaned his back against the trunk of the tree. His long legs were bent, and he rested his wrists on his knees. He was twisting a long piece of grass between his fingers, but he was looking at Mary, his blue eyes filled with love.

Mary moaned softly, then opened her eyes, wishing she could remain in that dreamy state forever. The dream was so much better than reality.

With a sigh, she sat up, then went to splash tepid water from the washbowl onto her face. It wasn't very refreshing, as warm as it was, but it did help a little. After drying her face with a towel, she glanced in the small, cracked mirror that hung on the wall. The reflection wasn't encouraging. Her cheeks were flushed with heat, her hair resembled a bird's nest, and there were dark circles beneath her eyes.

This after only two days of captivity. She might go mad before this was over.

Carson had brought food at noon and had told her the circuit judge would be in Whistle Creek in early September. Perhaps as early as the ninth, he'd said. But that was almost two weeks away. It seemed a very long time to one who was no longer free to come and go as she pleased.

She heard the creak of boards on the stairs and turned toward the door in expectation. She thought she might welcome a visit from Winston Kenrick himself, just to break the monotony of her confinement.

But it wasn't her nemesis. It was someone much more welcome but much more unexpected.

"Quaid?" she whispered in disbelief. It had been seven years since she'd seen her brother, and time had made a man of the youth she'd remembered. "Is it really you?"

"Aye, Mary, 'tis meself." He grinned. "And happy I am t' see you altogether, Mary girl. Happy I am."

A moment later, they were hugging and laughing. The years melted away in an instant, and it seemed they'd never been apart. For a short while, Mary forgot her worries. She was reunited with her beloved brother, and that was all she wanted to think about.

"How did you find me?" she asked him at last.

"I didn't find you, lass. 'Twas me that was found." He jerked his head toward the open door. "'Twas your friend who brought me here."

Mary hadn't noticed John Tyrell standing there until Quaid caused her to look. She knew immediately that Carson had sent John looking for her brother. With all the other troubles in the town and at the mine, he'd done this for her.

"Thank you," she whispered.

John smiled in reply.

"Now, Mary girl," Quaid said, drawing her gaze back to him, "I'm thinkin' it's time you were tellin' me why you're kept a prisoner in this room."

"'Tis a long story."

"And I've got nothing but time, me girl."

Mary heard the door close and knew John had left brother and sister alone.

And so she told Quaid all that had happened, sparing no detail, just as she had told Carson two days before.

There was something about the way Portia watched him lately that nearly drove Winston insane. If he didn't know better, he'd think she suspected him of embezzling from her. But she couldn't know. Portia couldn't possibly have guessed what he'd done. His wife wasn't a stupid woman by any means, but she had no grasp for the financial intricacies of the Pendergast empire, as much as she liked to think she did. Besides, he'd been careful not to leave any clues of his larceny, and he'd taken his time. Years and years of time.

Of course, all those years of working and waiting would be lost without the documents contained in the missing box. Those papers gave him access to all that money. They gave him a new identity. They were his future. He had to get them back.

And Mary Malone was keeping them from him.

"Winston dear," Portia said, interrupting his dark thoughts, her voice grating on his nerves, "you seem restless. Why don't we hire a buggy from the livery and take a drive, see some of the countryside?"

"In this heat?" he shot back, irritated by the very suggestion.

Her smile was tolerant. "Perhaps it wouldn't be so hot once we were in the forest. I understand there is a small lake not far from—"

With the sound of splintering wood, the door to their room flew open, crashing into the wall. Portia gasped. Winston spun around in alarm.

The man who stood in the doorway—his feet planted apart, his arms hanging at his sides with his hands curled into fists— was short but built like an oak tree, his chest, arms, and thighs heavily muscled. He had black hair and even blacker eyes, eyes that smoldered with barely controlled rage.

"Would you be Winston Kenrick?" the stranger asked, his accent marking him as an Irishman.

"See here," Winston sputtered, finding his voice at last. "What is the meaning of—"

"Answer me. Would you be Winston Kenrick?"

"Yes, but—"

With surprising speed, the fellow was across the room and had hold of Winston by the shirt. "Me name is Quaid Malone.... I'm Mary's brother."

Fear burned Winston's throat like bile.

"If you were t' hurt her, I'd have t' kill you. D'ya understand me, man?"

Winston swallowed hard, then managed to say, "You have no right to threaten me." Sweat trickled down the sides of his face. Moisture beaded his upper lip.

"I've got the right of any man whose sister has had unwanted hands laid on her."

From the doorway came another much more welcome voice. "Release him, Malone," the sheriff said with authority.

Quaid Malone didn't obey at once. He continued to stare hard into Winston's eyes, his gaze threatening even though his voice had been stilled.

"Sheriff Barclay...," Winston pleaded, the two words more of a whimper than a name.

"Now, Malone."

Quaid let go of Winston's shirt and, with a little shove, took one step backward. "You remember what I said, Kenrick. Hurt Mary and you'll have me to answer to." He turned toward the doorway. "So you'd be Barclay himself. 'Tis you I'd be talkin' to next, then."

"I reckon that's a good idea."

Quaid Malone strode from the room, Carson stepping back to let him pass. Then the sheriff glanced from Winston to Portia and back again before saying, "Mrs. Schmidt will see that someone repairs this door." He bent the brim of his black Stetson toward Portia before walking away.

Winston's muscles seemed to turn to water the moment the sheriff disappeared from view. His legs gave out, and it was merely good fortune the bed was directly behind him. He sank onto it, shaking all over, his innards in knots.

Through a buzzing in his ears, he heard Portia say, "Should I send for the doctor, dear? You don't look well."

"Shut up, Portia. Just shut up."

Carson liked Quaid Malone right off. His quick approval of the Irishman might have had something to do with the similarities between brother and sister. There was the same accent and the matching ink-black hair. There were also certain words they both used and the unique way they phrased their speech. They shared many of the same mannerisms, too, like the way they sometimes talked with their hands, punctuating their sentences with a gesture in the air.

Carson quickly learned that for a brother who had been absent and out of touch for seven years, Quaid was enormously protective of his little sister and dead set on making sure no one hurt her. He supposed that was the real reason he liked Quaid Malone so much. Both men wanted the same thing—Mary's safety and happiness.

His approval obviously meant nothing to Quaid. It took a bit of fast talking on Carson's part before Mary's brother was willing to believe him. Telling Quaid that he loved Mary, no matter what she'd done, seemed to be what threw the scales in his favor.

Half an hour after Carson took Quaid from the Kenricks' boardinghouse room, the two men stood in the shade of a large elm that grew near the northwest corner of the church. Carson stared at the running waters of Whistle Creek as he finished telling Quaid what he knew. "Mary's sure she had that box when she got to Idaho. She says she put it in one of the drawers at the saloon. That's the last she remembers seeing it." He glanced toward Quaid. "I think someone must've stolen it. Probably somebody who works there. We need to find it. Mrs. Kenrick is certain it will prove Mary's innocence."

Quaid's black eyebrows lifted. "Mrs. Kenrick?"

Carson nodded.

"And why would she be tryin' to help Mary?"

"Because she's nobody's fool."

"I'd not be trustin' her."

"I've got a gut feeling we'd better trust her." He looked down the street toward the sheriff's office, his gaze fastening on the window of his small apartment over the jail. "Mary's freedom could depend on it."

They were both silent for several moments, their thoughts unknown to the other.

After a spell, Quaid said, "What would ya have me be doin', Sheriff?"

Carson returned his attention to the Irishman. "First, I'd have you call me Carson. After all, we're going to be brothers." His smile was fleeting. "Then I think I'd like you to join John and Edith in combing the saloon from top to bottom for that blasted box. Other than Mac MacDonald, nobody who was working there when Mary arrived in Whistle Creek has left town."

"And if 'twas this MacDonald who took it?"

"I don't think it was Mac. I think it's still there. We just have to find it."

"You could be riskin' Mary's life on a hunch." Quaid's voice was solemn. "What is it you'll be doin' if we find nothing?"

Carson had spent most of the last decade trying to serve justice. Would he let a man like Kenrick twist the law for his own use and take Mary from him?

When dogs could fly.

"I won't let anyone take her away," he answered in a low voice, his gaze hard and unflinching. "No matter what."

Quaid held out his hand. "We won't let anyone take her."

The pledge was made, and the two men shook on it.

—

Darkness blanketed Whistle Creek, and with the night came a blessed cooling breeze. Mary lay on her cot, hoping for sleep, but her thoughts ran wild as usual.

She was worried about Quaid. After she'd told him what transpired in New York, he had stormed out of this second-story room in a splendid Malone fury. He hadn't returned. She hoped he hadn't gotten himself into trouble.

Edith had brought both food and the children around six o'clock. They'd eaten together, the four of them, and Mary had held and nuzzled her son, playing with him as if she hadn't a care in the world. It was a fine act she'd put on, but Nellie hadn't been fooled by it. The girl had seemed on the verge of tears the entire time. Before the three visitors left, Mary had pulled Nellie into her arms and promised her that all would go well, that Nellie would always be loved and cared for. She'd spent the rest of the long evening alone.

Now, as she stared through the darkness at the ceiling, her thoughts were on Carson, unhappily so. She didn't want to think about him. She didn't want to miss him. She didn't want to love him. It hurt too much. Too much altogether.

She groaned and pulled the pillow over her face, pressing down until she could scarcely breathe.

That loose board on the stairs alerted her to someone's coming. She held her breath in anticipation, knowing she shouldn't want it to be Carson and yet wanting it all the same.

He rapped softly, then opened the door. "Mary?"

Ah, she loved Carson's voice. Her name never sounded the same as when he said it.

"Are you awake? Can I come in?"

"Aye." She sat up. "Is something wrong?"

"No, I wanted to check on you, that's all." He closed the door behind him, then came toward her.

There was no moonlight for her to see him by, and yet it seemed she could see him clearly. Perhaps it was knowing him with her heart that made the difference.

Carson stopped beside the cot. "I've just left your brother."

"Sure and he isn't in any trouble, is he? You've not had to arrest him?"

"No." Carson chuckled softly. "But he's got a temper a lot like yours, so I suppose it might still happen."

She couldn't help smiling.

Unexpectedly, his hands closed over her shoulders, and he drew her up from the bed and into his embrace. She could hear the rapid beat of his heart as he dropped kisses onto the top of her head.

After a while, he gently tipped her head back with his index finger and claimed her mouth with his own. She surrendered to the heavenly moment, wanting to take with her whatever scraps of happiness she could, hoping to gather as many memories as possible.

At long last, Carson broke the kiss. "I love you, Mary. I wish I knew how to tell you how much."

She almost sobbed, the words both a balm and a torture.

"Reverend Ogelsby got into town today. I went over to talk with him." Once again he kissed her, long and deep. Then, with his lips brushing hers as he spoke, he said, "I've asked him to perform the wedding tomorrow. He agreed to do it. Right here in this room."

She gasped in surprise. "What?"

"Remember last week? I asked you to marry me when Reverend Ogelsby returned to Whistle Creek. Well, he's back, and it's time."

"Sure and I never gave you me answer."

She couldn't see his grin, but she knew he was smiling all the same. "How can you refuse me, Mary? You're my prisoner."

Mary didn't find his words or the subject amusing. "Are you completely daft, Carson Barclay? I can't be marrying you. Not now. Not ever." She pulled out of his arms and moved away from him.

"What do you mean, can't marry me now or ever?"

"Just what I'm saying. I can't marry you."

"Why not?" He stepped toward her, reached for her, took hold of her arm.

She shook him off. "You must be knowing why. I'm guilty of what Master Kenrick says. I'll be judged so and sent away. I could hang. What sort of thing would that be, a sheriff whose wife was hanged? 'Tis bad enough they'll all be knowing me boy's got no father to call his own. No, 'twould ruin you, having me for a wife. I'll have no part in it. 'Tis harm enough I've done as it is."

His voice was louder, harsher, when he spoke. "Do you hear what you're saying, Mary? What does one thing have to do with the other? Besides, you're not going to be taken from here, and you're not going to hang for anything."

"Are you still fooling yourself altogether, then?" she whispered sadly.

"Doggone it!" he shouted.

She jumped back in surprise.

"You might be the ruination of me, Mary, but it won't be because you took something from Winston Kenrick or because you hit him over the head like he deserved. It'll be because you drove me crazy!"

She couldn't form a retort.

Carson swore again, then spun away and marched to the door. "Make up your mind to one thing, Mary Malone. You are going to be my wife, and nothing's going to keep it from happening. Not even your stubborn, idiotic pride."

A moment later, the door slammed closed behind him.

Twenty-three

The Reverend Ogelsby came to see Mary the next day, offering gentle words of advice and comfort. He talked to her for more than an hour, reading words from the Bible, sharing about God's love. He explained that confessed sins were wiped clean by their merciful God.

For the first time in her life, Mary suddenly understood that God's forgiveness wasn't dependent upon what she did or didn't do but upon what Christ had done on her behalf. She realized that God hadn't turned his back on her. He wouldn't have withheld his forgiveness even if she'd been guilt of murder as she'd once feared. With that understanding came a strange peace.

But even her newfound peace didn't change her mind about marrying Carson, and she told the good reverend so.

After that, whenever Carson stopped to check on her, both of them acted tense and wary, and their frustration showed. By the time he left her alone—always with the same promise that they would be married, despite her stubborn refusals—Mary felt drained and exhausted.

But even those painful encounters were better than the monotony that shaped the hours of her captivity. It grew less bearable with each passing day, every one of them seeming a hundred hours long. The sleepless nights were little better. Quaid and Edith and the children came to see her often, their visits carefully interspersed throughout the day, but they didn't come often enough to ease the tedium that stretched in between.

Alone again in her upper-room prison following her afternoon visit with the children, Mary stood at the window, thankful that the heat of late August had vanished with the coming of September. Thin clouds drifted across the sky, swept along by a cool, brisk breeze. Small eddies of dirt whirled down the center of the street. Women fought to keep their skirts down and their bonnets on. Horses lifted their heads, pranced and snorted, made nervous by the changing weather. Even Abe Stover's lazy hound had crawled out from beneath the boardwalk; now the dog was lying in the sun near the corner of the livery stable.

Mary didn't turn when she heard the door open behind her. She knew her newly arrived visitor must be Quaid. It was his turn.

She was mistaken.

"Hello, Mary."

With a gasp, she spun around, her gaze clashing with Winston Kenrick's. "What is it you're doing here?"

His face looked gaunt, his eyes somewhat glazed, and Mary suspected the strain of the past five days had been harder on him than on her.

"I came to give you one last chance. I'm not going to ask again. After the judge comes next week, it will be out of my hands. Just tell me where you've hidden what is mine, and I'll have the sheriff release you."

Reflexively, she stiffened her back and held her head high. She refused to let him see how much she dreaded the day the judge would arrive, certain as she was that she would be found guilty. She refused to give Kenrick an ounce of satisfaction by cowering before him. Silence was her only reply.

He surged forward, crossing the room quickly. She backed away but couldn't escape him. In a voice hardly human, he growled obscenities at her. When she still didn't speak, he slapped her with the back of his hand. The force of his attack knocked her head against the wall. She covered her cheek with her fingers, felt her skin grow hot where he'd struck her. Unwelcome tears—from both anger and pain—blinded her, and they only served to increase her fury.

"I want that box, Mary," Winston ground out through clenched teeth. "Give it to me so we can be done with this."

"I...don't...have it." She emphasized each word, obviously frustrated, but her voice didn't rise above normal.

He didn't enjoy the same control. Almost shouting, he shot back, "Liar!"

Suddenly, she'd had enough. With a quickness he wasn't expecting, she shoved him away from her. "I'll not be listening to your threats. You'd better be leaving me alone, or you'll be the next one the sheriff arrests." She pointed an accusing finger toward him. "'Twas your fault I hit you that day. 'Twas you who tried to force yourself upon me. You with your money and your fancy house and your fancy clothes. You're thinking you can take what's not yours. You're thinking you're better than the likes o' me. 'Tis a fine name, Kenrick, you're thinking, and you puff up your chest like a grand peacock. 'Tis a fool you are, and a fool you'll always be. The Malones might be poor, but they're a finer family than yours, and proud I am altogether to be one of them. Sure and you wouldn't measure up to the worst in the lot. Me son is already worth more than you'll ever be."

Winston's face turned bright red. For a moment, she thought he might strike her again. But he didn't. Instead, he turned and walked to the door. Once there, he paused, his hand on the doorknob.

"You're not going to ruin me." He glanced over his shoulder. "Hanging would be too good for you." Then he yanked open the door and left.

—

Word on the street was that the other two mine owners— who had never before, in anyone's memory, visited the Lucky Lady—would arrive in Whistle Creek the next day. It was anticipated that they would approve Halligan's plan to send scab labor into the mine. In midafternoon, striking miners swarmed into town to search out those who'd been hired to take their jobs. Tempers were high, and there were more than a few men carrying weapons, a sure recipe for disaster.

Carson and his small band of deputies were hard-pressed to keep order. Since the jail cells were already full, the livery had to be commandeered for the new prisoners. With hands bound behind their backs, they were locked up in stalls to await the same judge as Mary.

Carson kept praying help would arrive on Friday's train. If it didn't...Well, if it didn't, heaven help Whistle Creek, because he was pretty sure he couldn't.

It was 4:00 A.M. when Carson finally fell, exhausted, onto the bed he'd made for himself behind his desk in the office. He didn't bother to undress. He settled for removing his hat and boots.

As soon as his eyes closed, he thought of Mary. He hadn't seen her since he'd taken her lunch the previous day. He missed her, but he wasn't about to awaken her at this hour just to say good night. Although maybe if he surprised her out of a sound sleep, he'd be able to talk some sense into her before she realized what he was doing.

Blasted woman! He loved her more than his own life. Why was she being so stubborn? Where'd she get this fool notion that she had to save him from himself?

"Ah, Mary," he said with a sigh. "Don't make this so hard on us."

Maybe tomorrow he'd be able to make her see reason. Maybe he'd visit her first thing in the morning, and she'd decide not to torture them both any longer.

Maybe in the morning...

Before the thought was finished, he was asleep.

But Carson didn't get to see Mary in the morning. He was awakened after only two hours of sleep to the sounds of gunfire. Instinct brought him out of bed and had him reaching for the gun belt that lay beside his pillow. Assured that the jail itself wasn't under attack, he yanked on his boots, slapped his hat over his head, and was out the door in a matter of seconds.

Near the rear of the Painted Queen, he found John Tyrell leaning over a bleeding man, one of Halligan's scabs. "What happened?" Carson demanded as he approached.

"Clyde Pugh shot him. When they saw me comin', him and Aldo Hirsch took off up the canyon there toward your old place." John motioned toward the injured man. "Looks like he was unarmed."

"Get the doctor for him. I'll head after Pugh and Hirsch."

"Do want me to come along?"

Carson shook his head. "No, the more deputies we've got in town the better. I can handle those two by myself."

"Right."

Ten minutes later—in the pewter light before dawn, when the whole world is painted in shades of silver and gray—Carson galloped out of Whistle Creek astride Cinnabar, unaware that the greatest danger lay behind him.

———

Your son will die like his father before him unless you turn over what is mine.

Winston Kenrick

Mary stared at the note, her mind screaming denials, her blood running cold through her veins, her hands shaking. Winston Kenrick had Keary. He was threatening to kill her son.

Edith whispered, "I don't know why I didn't wake, why I didn't hear him. How could he come right into my room and take Keary like that?"

Mary glanced up. Edith's face was colorless, and tears traced her cheeks. She twisted a handkerchief between her hands. Nellie stood behind her, looking just as lost and frightened.

"Carson?" Mary said. "Does he know?"

Edith shook her head. "Somebody got shot this morning outside the saloon. The sheriff's up in the mountains, looking for the men that did it. Johnny said he'd go after him. Oh, Mary, this is all my fault!"

"No, 'tis not your fault. 'Tis Master Kenrick's fault, the devil take him."

Your son will die like his father before him unless you turn over what is mine.

As the words ran through her mind, Mary felt as if she should understand something. A clue of some sort. It was there, yet she couldn't quite grasp hold of it.

Your son will die like his father before him unless you turn over what is mine.

Winston Kenrick hated her. Beyond all reason, he hated her. She had seen it in his eyes, heard it in his voice. She had recognized desperation yesterday. But what—

...will die like his father...

"God have mercy," she whispered as the note fell to the floor.

"Mary?"

Wide-eyed, she stared at Edith. "The mine. He's taken Keary out to the mine. That's how Seamus died. In the mine."

"You can't know that for sure."

"Where else would he be hiding him? Keary'll be crying. He'll be wanting me. Oh, God, protect me boy!" Before the prayer was scarcely out of her mouth, Mary was across the room and racing down the stairs.

"Wait!" Edith cried from behind her.

But Mary paid no heed. She had to find Keary.

She grabbed the reins of the first saddle horse she came to on the street. It was sheer panic that got her up and onto the saddle without breaking her neck, and good luck over riding skills that the horse didn't throw her off before they were out of town.

Perhaps the animal sensed a mother's terror. Or perhaps it was just ready to gallop after being tied to a hitching post for too long. Whatever the reason, once it was on the road to the Lucky Lady Mine, the horse stretched into an all-out run, ears flat against its head, hooves pounding a relentless beat against the road. Mary gripped the saddle horn and clung to it for all she was worth. Her only thought was to reach Keary before it was too late.

Please, God, don't let me be too late.

The site of the Lucky Lady Mine was drastically different from the last time Mary had been there. Deserted by the striking miners, the place was silent. Eerily so. The only sign of life was a horse and buggy, standing unattended near the mine entrance.

Somehow, Mary stopped her mount, then half slipped, half fell from her precarious perch. Her knees buckled, and she pitched forward into the dust and rocks.

"Keary," she whispered as she scrambled to her feet. Then she shouted it. "Keary!"

She ran toward the entrance. She stopped when she saw Winston Kenrick, standing alone in the elevator cage. There was no sign of Keary. Another man stood near the controls of the hoist. Steam hissed from somewhere within the complex machinery, a fitting sound for this nightmarish moment.

"Good morning, Miss Malone," Winston said in that smooth, cultured voice of his, drawing her gaze. He no longer sounded desperate or panicked. He was in control again. "I wondered how long it would take you to figure out where we would be."

"Where's Keary?"

"Where's my property?" Winston raised an eyebrow. "Don't tell me you came without it." He clucked his tongue. "Now that was a very foolish thing to do. You know what it means to me."

"I'll not be giving it to you until I have me son." She was surprised by how calm she sounded when all she wanted to do was shriek and scream.

"I don't trust you, Miss Malone."

She moved forward, hoping and praying her legs wouldn't give out on her as they had when she'd dismounted. "Sure and I don't see what choice you'd be having, Master Kenrick. If anything was to happen to Keary, I'd not ever tell you where I hid it, and well you'd be knowing it."

"Aha!" He grinned. "Then you do have it!"

"Aye," she lied. "And I'll be givin' it to you as soon as I've got me son back. You've got me word on it."

"Your...word...," he echoed softly, drawing the words out. "Hmm."

Mary glanced toward the man at the controls, then back at her tormentor.

As if she'd asked a question, Winston said, "I paid Armstrong there a handsome price to run this cage for us." He grinned.

Mary thought the look an evil one.

"He'll have to run it again if you're going to get your son."

"You've left him below?" Sick horror twisted her stomach. "By himself?"

Winston motioned her forward. "I'll take you to him, Miss Malone, but understand this." His smile vanished. "If you betray me, you won't get another chance. I'll see you hang. You know I have the power to do it. You'll die knowing I'll do even worse to your boy. He'll suffer, and you won't be there to save him. Do you understand me?"

She nodded.

"Very well." He reached for two lanterns on the floor near the cage. He took one in each hand, then offered one to her. "You'll need this. It's dark where we're going."

Keary, me darlin', don't be afraid. Your ma's coming. Don't be afraid.

"Go ahead, Armstrong. Lower us to the same level as before."

—

Exhaustion pulled at Carson like lead weights. His eyelids were heavy from lack of sleep, and weariness caused the muscles in his neck and shoulders to ache.

He followed his two prisoners along the narrow forest track. They were on foot, their horses having bolted during a brief gun battle with Carson. The slow pace they'd set as they walked toward town was almost enough to lull Carson to sleep.

"Sheriff Barclay!"

The distant shout instantly revived him. He didn't know what had brought John looking for him, but whatever it was, it couldn't be good.

"Here, John!" he yelled in return. Then he glared at his prisoners who had stopped in front of him. "Get moving and be quick about it."

John found the three of them a few minutes later. "It's Keary," he said without preamble as he brought his horse to a stop a few yards up the trail. "Kenrick's taken him. Edith sent me—"

Carson didn't need to hear more. He spurred Cinnabar, and the trusted animal shot forward instantly. Pebbles and dirt flew up behind pounding hooves. Carson leaned forward, wanting the horse to go faster, demanding it from him.

He prayed. Prayed as he'd never prayed before in his life.

Edith and Nellie were waiting for him at the bridge over the Coeur d'Alene. The moment she saw him, Edith began frantically waving her arms above her head.

Carson reined in as he drew near.

Edith's eyes were wide with fear. "She's gone after him."

He didn't need to ask whom she meant. "Where?"

"She thinks he's taken Keary up to the Lucky Lady. The note said Keary was going to die like his father if Mary didn't give him what was his."

Like a sledgehammer, dread hit Carson square in the chest, knocking the air from his lungs. The mine. Kenrick had taken the woman and boy Carson loved into that mine.

Before he could recover his voice, he heard a deep rumbling noise. He would have sworn the ground shook beneath his horse's hooves. His gaze shot north...

Toward the Lucky Lady.

Don't let it be what I think it is, he thought as he spurred Cinnabar into a gallop once again.

———

It happened in one horrifying instant.

Mary knelt in the mine shaft, holding Keary tightly in her arms, pressing her face against the downy hair on his head, weeping tears of relief. A frightened Keary, who had been tied with a rope around his waist to a large timber, sobbed and hiccuped. Winston stood no more than five feet away, saying something about going back to the cage.

Suddenly, an enormous roar blasted through the tunnel, deafening Mary. She was knocked onto her side as the earth bucked and rolled. A violent rush of air blew out the lanterns, plunging them into complete darkness.

It lasted an eternity. It was over in the blink of an eye. The silence, when it came, was more deafening than the explosion had been.

Mary righted herself, clutching Keary ever tighter. "Master Kenrick?" she whispered, her throat choked with thick dust and the smell of water-soaked timbers.

There was no reply.

For a moment, Mary was frozen by her own terror. Had she come all this way—across an ocean, across a continent— only to perish in a mine? Would she die in this horrible blackness, she and her son, too?

She felt a scream rising up from inside, the sort of scream that would never stop once it began. It was Keary, straining against her, that pulled her to her senses.

"You're right, Keary me boy. I'm thinking we should be getting ourselves out o' here."

She was thankful now for the rope that was tied around her son's waist. The thought of losing him in this blackness had the power to paralyze her again. She quickly shook off the feeling. She tied the opposite end of the rope around her own waist, then rose to her feet, bringing Keary with her, holding him on her left hip.

As she reached out with an arm, feeling for the wall of the tunnel, she cleared her throat. "Master Kenrick?"

It took a few moments of groping in the dark, but she found him, nearly stumbling over his prone body. Kneeling again, she touched his face and hair. She felt the warm, damp blood near the crown of his head. Then she felt for a pulse. There was none.

"May God have mercy on your miserable soul," she whispered.

Twenty-four

Mary moved away from Winston's body and felt her way toward the wall again. Once there, she took a moment to get her bearings, forcing herself to think clearly. Both her life and that of her son could depend upon it.

The cage had been lowered deep into the mine shaft—or so it had seemed to Mary. Once the cage stopped, Kenrick had led her along a dark passage until it branched. Perhaps three hundred yards or so. He'd taken the right fork. They hadn't walked very far from that point before Mary had heard Keary's cries. She'd hurried ahead of Winston then, filled with joy and relief to have found her son. Winston had still been behind her when the explosion took place.

Therefore, she reasoned, keeping in mind where she'd been and where his body was now, she was certain she knew in which direction she would find the elevator shaft. She had only to make her way along this tunnel, take a left at the fork, and find her way to the main shaft. Then she and Keary could be rescued.

"Carson will come for us, Keary." Saying Carson's name aloud made tears well in her eyes. She blinked them away. "We'll be out of here in no time at all. And won't that be grand altogether?"

She drew a deep breath, then began her slow walk in what she hoped was the right direction, feeling her way as she went. The walls were damp, and every so often, drops of water fell from the ceiling onto her head. Worse still, she thought that she heard the scurry of tiny feet.

An image of rats, surrounding her and Keary in this dark mine tunnel, flashed in her mind. She could almost feel their teeth biting into the flesh of her legs. Her stomach turned, and she tasted bile on her tongue.

She hated the large rodents. Rats lived in the poor villages of Ireland. They traveled across the ocean in steerage with immigrants. They dwelled in the tenement houses of New York City. Mary detested the sight of them. In this total darkness, she feared them.

To calm herself as well as her son, she began humming softly. The melody was from a lullaby her mother had sung to her when she was little, the same one Mary had sung to Keary from the day he was born. Strangely enough, she couldn't remember the words now. Only the melody came to her.

She pressed on, still humming, reassuring herself that it wouldn't be long before they reached the main tunnel. It only seemed to take forever because of the darkness, because of the strange smells of the mine, because of the horror of what had happened.

Keary grew heavier with each step she took, but she wasn't about to set him down, not even for a moment, not even with the safety rope around his chubby waist. She shifted him to her other hip and continued walking.

Pebbles crunched beneath her feet. Then she found herself stumbling over progressively larger rocks. At first she was merely surprised by them, knowing she hadn't had to step over any rocks that size on the way in. She supposed the lantern could have made the difference, but...

And then, just a second before her hand touched the solid rubble, she understood what had happened. Her way of escape was blocked. The mouth of the tunnel had collapsed.

Mary and Keary were trapped in tunnel number fourteen of the Lucky Lady Mine.

———

Waiting for a rescue party of experienced miners to be organized was the hardest thing Carson had done in his life. If he could have operated the elevator controls and gone down in the cage at the same time, he would have done so.

Horrible scenarios played in his mind as he waited. He imagined Mary and Keary buried beneath rubble. He imagined them falling down a bottomless shaft. He imagined them alone and frightened.

There was no one to tell him exactly where to find Mary, which only made matters harder for him. Whoever had operated the steam-driven hoist had disappeared before Carson arrived. He was certain it hadn't been Kenrick running the elevator, for it took a skilled operator to run the machinery, enough skill that hoistmen earned a dollar more a day than their colleagues who worked below ground. Besides, Kenrick's horse and buggy—rented from the livery—were still outside, along with the horse Mary had ridden from Whistle Creek.

Kenrick must be in the mine with Mary and Keary. Carson didn't know whether that possibility made him feel better or worse.

After what seemed a lifetime, he stepped into the elevator cage with Quaid Malone, John Tyrell, and a dozen other men, everyone wearing hats with carbide lamps on top of them, everyone carrying shovels and picks. Expressions were grim and determined. For now, the strike—and all the anger that had gone with it—was forgotten. These miners were joined by a common cause, and they wouldn't rest until they'd found those who were trapped below.

As the men closed in around him, Carson thought his heart might stop. Then his pulse began to race, causing a buzzing sound in his ears. He felt the oxygen being sucked out of his lungs. His hands perspired, making the handles of the tools slippery. The cage started its descent with a jerk amidst the hiss of steam and a rattle and clang as gears and pulleys turned.

Like the serpent whispering lies in the garden of Eden, a voice of doom warned him, *You're going to die below. You'll never see daylight again.*

"Get behind me, Satan," he whispered to the enemy.

John leaned toward Carson. "You okay?"

He nodded. "Yes."

"You don't have to do this. There are plenty of others who're willing."

Carson met John's gaze. "I do have to do this. It's Mary and Keary down there."

John nodded in understanding.

"Here!" someone shouted. "This is the level."

The cage jolted to a stop, and the miners spilled out.

"How do they know we should be on this level?" Carson demanded of John as they moved forward. He looked toward Quaid on his other side. "What if they're wrong?"

It was Mary's brother who answered his question. "They brought the cage up from this level. 'Tis here we have to suppose they'd be. Your Mr. Christy showed me the map of the mine. This tunnel drifts to the left, then breaks into three stopes. We'll be dividin' up there and followin' the tunnels till we find Mary and Keary."

Up ahead, someone shouted, "We've found someone!"

Carson shot forward, pushing his way through the miners who had come to a halt in front of him. Hope. Fear. Despair.

He felt them all before he broke through the crowd and saw one of the search crew bending over a man on the floor of the tunnel.

A man. Not Mary.

"Who is it?" he demanded.

"Bart Gibson." The crew member lowered his voice. "He's lost a lot of blood. Hurt bad."

Carson knelt.

Gibson grabbed hold of Carson's shirtsleeve. "I didn't know anybody'd be down here. Halligan swore the mine would be deserted today. Nobody was supposed t' be in here when I set the dynamite."

Carson's gut tightened. Halligan. Halligan had hired someone to blow up a section of his own mine. And now it was Mary and Keary, innocent victims, who could be paying the price of his treachery.

Gibson's eyes reflected the glow of Carson's carbide lamp as he pulled Carson's face closer to his own. "I don't hear so good after all the years of blastin'. I thought I was imaginin' things when I heard a youngster's cry." He grimaced, then shuddered. "But when I saw the cage'd been lowered, I knew it was real. I tried to get back in time to stop the blast, but it was too late. I heard a woman's voice. Then it blew."

Carson caught a glimpse of the extent of the other man's pain. "Hang on, Gibson. We'll get you out of here."

"Never mind...me. I'm dyin'...anyways." It took a lot of effort, but Gibson managed to roll his shoulders off the ground and point. "That's the way. The stope ain't...deep yet. If they're alive...there won't be...much air for 'em. She'll be... sealed up tight. Get 'em...outta there...quick." He dropped back onto the hard rock ground and closed his eyes.

Carson felt for a pulse, then glanced up. "He's dead."

The rescue party surged forward and around Bart Gibson. There was nothing anyone could do for him now. The moment they reached the wall of rubble and debris, they set to work with shovels and picks.

Someone shouted, "Miz Malone, can you hear us?"

But the only sounds were those made by the rescuers as they hacked away at the sealed tunnel.

Working beside the other men, Carson sent out a silent cry of his own. *Jesus, hold them in your hands. Keep them safe, I pray. Give me a miracle, Lord, 'cause only you can deliver them to me.*

———

The air was thin, dank, and hot.

In the complete blackness that surrounded her, Mary had difficulty knowing for sure when she was awake and when she was dreaming. Her thoughts sometimes meandered, sometimes raced. Some made sense. Some were a mystery.

She saw Fagan Malone standing before her, smiling sadly, heard him say, *Ah, Mary, me girl. Would ya never be larnin' t' keep that temper o' yours? Always fightin' with your brothers. Will ya be provin' all by yourself the sayin' that an Irishman is never at peace except when he's fightin'? Sure and 'twill be the death o' you. Mind me words now. 'Twill be the death o' you, Mary girl.*

Her da was right. It was her temper that had led her into disaster time and again.

"I'm sorry, Da," she whispered. "I'm sorry I wasn't listening to you."

Fagan shook his head, but there was a twinkle in his eye. *'Tis a fine lad you're holdin' in your arms, Mary, me girl. You tell him his grandda said so when he's old enough t' hear it. A fine lad altogether.*

She felt the sting of tears in her throat. "Aye, I'll tell him, Da."

Maeve Malone came to stand beside her husband. *'Tis your heart I worry about, me darlin' daughter. You've a stubborn pride, that you have. Don't be breaking a shin on a stool that's not in your way, Mary Emeline.*

She thought she felt her mother's fingertips stroke her cheek. "Ma…" She reached to take Maeve Malone's hand, but all she grasped was air.

Her brothers appeared next. They talked amongst themselves, laughing and poking and punching and shoving as boys were prone to do. They called to her in teasing voices. Ah, how they loved to prod their little sister into a fight. But they loved her fiercely, of that she was certain, and so she didn't mind it much. She wanted to join them now but couldn't make herself rise. She felt altogether too tired.

Mary.

She gasped.

Carson was there, watching her with those brilliant blue eyes of his. She saw the tiny scar that split his left eyebrow, saw the golden highlights in his thick brown hair, saw the slightly crooked curve of his smile.

"Me ma was right," she said to him. "Ah, me darlin', I wish I could be telling you how much I love you. You've held me heart in your hands almost from the first. Forgive me stubborn pride."

Hold on. I'm coming. I love you, Mary.

A weak smile played across her mouth, then she slipped into a well of nothingness.

———

"We're through!" someone shouted.

But Carson had already tossed aside his pick and was digging at the small hole with his bare hands, working to make it larger. Large enough for a man to crawl through. He pushed and scratched at the rock and rubble. He didn't stop to yell her name. He had to get to her. He felt it in his heart. He had to get to her now.

Quaid joined him. "Mary!" he called through the opening. "Are ya there, lass?" After a moment, he laid a hand on Carson's shoulder. "Listen!"

Carson stopped his frantic digging. Everyone in the tunnel stilled, waiting breathlessly. And then they heard it. The soft whimper of a child.

"Keary!" Carson, with Quaid's help, lit into the wall of dirt, rock, and shattered timbers with double the effort. "Mary, I'm coming!"

Within a few minutes more, he and Quaid had widened the hole to almost shoulder width. Carson didn't stop to ask if it was safe. He didn't ask if more of the tunnel might come crashing down at any second. He wasn't even thinking of the dangers he'd always known lurked in the mines. Mary and Keary were inside. That was all he knew. That was all he cared about. He had to get to them.

Please, God. Please.

Sweating profusely in the intense heat, his hands torn and bleeding, he squeezed through the tight opening. Jagged pieces of rock snagged his shirt and scratched his skin. He didn't notice. On the other side, with nothing to grasp onto, he fell headfirst toward the ground, breaking his fall with his outstretched arms. His miner's hat fell off and rolled a few feet away, but the lamp stayed lit.

There, in the light of that blessed carbide lamp, was Mary, curled up in the corner against the rubble, Keary held tightly in her arms. Nothing had ever looked so good to Carson in his life as the sight of mother and child.

Thank you, Lord. Thanks for the miracle.

"Mary?" he called softly as he crawled toward her.

Her eyes were closed. She looked ghostly pale, but he could see the gentle rise and fall of her chest. At least he knew she was alive.

Keary began to cry weakly, drawing Carson's attention to him.

"It's okay, little fella. It's okay. Your dad's here now."

He untied the rope around the toddler's waist, then rose and carried him to the opening.

"Quaid," he called, "take Keary. Get him up to the doctor." He passed the child through to his uncle's waiting arms.

"How's Mary?" Quaid asked.

"She'll be okay." He hurried back to her, kneeling down and taking hold of one of her hands. "Mary? It's me. Carson."

Her eyelids fluttered, then opened. For a moment, she seemed disoriented. Finally, her eyes focused on his face, and a gentle smile played on her lips.

"Ah, 'tis you, me love. I thought you were gone."

"I've come to take you home, darling."

"Aye, take me home, Carson."

He drew her into his embrace.

"'Tis finished I am, breaking me shin against a stool that's not in me way."

Carson smiled, not knowing what she meant but not caring. He was holding her once again in his arms. That was all that mattered for now.

Twenty-five

Bryan Halligan was apprehended in Spokane a few days after the explosion in tunnel number fourteen and was destined to spend many years in prison. His former business partners, Michael King and Stephen Smothers, brought an end to the strike, promising not only fair wages but better working conditions for the miners.

Accompanied by Tibble Knox, Winston Kenrick's body left Whistle Creek, shipped in a pine casket to New York City, where he would be interred beside other members of his family. In the casket with him was the silver filigreed box he had sought so desperately in the final weeks of his life. It had been found in Lloyd Perkins's old room, apparently stolen while Mary still lived above the saloon.

Portia Kenrick did not go with her husband's remains. The evidence of Winston's betrayal, discovered in a cleverly disguised secret compartment of that silver box, had dispelled any remnants of responsibility she might have felt toward her husband of twenty-four years. Now, she decided, it was time to live for herself, and that was precisely what she intended to do, immediately following the anticipated nuptials of Whistle Creek's sheriff and the owner of the newly established Blanche Loraine Refuge for Women and Children.

There were so many people who came to the wedding on that Saturday in late September that they couldn't all squeeze into the Whistle Creek Methodist Church. So they gathered—men and women who had been bitter enemies a few weeks before—beneath the open windows on the sides of the building and listened from the narthex at the rear of the church.

Around and behind the bride and groom stood those dearest to them. Quaid was there, beaming at his little sister. Edith Tyrell, a recent bride herself, watched it all with a bloom of happiness on her cheeks. Claudia Hailey, Carson's foster mother, had traveled from San Francisco to be there for the occasion; Carson had been surprised and pleased beyond words to see her again.

John Tyrell served as Carson's best man, and he held himself with pride, no longer ashamed of the scars on his face or his useless arm. Beth Steele had come with her family from Montana to serve as Mary's matron of honor. The reunion of the two young women who'd come all the way from England together, their futures unknown, had been a joyous one.

But as the wedding ceremony began, Mary forgot the presence of others. She had eyes for Carson alone. He stood beside her as the parson read from the prayer book, looking tall and rugged and incredibly handsome. He held a smiling Keary in his arms while Nellie stood beside him.

Her heart welled over with joy and love at the sight of the three of them. Never in her wildest dreams had she imagined she would find so much happiness in the wilderness of Idaho. She thought of the many small steps that had steered her course in this direction and knew it was a miracle of God, indeed, that had brought her to this place, to this man, to this moment. Things that she had thought were disasters and insurmountable mistakes had all been used by a loving and divine hand to send her toward her destiny. She could look back at everything now and see the path so clearly.

Fighting's not the only place an Irishman finds peace, Da, she thought, staring into beautiful eyes of blue. *Sometimes we find it in love. And I'm thinking I'll be proving that with Carson.* She smiled as she mentally added, *Though I suppose we'll do our share of fighting, too.*

Reverend Ogelsby's thin voice continued to lead them in their vows.

I'm thinking you'd be fond of me Carson, Ma. Sure and I know you would. I'll not be breaking me shin again, I'll promise you that.

"And so, by the power vested in me..."

As the parson proclaimed them man and wife, Carson handed Keary to Quaid, then placed the fingers of his right hand beneath Mary's chin and tipped her head slightly backward. With infinite tenderness, he kissed her for all to see.

For a moment, there was only silence and the rapid beating of Mary's heart. Then the church erupted in shouts as miners and townsfolk, family and friends, cheered the bride and groom. Men tossed hats high into the air and whooped and hollered like drunken cowpokes. Mary found herself separated from Carson, passed from one person to another, hugged and kissed on the cheek and wished well by those she knew and those she didn't.

It seemed far too long before she returned to Carson's side. When she did, he put an arm around her waist and held her close, and she knew he'd been feeling the same. She knew he wasn't going to allow her to be swept away a second time.

It was dusk by the time Carson carried his bride across the threshold of his cabin. He stopped in surprise at what awaited them. Ferns and pine branches and late summer flowers filled the room, changing the interior from a rustic cabin to a sweet-smelling bower. His old bed had been removed, replaced by a new wider one with a thick, soft mattress covered in smooth sheets. A lamp burned low on a stand beside the bed.

"Someone's been mighty busy," he said as his gaze turned to Mary.

Her cheeks were flushed, and he realized with more than a little surprise that she was nervous.

Carefully, he lowered her feet to the floor, then drew her into his arms. "Are you hungry? Do you want me to rustle up something to eat?"

She shook her head, her gaze never leaving his.

"Would you like me to leave you alone for a while?"

Again she shook her head. There was a light in her brown eyes, a light that revealed the hidden corners of her heart. With her gaze, she told him she loved him, she trusted him, she would be forever a part of him. Her eyes told him that together they would face whatever came their way, that they would be one for the rest of their lives.

He searched his mind for the right words, regretting that he wasn't an educated man, a man who could quote sonnets and poetry. Mary deserved those things.

And because he hadn't the words, he kissed her instead.

"Can you feel me heartbeat, Carson?" she asked when their lips parted.

He nodded.

"'Tis beating for you."

"Ah, Mary. My life. My love."

She pressed her cheek against his chest. "Would you be knowing I was afraid of you when first we came here, Keary and me?"

"Yeah, I knew. But not why."

"'Twas because I thought I was running from the law." She looked up at him again, her eyes filled with love beyond measure.

He smiled tenderly. "And you ran straight into the arms of the sheriff of Whistle Creek."

"'Tis a good thing," she said with a sigh. "For 'tis in his arms I always want to stay."

~Epilogue

Whistle Creek, Idaho
April 1907

It was late afternoon on one of those perfect spring days that made a person want to dance and sing for joy just for being alive. The sun was a golden orb in a cloudless heaven. A warm breeze carried the kiss of summer yet to come. The pines seemed greener, the earth more umber, the sky a crisper shade of blue.

Mary laid her pen next to the two completed letters and felt another wave of contentment wash over her.

Ten years. It had been ten years since she, Beth Wellington, and Inga Linberg had arrived in America. She closed her eyes and envisioned those three young women who had rushed to the railing of the RMS *Teutonic* for their first glimpse of the Statue of Liberty and New York harbor.

There was Beth. Lady Elizabeth, as Mary had called her then. So beautiful and fragile in appearance. So recognizable as a member of the English aristocracy.

There was Inga, tall and willowy, with hair as pale as prairie wheat. Inga, the minister's daughter, who had always thought of others before herself and who had told stories in her splendid quilts.

And there was Mary, headstrong, stubborn, and fiery-tempered, always breaking her shin against a stool that wasn't in her way.

Would any of them have guessed where they would be on this day, a decade into the future? No, she answered herself with a smile. Those three immigrant girls could never have imagined what lay ahead.

These days, Beth Steele helped her husband run a thriving cattle ranch in Montana. From her letters, it was clear there was little, if anything, left of the English noblewoman who'd arrived ten years before. Beth rode, roped, and branded right alongside Garret, a true woman of the American West.

Quiet, submissive Inga Bridger had become famous because of her quilts. Requests and orders poured in from around the country, far more than she could fill. Dirk Bridger had also made a name for himself and had great hopes for one of his fine thoroughbreds in this year's Kentucky Derby.

As for Mary herself...

"Penny for your thoughts," Carson said softly, his breath whispering against her neck.

A delicious shiver shot up her spine as she twisted on her chair. "I didn't hear you come in."

"I know. Where were you?" With possessive but gentle hands, he drew her up from the chair.

"Sure and I was thinking of Beth and Inga. 'Twas ten years ago today that we arrived in America."

"I wish I'd been there. In New York, I mean. I wish I'd seen you when you first walked off the boat. We'd have had ten years together instead of only eight and a half."

"Oh, that would've been perfect altogether, me belly big and round with Keary." She laughed. "You'd have wanted me for sure then."

His smile faded, replaced by the intense, loving look she cherished so. "Yes, I would have wanted you for sure then, Mary Emeline Barclay. I would have loved you immediately."

There was no point arguing with him. Carson had forgotten long ago what he'd thought of her when she'd arrived in Whistle Creek, and she was willing to let him forget if it made him happy.

Her husband glanced toward the hallway. "The house is quiet. Where is everyone?"

"They've gone to stay the night with the Tyrells."

"All of them?" Carson raised an eyebrow in surprise. "Even David?"

He was referring to their two-year-old son, the youngest of the Barclay children. It caused Mary to do a quick count of the blessings of her full quiver. Nellie was a woman grown; she'd married the previous summer and was expecting her first child. Keary Barclay was almost ten and growing more like the man who had adopted and raised him with every passing day. The twins, Fagan and Maeve, were nearly seven, and if ever there were children filled with blarney, it was those two. Claudia, at five, was as sweet and loving as her namesake. David, as was true of any child his age, kept his mother running from dawn to dusk.

And there was Carson, her greatest blessing, the man who held her heart.

"Just what will we do with all this peace and quiet, Mrs. Barclay?" he asked with a twinkle in his eyes.

She smiled, her joy uncontainable. "Whatever it is, Mr. Barclay, I'm thinking it will be perfect altogether." She stepped closer into the circle of his arms. "Aye, perfect altogether."

Share Your Thoughts

With the Author: Your comments will be forwarded to the author when you send them to *zauthor@zondervan.com*.

With Zondervan: Submit your review of this book by writing to *zreview@zondervan.com*.

Free Online Resources at
www.zondervan.com/hello

 Zondervan AuthorTracker: Be notified whenever your favorite authors publish new books, go on tour, or post an update about what's happening in their lives.

 Daily Bible Verses and Devotions: Enrich your life with daily Bible verses or devotions that help you start every morning focused on God.

 Free Email Publications: Sign up for newsletters on fiction, Christian living, church ministry, parenting, and more.

 Zondervan Bible Search: Find and compare Bible passages in a variety of translations at www.zondervanbiblesearch.com.

 Other Benefits: Register yourself to receive online benefits like coupons and special offers, or to participate in research.